# EXPULSION
## & Other Stories

ESSENTIAL PROSE SERIES 112

**Canada Council    Conseil des Arts
for the Arts      du Canada**

ONTARIO ARTS COUNCIL
CONSEIL DES ARTS DE L'ONTARIO

an Ontario government agency
un organisme du gouvernement de l'Ontario

Canadä

Guernica Editions Inc. acknowledges the support of the Canada Council
for the Arts and the Ontario Arts Council. The Ontario Arts Council
is an agency of the Government of Ontario.

We acknowledge the financial support of the Government of Canada.
*Nous reconnaissons l'appui financier du gouvernement du Canada.*

# EXPULSION
## & Other Stories

## MARINA SONKINA

GUERNICA
EDITIONS
TORONTO • BUFFALO • LANCASTER (U.K.)
2015

Michael Mirolla, editor
David Moratto, cover and interior design
Front cover image by Vladimir Osherov
Guernica Editions Inc.
1569 Heritage Way, Oakville, (ON), Canada L6M 2Z7
2250 Military Road, Tonawanda, N.Y. 14150-6000 U.S.A.
www.guernicaeditions.com

Distributors:
University of Toronto Press Distribution,
5201 Dufferin Street, Toronto (ON), Canada M3H 5T8
Gazelle Book Services, White Cross Mills, High Town, Lancaster LA1 4XS U.K.

First edition.
Printed in Canada.

Legal Deposit—Third Quarter
Library of Congress Catalog Card Number: 2015940391
Library and Archives Canada Cataloguing in Publication
Sonkina, Marina, 1952-, author
Expulsion & other stories / Marina Sonkina.
Issued in print and electronic formats.
ISBN 978-1-55071-945-1 (paperback).--ISBN 978-1-55071-946-8 (epub).--
ISBN 978-1-55071-947-5 (mobi)
I. Title. II. Title: Expulsion and other stories.
PS8637.O537E96 2015      C813'.6      C2015-903516-3      C2015-903517-1

*For my sons,*
*Theodor and Yuri Kolokolnikov*

*The author gratefully acknowledges*
*the support received through a grant of the*
*Canadian Association of Independent Scholars.*

# CONTENTS

*FACE*, THE NOVELLA that opens this collection, is set in modern-day Vancouver, imagining the cataclysms befalling this chaotically-growing metropolis on the Pacific Rim of Canada. The short story "The Hand" is not attached to any physical place and is inspired by a small photograph glimpsed by the author in an edition of Jorge Luis Borges' work.

The stories in the second part of the book take us to Russia. The main protagonists of this part are girls and women living in Moscow before *Perestroika* when the Soviet system still seemed monolithically solid.

The ideas and themes for this part of the collection were born out of a seemingly simple question that my students had asked after studying Russia's cultural history: "How was it possible for people to conduct their daily lives under such circumstances?" They meant revolutions, wars and brutally oppressive regimes that characterized the history of the country.

The ordinary fabric of life is elusive and much harder to describe than the manifest acts of dissidence, heroism, or sacrifice. Yet, my students somehow ruled out any normality, suspecting that Russians must have been sort of extra-terrestrials, thinking and breathing differently from any known species. Being born and raised in Russia, I of course never considered people that I knew — or myself, for that matter — as aliens. Just as everywhere else, there were cads and cowards, bureaucrats and secret sadists, against whose grim moral background the small acts of kindness and grace and mercy shone with a brighter, more treasured light.

When I embarked on the first "Russian" story in the collection — about seven years ago, the preoccupations and circumstances of the characters seemed somewhat dated. After all, there was no more Soviet Union, and the new emerging Russia, even if haltingly, was moving towards democracy. Has Russia made a regrettable detour or is the resuscitation of an increasingly authoritarian regime at the hand of the KGB operative permanent? Whatever the answer, the stories examining the fabric of Soviet life, its mores and customs, now seem timely.

*Marina Sonkina*

# PART I

**FACE**

*I shall give you what no eye has seen and what no ear has heard ...*
      *— The Gospel of Thomas*

# 1

SHE WAS THE first one to respond to my ad and, when I saw her on my porch, her head and face completely covered with a scarf and veil, I was slightly taken aback. In a city of more than a million Asians, I had expected not a Muslim but a young Chinese woman to knock on my door. I wouldn't at all have minded meeting any of those Daisies, Irises, Lilies, Violets, and other flowers brought by Chinese handlers to our shores.

But a girl in a hijab or chador or whatever they call it?

My imagination immediately had all her male relatives — brothers, uncles, first cousins, second cousins — sitting cross-legged around a hookah in my backyard and happily trading glottal stops. Goodbye to my precious solitude!

I scrutinized the visitor, or rather what there was of her to scrutinize, since besides the black veil that concealed her nose, mouth, and chin, her eyes were hidden behind big retro sunglasses, à la Sophia Loren.

"Did you come to see my basement?" I asked.

She nodded. I took a closer look. Except for the black scarf and veil, she was dressed like any other teenager: faded jeans and a flimsy top that barely covered her midriff. It occurred to me as I looked at her that I would be much better off with a man from the university. After all, I lived not much more than a stone's throw from the campus.

"I have to warn you," I said. "There's no real kitchen, just a hot plate and a sink. Do you still want to see it?"

Another nod, although I couldn't tell how decisive it was.

"And there isn't any dryer, either. Just a washing machine."

I paused, but she still didn't say anything. As if I were merely kicking a ball against a wall while she examined me to her heart's content far beyond the usual conversational interval between a man and a woman, which probably lasts three or four seconds before the woman starts to get nervous.

"All right, then," I said reluctantly. Her silence was actually starting to annoy me. "The basement has a separate entrance from the backyard."

I took her around the house past the thick cedar hedge and bushes of Portuguese laurel. I politely let her walk ahead, although not without the hope of gaining a better vantage. Whichever god or spirit made her had certainly applied himself. Her tight jeans outlined a well-shaped rear, and her tank top revealed an extraordinarily slender waist. Heeled sandals, slim ankles with a small leaf-shaped tattoo on the inside of one, and vampire-black nail polish on her toes completed the picture. Her hair and face were hidden, but her body was assertively on display, clamouring for attention. What was I, a man of 24, to make of that?

She stopped for a moment and pushed a strand of hair back under her scarf. It was unmistakably blond. More mystery. A convert? Or maybe a foreign student from Bosnia? I had a brief affair with a blond, green-eyed Bosnian once. But converts to any religion scare me. I'll take a foreign student over a convert any day.

"As I said, nothing fancy."

"I don't mind," she replied, and for the first time I heard her soft, resonant voice. No foreign accent. But not a Vancouverite either. A Muslim girl from Winnipeg or Moose Jaw? Again my imagination took off. A Canadian-born mole hiding out in my basement to recruit terrorists? A sleeper agent who one day ... Paranoid nonsense, obviously. She was probably just an ordinary Muslim girl trying to look like others her age. I'm not prejudiced. I don't give a damn about the labels we hang on each other.

"Aren't they pretty!" she exclaimed, pointing to the crocuses that had spilled over the brick border of my scruffy flowerbed onto the grass. "Like tiny elves with lanterns! Just look! Lavender, purple, all kinds — how beautiful they are! I wish I could fly over them so I wouldn't hurt them."

That caught me up. "Tiny elves." You don't hear people talk that way very often. I was sure she was smiling under her veil. I had a sudden desire to see that smile. How many times had I gone into the backyard without paying any attention to those "elves"! But she was right. The crocuses had become so abundant, growing here and there in random bunches of two or three flowers, that it was hard to find a place to put your foot down without stepping on them. The childlike excitement in her voice was captivating, as if she were discovering a newly created world. But how old was she? Seventeen? Eighteen, maybe?

Enchanted by her voice, I imagined that her face would have to be just as lovely. I bent down and examined the flowers more closely. There was an affinity between the lilt in her voice and the way the flowers seemed to hold tiny lilac suns in translucent cups: a similar joy, perhaps.

As I moved toward the basement entrance, the girl stopped to look at the large alder standing near the rear edge of the backyard. It was an unusual specimen, even by lofty Vancouver standards. Its lower branches reached across the yard as far as the kitchen window and, at night when a breeze stirred them, I could hear their light tapping against the windowpane, as if the tree were asking to come inside.

"It's a real giant!" the girl said as she walked over to it and then pressed her pale slender fingers against its smooth speckled bark. The muscular roots she stepped on to reach the tree raised her well above the ground and made her quite tall. "Doesn't this look like an eye? Maybe of a pre-historic lizard or an iguana?"

And in fact the knot where a massive low branch had been cut off long before was enclosed in three thick bark folds that did make it look like a reptile's eye or perhaps a rhino's. The girl now intrigued me even more. She obvious-ly was highly observant. Yet the instrument of that observa-tion — her eyes — she kept hidden.

"The alder is like a whole forest," I said. "If you look at a satellite image of our neighbourhood, it's the greenest spot."

Invisible in the tree's high branches, a bird began to warble a pure and lonesome melody. The girl immediately reproduced it with amazing accuracy.

"Are there children living here?" she asked, pointing to the swing, an old board hanging from a branch on two frayed lengths of rope.

"The original owners may have had kids. But that was a long time ago. The swing is pretty old."

The braided rope had formed deep grooves in the branch above, and over the years bark had grown over them, partly incorporating the rope into the tree.

"Dee-dah-dee," the bird warbled again.

"I'd like to rent the room," the girl said.

"Don't you want to look at it first? It's not Buckingham Palace, you know."

"I love the tree," she answered — and that seemed to be enough for her.

# 2

My bungalow, bought for me by my father, was old by any Vancouver reckoning, having been built long before the Burrard and Granville bridges connected the downtown area with the part of the city now spread along the southern shore of English Bay. Most likely, the first owners had used the house as a summer cottage, which at the time would only have been accessible from the centre by boat across the bay to Spanish Banks. The house sat across from the large forest tract that later became the University Endowment Lands near West Point Grey, now the most desirable and expensive area in Vancouver and therefore in all of Canada. When my father put down one and a half million for it, he was buying the property, not the house, which was assessed by the city at a mere fifteen thousand. I'm 24 and owe nothing. My father's a millionaire and purchased the house for a fraction of his net worth. Does that make me uncomfortable? Not in the least.

He had two good reasons for spending his money. First, he wanted to get me out of his home and into my own place; and second, he saw the purchase as an investment. One day, he told me, we'll tear the house down, build a much bigger one, and resell it at triple our purchase price. With nouveau-riche Chinese gobbling up the city's real estate and its old Victorian-era houses regularly becoming bulldozer bait, my father's idea was by no means foolish. On any given day on nearly any block, two or three sturdy old houses are being torn down.

I wasn't going to argue with my father, but I had no intention of taking part in any of that madness. I fell in love with the house the moment I saw it. With its steep roof and dark cedar-shake siding, it looked like a gnome which had just stepped out of the forest. After dozing a century or two under some stump, the gnome still carried traces of that green kingdom on its shoulders: moss around the gables and ivy creeping up the siding to the house's forehead — three bay windows with stained-glass transoms. Lilac wisteria grew on the pillars of the veranda that skirted the rear of the house. Two dour sentries — tall dark cypresses — guarded each side of the front porch, while a hedge of Pacific yew formed the next line of defence between the house and the street, with tall foot soldiers of azaleas, hydrangeas, and rhododendrons deployed along the near edge of the lawn and completely hiding the lower part of the gnome. From long neglect, the shrubs and hedges had all lost their shape, but in the spring the old rhododendrons, some of them the size of small trees, would burst into vivid crimson, yellow, and white against the dark-green background of their leaves.

Early in the season when I first saw the house, the front yard was dotted with hyacinths, dandelions, and tulips. Untamed, they came all the way down the street and a line of old cherry and plum trees in bloom.

With its oak floors and panelling, two ornate fireplaces, and intricate cornices, the main floor was exceptionally dignified. Structural subversion had gained an ugly foothold in the basement, however. The amateur zeal of the previous owners had turned what had been a decent space into a warren of crooked partitions and passageways. As a result, the kitchen area was reduced to a counter above where the presumably broken dryer had once stood. The clumsily installed plywood ceilings were not everywhere parallel to floor, and their corners were stained with mildew. The fans and large trays I found buried among the basement clutter clearly indicated that it had once been the scene of a tidy little cannabis operation. In short, the house had a past, a history all its own.

Buying me the place was generous of my father and it provided me with long hoped for freedom. An easy-going man with a lively sense of humour, he had made his fortune from the sulphur mines and gravel and sandstone quarries he owned. It wasn't old money like my mother's, but it had been earned by hard work and the sweat of his brow.

I loved my father. And ever since he had pointed out to me at the age of five an enormous bright-yellow pyramid of sulphur waiting across the bay for export to China, the Philippines, and other Eastern lands, I believed that he was a magician, a king and master of underground treasures. And I don't think I've ever quite let go of that belief.

My mother, however, found the dirt, her husband's crude off-colour jokes, and his visits to his quarries with their mostly immigrant workers more than a little vulgar. His activities seemed to her to be a caricature of the noble toil of her own forebears who had come to the Colonies to force the Wild West to its knees through sheer will power — in their case, the construction of the Canadian Pacific Railway. The men had courage, daring, and above all vision. They had tamed rivers, blasted through mountains, and vanquished dangerous gorges. Kicking Horse Pass over the Rockies at 5,300 feet had been built with her great-grandfather's help and was the steepest stretch of main rail line in North America. The men had a sense of entitlement and continuity, a sense of history and their place within it. But they were also romantics and even aesthetes. It was no accident that they erected at various places in the country majestic Victorian hotels, jewels that still stand today. When we vacationed at Chateau Lake Louise in Banff, my mother's famous maiden name would have entitled us to a significant discount, although of course we never mentioned it. Our large home in Shaughnessy, the exclusive Vancouver enclave built by the Canadian Pacific Railway, was crammed with old furniture passed down through many generations: mahogany card tables, oak armchairs with straight backs, squeaky rosewood sofas — the antique ghosts that haunted my childhood. But my mother didn't flaunt her distinguished pedigree. Genuine wealth doesn't shout. Rather it wears, at least in her case, a demure, sombre palette sorted out on hangers in vast closets according to colour: grey skirts, brown jackets, black dresses with high necks and long sleeves. My mother's plain appearance was as deceptive as the little game she liked to play: revealing her maiden name to enjoy the surprise on people's faces. She would lend that name to committees, charities, and fund-raisers, but selectively; people had to make an effort for the privilege of using it and then lavishly express their gratitude. My mother was a collector of admirers at the meetings of the boards of the Vancouver Art Gallery, the Vancouver Playhouse, and the Bard on the Beach Shakespeare Festival. But the real reason, the true reason for her participation in all those activities was to make the city blossom with art.

Road work seems to be ubiquitous in our city. A special stimulus package has virtually ensured that half of the roads will be under repair at any given time. My mother had hoped to use her influence to divert some of that money to badly underfunded art projects and enterprises. It wasn't money or influence or even her children and husband that she considered to be her real vocation, but art.

Artistic circles, as my mother called them, were invited to the catered parties in our grand house. The members of those circles admired my chestnut locks as I sat on their knees at the age of five. After elaborate meals the guests would praise my mother's creative talent, manifest in the two watercolours that hung next to each other in our dining room. One depicted the sadly drooping leaves of a bamboo tree after a rain, while in the other the same leaves stood at attention under a bright sun. It was the difference in the leaves' attitude that my mother's brush was supposed to have caught in her very first class with her Japanese art teacher. But social responsibilities had deprived her of the leisure necessary for such sublime art, so the teacher had not only begun the painting for her but had masterfully finished it too. Eventually, however, his authorship had somehow been washed away, perhaps by the very rain he had sprinkled on those leaves. My mother didn't mind encouraging belief in the power of her brush, and occasionally would even wear an antique kimono to her soirées, as befitted an artist of such wonderfully refined Japanese sensibility.

Next to the figure of my mother, my father looked rather ordinary. A stocky man of Mennonite descent, he was a good sport to his children — there's no denying that — but also an uncultivated bore, insensitive to art. Though firm with his subordinates, he was a "yes, dear!" man at home. That was his main flaw. How could any woman respect such a husband? Although he worked hard, my mother suspected that he didn't really care about money at all. The smell of dirt, the rumbling of excavators, that's where his heart lay. Money was an accidental by-product of that gritty, grimy passion. With such a husband my mother had no choice but to become a tireless watchdog over our wealth, our servants, me, and especially my older sister, who had to report to her daily, even after she was married and had a baby of her own. I was the only one in the whole family who managed to escape.

In high school, I was expected to choose from my mother's list of desirable professions: law, medicine, business,

engineering (if worse came to worse), but certainly not acting, which had infected me like a virus, as my mother put
it, since the tender age of six, and of which I would, she
believed, sooner or later have to be cured.

Whenever Monsieur Leblanc, the former director of a
small Parisian theatre and my mother's closest friend,
would tip his head in my direction and say: "Janet dear,
there's a spark in this boy! Look at the way he moves," my
mother would grimace as if she had just eaten a raw onion.
"He loves to show off, the little rascal, that's all," she would
reply. "Why does he always want to be the centre of attention? It's unbearable, really."

Later, when I was old enough to understand, she finally presented her argument. Art was the highest calling in
life, but unless you had real talent, it was silly to pursue it
as a career. In the absence of talent (which she didn't doubt
applied to me), how may one outdo the crowd, the multi-
tudes, and outdo them one surely must if one was to have
any hope for material success, the only true measure of a
person. I ignored such talk and refused to enter a university.
Instead, I got a job as a carpenter building theatre sets,
which was, as my mother used to say without trying to be
funny, another nail in her coffin. She was convinced that I
would end up badly because of what she called my anti-
social, anarchist tendencies.

But she had misunderstood me. I had from early ado-
lescence fully appreciated the magnetic power of money.
The kids who came to play with me at our home in Shaughnessy may have taken for granted the meals prepared by
our staff and the swimming pool we all played in, but their
parents certainly didn't, and I saw that. Sensitive since

early childhood to the moods of others, I was aware too how much people were drawn into that vortex of power and wealth. From remote acquaintances to the relatives of our servants, everybody seemed to want to be close to it, as if the confidence and ease of our world might rub off on them, or perhaps aid them in a later time of need.

"He's the spitting image of Uncle Claudius," my mother would say of me, having in mind a mad architect relative who had spent much of his life researching the construction of the great theatres, from ancient Greece to La Scala, and who had ended up in a London mental hospital at the turn of the last century. The only thing I had inherited when he died was a splendid collection of lithographs of famous opera houses at different stages of their existence: the Teatro La Fenice in Venice, the Royal Opera House in Covent Garden, the Staatsoper in Vienna, the Bolshoi in Moscow, and so on.

It was in the Spring of 2006 that my mother announced that we were selling our home in Shaughnessy and moving into the recently built 62-floor Living Shangri-La, the tallest building in metropolitan Vancouver. Two of her acquaintances had already moved in, as had some Russian Mafiosi, according to rumours, since this particular Shangri-La had the tightest security of any building not in fact a prison. My father pulled his head into his shoulders (a sign of unconditional surrender) and paid seventeen million dollars for one of the penthouses. I think he was relieved when I said that I would rather sleep under a bridge than live in that sealed fish tank, despite its panoramic view of the Georgia Strait and Vancouver Island. After they moved in, my father called me up and told me in mock excitement that the kitchen and the bathrooms were fully programmed. The shower door, for example, automatically closed the moment you stepped in, and then, *voila!* it opened again after you were done. When he got into it, he said, he felt like Charlie Chaplin in *Modern Times*. "But what if the shower mechanism breaks down? How will you get out?" I said. "Your mother would have to save me," he said. "She loves those gadgets!"

# 3

To many people, I'm a high-strung, irritable, easily distracted person. But that's another misconception. In fact, I'm always alert, calm, and collected. Or maybe that's what I want to be, or at least mean to project. And I'm focused when it comes to work, the unpaid one, which in my case is observing people. In order to know, as any actor needs to, how they move, talk, and live in their own skins, I have to pay close attention. Suppose there's a little girl sitting with her mother in an outdoor café. She's sticking out her tongue as far as she can, trying to get as much of her ice-cream cone as possible in one lick, while her text-messaging mama completely ignores her. Or there's a young guy standing on a corner with a baby clinging to his chest. He impatiently pats the baby's diapered bottom as they wait for the light to change. Sometimes I'm in awe at the strange vulnerability of our bodies: two legs, two arms, a protruding nose on the flat plane of our faces. How arbitrarily we're stuck together, how helplessly, yet how supremely beautifully. That's what's so bizarre. You watch the crowds, all those strangers in their almost identical clothing: drab pants and jackets and T-shirts, their arms, legs, and chests covered with tattoos. Are we really to believe that those mannequins all lead equally drab, unimpressive lives, all rolling along identical tracks, their faces closed and expressions impenetrable? Or are their faces just masks with a mystery lurking behind each one? It's my task in life, my vocation, to discover that mystery. What impels my desire to do so? I don't know. From an early age I've yearned to know what it's like to be someone else, to breathe the way another breathes, to dream another's dream. As if the core of my existence were a liquid and I had to pour it into the vessel of someone else to give it form and life. Once I even tried to walk like a cripple out of sheer curiosity, merely to see what it felt like. Another time I taught myself to write and do everything with my left hand in order to imitate people who had lost their right ones in a terrible war or accident.

At the age of 15 I became obsessed with the idea of owning my own theatre. Mad Uncle Claudius was my hero. I fell in love with opera and decided that I would one day recreate the original productions of some of the more famous ones. I would, I decided, call my theatre *RetroArt* to celebrate its unapologetic affection for the past. Modernism didn't appeal to me. Minimalism, I decided, had had its day. Audiences were sick of theatre interiors that looked like urban slums with exposed plumbing and wiring against black walls and ceilings, and they were sick of Brünnhildes in rags too. It was time to revive the beauty of the old, to reproduce the splendour of the great opera houses: La Scala, Covent Garden, the Palais Garnier, with their brocade curtains and upholstery and gilded furnishings. My theatre would be a feast for the eyes, a unique experience for this city on the Pacific rim.

Under the circumstances, then, my father's gift of the bungalow couldn't have been more timely. I decided to rent out the basement and quit my job at the theatre, or at least to stop working there full time. All my free time would be now devoted to achieving my dream: leasing the building, finding a cast and artistic director, making costumes, designing and constructing sets, hiring an orchestra, and so forth. My rough estimate of what would be needed to get my project off the ground was at least two million dollars. An ambitious plan, indeed! I spent many sleepless nights thinking about fund-raising, about philanthropists my parents might know.

In the meantime, however, I had set about decorating my new home. I got some of the family heirlooms from the Shaughnessy house: a Biedermeier secretary and a table made of birch went into the room that served as my study. Uncle Claudius' lithographs of the great European theatres naturally found a place on the walls of the living room. And rattan furniture with designer pillows secured a spot on the rear veranda.

I cleaned up the basement, threw out all the junk, removed the flimsy partitions, painted the walls a cheerful light-green, and highlighted the window frames and floor mouldings in red. I also picked up a bed, a desk, and some shelving and kitchen essentials at a garage sale and hung a new shower curtain in the bathroom, thus making the basement apartment quite rentable.

# 4

My new tenant in her jeans, scarf, veil, and retro sunglasses moved in with two duffel bags, a small suitcase, and two clay pots of geraniums — the full extent of her earthly possessions, apparently. She identified herself as Erythia.

"A very unusual name," I said jokingly. "Kind of airy or ethereal."

"Call me Erin. Everybody else does."

The next day as we were examining the so-called kitchen — really no more than a counter with a hotplate, electric teakettle, and aluminium basin, she said: "I could use a microwave too, although I'm not sure where I'd put it."

I loved the sound of her voice: diffident, uncertain. She drew out her vowels, finding the melody in each.

"I'll have to ask the owner," I said. "But I don't think he'll object."

"Oh! I thought ... But aren't you the owner?"

"I'm just renting the main floor," I said. "The owner lives in Hong Kong. I'm managing the place for him."

Why did I lie? Having suddenly acquired property through no effort of my own, without lifting a finger, I felt a little like a con artist. Besides, my assuming the status of owner would have raised a barrier between us and I wanted to avoid that. I had already realized that I would be spending a good deal of time improving the kitchen just to be around her, just to hear that voice.

But Erin wasn't the talkative type, and from her vague mention of the Prairies and of Nova Scotia, I concluded she had lived all over the country before arriving in Vancouver the previous year. What had brought her here? She waved her hand vaguely. "Trees. I love trees."

That seemed an improbable reason to move to the most expensive city in Canada, but Erin assured me that she had already found a part-time job in a thrift store, with good prospects for something better later on. What about her family? Another vague gesture.

How does one get to know a woman without seeing her face? Something in Erin's posture, in the languor of her movements, suggested that hers was a lonely, melancholic character, the naïve delight she took in the smallest things notwithstanding. That strange combination of melancholy and delight was accentuated by the way she spoke: answering after a delay, after a little pause, with a sort of question mark at the end of each sentence as if she weren't completely sure of her own words.

She never seemed to have any visitors. She didn't own a cell phone or have a separate land line, either, and nobody called her on my phone. She asked me once if I would consider sharing my cable TV hookup with her. I said I would get a splitter, and so I did. But I never heard the sound of a TV in the basement apartment, even though I had earlier provided it with a small one and some rabbit ears.

I was fascinated by my new tenant, in large part, I now realize, because I couldn't see her face. I didn't doubt that it was exquisite, just like the rest of her. Lying in the darkness, I tried to imagine it, without knowing exactly how to direct my thoughts. Dark, almond-shaped eyes? Or perhaps blue, or light-green, my favourite in women. What does it feel like to be always hiding your face, I wondered. The actors of classical Greek tragedy performed in masks. Japanese Noh theatre uses masks too, as do contemporary Venetian masquerades, but only for a short time during the performances. Erin, however, hid her face all the time. Once

I put on dark glasses, wrapped my head with a scarf, and covered my face with a veil to see what it would feel like. I broke into sweat and found it hard to breathe. I tried to reproduce her way of speaking too: brief, halting sentences with pauses in unexpected places. But of course none of that helped me get a better grasp of who she really was. Erythia, Erin. I could also have called call her Airy for being so light on her feet, or Dee-dah-dee, for imitating chicka-dees so precisely.

Once I dreamt that I was making love to her, gently kissing and caressing her body inch by inch up to her neck and then slowly removing her scarf. But just before her face was finally revealed, I woke up.

# 5

In the summertime, I often found Erin on the swing in the backyard. Her slender body gently swayed thanks to subtle propelling movements I never quite managed to catch, as if the air itself were moving her. The way her small bare feet dangled in the air was somehow touching, too. When she saw me, she would wave her hand, and I would notice the pale, almost translucent skin of her arm, bare to the shoul-der. She loved wearing bright summer dresses. The black headscarf I first saw her in had been replaced by azure or lilac or pink ones to match her outfits. Only the dark tri-angular veil that covered the lower part of her face re-mained unchanged, as did her sunglasses. I complimented her once on a blue sundress with a pretty pattern.

"You like it? I made it myself. I make all my clothing."

Dressing up for me then, I thought not without pleasure.

"Careful with these ropes though," I said. "They're rough. And probably as old as the house itself. I should put some tape on them so you don't hurt your hands."

"Where are you going?" She jumped down from the plank as I was about to go back inside. It was like her to ask personal questions with innocent faith that they would be answered.

"I have some work to do and then some people to meet."

"Do you manage other houses too, or only this one?"

"Managing houses? No, I mean yes, on a part-time basis. But I'm also trying to start my own theatre."

"Really?"

"Yes, really."

"Can I see it then?"

"There isn't anything to see yet."

"But when there is?"

A regal Steller's jay with a dark crest and deep-blue breast, wings, and tail landed on the branch above Erin where the swing was attached and began to examine us with a quick, bold gaze.

"Maeterlinck's Blue Bird of Happiness," I said, pointing out the jay to her. "Do you know Maeterlinck?"

She shook her head.

Perhaps commenting on our presence, the jay produced a raucous, scolding cry.

"They only pretend to be magical. They're really nothing but crows in a fancy disguise," Erin said with a soft laugh, and I imagined her scattering small translucent pebbles..

# 6

For the previous two summer months there hadn't been a drop of rain, and our alder was already starting to lose its leaves. From an upstairs window, I watched Erin working with a rake to clear the already carpeted backyard. She had filled three large lawn bags and lined up their amputated human-like forms against the backyard fence. A pile of leaves at the alder's base remained to be collected. Unaware she was being watched, she put down her rake and sat down in the pile, immersing herself in it, motionless for a moment. Then she picked up a leaf and held it against the sun, carefully examining it. After pressing it flat on her hand, she put it into the remaining lawn bag. She continued in that manner until the bag was full. Then she got to her feet, shook out the back of her dress, and went to her basement, dragging the bag of leaves behind her. What could she possibly want the leaves for? Puzzled, I stepped away from the window.

A few days before Christmas I almost tripped over a small parcel by my front door, a present from Erin. It contained two puppets, a traditional Neapolitan Punchinello and the Muppet Gonzo, with a postcard written in a childish scrawl, with the letters moving in different directions: "Dear Mathew! I hope that your dream for a theatre will come true very soon." I racked my brain about the best way to respond and finally decided on the microwave that she had mentioned but which she never got. With the gift I included a note: "Dear Erin, I hope that the microwave helps. But if you ever want to use a real oven, you're welcome to use mine anytime. Perhaps we could even cook something together?"

Three days later I found a folded piece of paper stuck under my back door. "Thank you for your thoughtfulness! Yes, I'd love to make dinner together sometime. But right now I need to ask a favour. Would the owner give me a two-week rent delay? I'll pay as soon as I get a new job. Thanks again, Erin."

"Oh, hell!" I muttered, referring not so much to the state of her affairs, as to disappointment in myself. I was suddenly sure that I had foreseen this scenario all along, although in fact I hadn't suspected anything of the sort even a minute before. "How do I know," I said to myself, "that it wasn't all planned beforehand and that she was looking for a free ride when she moved in? What should I do now? Give her an eviction notice and look for somebody else?" Although I did need the money, I didn't want another tenant. I wanted her.

Two days later, I left a note under her door: "Don't worry about it. I'll cover your rent for the next month. You can pay me back when you get a new job."

I don't know exactly what inspired that sudden generosity, but somehow I had managed to overcome my suspicion, no small feat for somebody like me. I got yet another "thank you" note, this time explaining that she had lost her job but was sure to find another one and that the landlord shouldn't worry as she was entitled to welfare in the interim. The naïve openness with which she revealed what other people would certainly try to hide — going on welfare — painfully reverberated in me.

Now I felt bad for her. I had unfairly suspected her. She had, indeed, lost her job. Where would she find a new one? She didn't seem to know anybody in the city. For no apparent reason, I remembered her bare feet suspended above the ground as she sat on the swing, and the way she covered her ears when the jay scolded us.

If I could, I wanted to help her.

# 7

Our city is usually protected from the cold continental climate by the Coast Mountains, but for two or three days around the middle of February, it snows heavily as warmer masses of air start to move inland. Then come winds that rampage all night long, leaving the backyard strewn with dead alder twigs and branches. Soon after that you begin to smell the ocean salt air again and hear the first birds of spring. And then, after another week or so, the cherry trees, still leafless, burst into bloom, adorning the city in a sublime pink. And then one morning you wake to find light-brown catkins dangling from the alder's bare branches. From a distance you might take them for furry caterpillars.

"What are these for, Erin?" I asked as she held out to me her open palm filled with newly gathered "caterpillars."

"The tree asked me to gather them," she said, bending to pick up more of the fallen catkins. I gave her a puzzled look.

"Our alder won't put out new leaves until I clear all the catkins from around its base. I'll give some to the birds too."

"You mean to say the tree cares what you do?"

"Yes, alders love order," Erin replied. "First they rid themselves of dry twigs and branches. Then they let the catkins out. Once I remove them, new leaves will come."

I chuckled.

"The tree has no hands," she said, "so it asks the wind to help. An alder's dead branches are brittle. Even a fledgling breeze, one that has only just barely learned to fly, can do a decent job."

"I see ... The wind is more like a bird, then, alive in some way?" I smiled at the whimsy of her new game.

"Yes, of course it's alive."

"So following your logic, the tree brings the wind into existence, then?" I said, adding more than a little irony to my voice.

"When the alder needs to clean itself, it calls the wind, and the wind comes," she explained. Then she put the catkins she had gathered in a plastic bag and sat down on the grass under the alder. Her skirt flared around her, forming a bright sun-dappled disk. I caught a glimpse of her bare legs.

"Come over here, Mathew, come! Let me show you something!" I took a few steps toward her.

"No, we have to lie down to see it." Without the slightest self-consciousness, she stretched out on her back under the alder.

Perplexed, I leaned over her. She waved her hand impatiently.

"No, you lie down on your back too, just like me, and look straight up." She pointed to the tree above us. I obeyed.

We were now so close to each other that, if I had moved an inch or so, our hips would have touched. It was those few inches — that forbidden space — that now occupied my attention. My senses suddenly sharpened. I inhaled her body's mild fragrance of lavender and damp moss.

"There!" she murmured.

Looking into the tree spread out above us, I marvelled at the skyward thrust of its trunk and the peculiar geometry of its branches. I had never seen the tree from that angle before, in the wholeness of its architecture, so to speak, and now located within it, it seemed for a moment that the tree was growing out of me, that the tree and I were one.

"The branches are like the arches of a Gothic cathedral," I said, hoping somehow to match to the uniqueness of the moment.

"Or like arms raised in supplication," Erin said, lifting up her arms. "Parallel to each other, but not exactly. Like a choir, with each branch a voice. They all pray, each its own prayer, without getting in each other's way."

"Pray?" I gently squeezed her hand. She didn't remove it.

"Yes, they're praying. I can hear them."

"What are they praying for?"

"For us," she whispered. "Every tree prays for us, even though each tree is different. This one has a sad, brooding intelligence." I put my arm across her body and brought my face close to hers, that is, to her veil.

"You're so sweet. Take this off, let me kiss you."

She quickly moved her head away.

"Why don't you at least remove your sunglasses? I want to see your eyes." I tried to embrace her, but she wiggled out of my arms.

"For now we see through a glass, darkly; but then face to face," she whispered, quoting St. Paul.

"Is she a Christian, then?" flashed through my mind. I took hold of her hand and gently stroked it.

"That tickles!" she said laughing, pulling her hand away and then putting it back.

"Here's an experiment," I said and lightly pinched her palm.

"Ouch!" she cried.

"See? The same thing happens in nature, in trees: a stimulus response, a chemical reaction, even if science can't explain everything yet." I drew her close to me. This time she didn't resist. Her strange talk and behaviour both excited and annoyed me. But I desired her and sensed that I would stand a better chance if I didn't contradict her.

"It looks like the tree has intelligence because it can do all kinds of things, such as lowering the temperature in its leaves, for instance, if it gets too hot outside," I said, while stroking her hand. "But that's just chemistry, not intelligence, you see."

"Trees have organs, like us," she said quietly without moving her hand away. "Leaves are their lungs."

"Oh, sure! Dozens of tiny lungs hanging from each branch. What a sight!" I laughed to hide my frustration.

"Not dozens, hundreds," she said quite seriously.

"Well, maybe. Nobody can know for sure how many leaves there are on a tree."

"Last year, the alder had nine thousand, three hundred and thirty-two."

"You didn't count them, did you?"

"Of course I did. We always do."

"We? Who is 'we'?" I suddenly felt like grabbing her and shaking that mystical hooey out of her once and for all.

"On some leaves," she went on, ignoring my question, "God's writing comes through clearly. On others, you can barely make it out. You pick the ones where it's clear and preserve them through the winter."

"Is that why you're stashing leaves in the basement?"

She took my palm and looked at it closely with real interest.

"Your hand is beautiful," she said, stroking my palm with her fingers. "You knew a lot in the past but have now forgotten it. That's what your palm is telling me. If you like, I can remind you."

"Remind me of what?"

"Of the stories you've forgotten." Was her strange talk meant to be seductive? With me playing along? "Every tree is a book, and every leaf, a page. All that has ever happened to the human race is written on the leaves of this alder."

"I wouldn't call that new, but I like it anyway," I said. "Nobody can see us here. Why don't you take off your veil and let me kiss you."

In a single quick movement, she freed herself and jumped to her feet.

"What's the matter, Erin? You don't want me to touch you? Just say so, then. Don't play these games!"

"I'm ... I'm not playing ... We're not supposed to, you see?" She was sitting on her haunches like a squirrel, a short but safer distance away.

"Look," I said, completely confused. "I'm a stranger. I understand there may be certain rules in your family, in your community. I know you don't want to get into trouble because of me. And that's just fine. Only say so, instead of ..."

"I have no family or community. I like you very much, Matthew, but I'm not allowed."

She reached for my hand again and kissed it. A strange, pitiful gesture. Though her tone of voice had disarmed me, I drew my hand back. What did she want from me? How old was she? For all I knew, she might not even be 18. A teenage

Muslim girl, taken advantage of by her landlord, who pretended to be somebody else for the purposes of ... In my mind's eye I saw the headlines. I got to my feet.

"You're leaving? Just like that? Didn't you want to hear my tree stories?" There was a childish plea in her voice. She got up and put her hands on my shoulders and pulled me back down beside her. I let her.

"Look, I'm not really interested in tree stories!" I said harshly to punish her.

"You should know that not everything dies," she whispered, her covered face so close to mine I could smell that moist, mossy flowery odour even through her veil. Her hands were on my chest. "Humans do, books perish, but trees ... When a tree's cut down, it ceases to be a tree to ordinary human understanding. Yet it lives on."

"As a ghost?"

"As a soul and keeper of all the secrets of the world. And as an agent."

"What agent?"

"An agent of change ... it can affect the life of one man, or many people, or the destiny of the city..."

*Is she a member of some Celtic tree cult?* I wondered. *There's nothing you won't find in Vancouver. And a Muslim, too?*

"Let me tell you a story, then. It's my favourite. About Abraham and Isaac. I feel sorry for Abraham and always pray for him."

*Do Muslims venerate Abraham? The New Testament? The Old Testament? Who is she?* — raced through my dazed mind.

"I know the story," I said. "And the sacrifice part of it doesn't make a whole lot of sense to me. But if I have to take sides, then why would I want to feel sorry for a stupid father who's ready to slaughter his own son because some stupid God said that's what he should do?"

She recoiled as if I had struck her. "God did save Isaac in the end, but he gave Abraham no release. He was left to struggle with his guilt for the rest of his life. That's why I pity him."

She rested her head on my chest. "I love you, Matthew, even if that means ..."

Almost in spite of myself, I put my arms around her, but she freed herself again, jumped to her feet, and was gone.

# 8

The next day I felt miserable, my whole body aching for some reason. I was deeply attracted to a girl whose face I had never seen, a loopy, babbling Muslim who was trying to break free of the ways of her people. Shouldn't I put an end to all that nonsense and concentrate on my own project before it was too late?

When evening came and I saw that the window of her basement was dark and that she still hadn't returned, I felt even more miserable. The whole day had passed without my seeing her. I could only hope that I would the next morning.

She was naïve and foolish, but her melancholy and childish notions and games were somehow endearing. I was enchanted by her. As if she knew something about life that no one else did — something that was the source of a gentler, softer, yet more vibrant, more genuine existence hidden deep within her that would now and then bubble to the surface in her wonderment and delight.

Where had she gone? How did she spend that day and

the ones that followed? Was she out looking for a job? If so, her chances had to be slim. She said that she had made all her dresses herself. Would she be able to design costumes for my theatre? I wanted to talk to her about that. I imagined us walking along a jetty or the beach, and my explaining to her about my theatre and listening to her naïve questions and delighted exclamations. She would bend over to pick up a shell or something, and her sunglasses would fall in the sand and a sudden gust would blow off her veil and at last, at last I would see her face.

When I saw her innocently swinging on a swing next day, I was relieved but didn't dare to ask her where she had spent the day before. I needed to talk to her, I said. She happily agreed.

On the beach we watched the gulls searching for crabs and shells in the puddles formed by the receding water of low tide, laying bare the ocean floor. At the pier, the Chinese were fishing for the crabs. Using a toothbrush, an old woman cleaned dirt out of the crab's paw before dropping the creature into the bucket of water.

Across the bay, the skyscrapers of downtown huddled together on a narrow strip of land. The setting sun hit their glass surfaces turning them into a phantasmagorical growth of cubes and parallelepipeds, now set on fire by some extraterrestrial flame. "See that tall building over there?" I pointed across the Bay. "Called Shangri-la. By the way, I know somebody ..." I quickly checked myself. "Some friends of mine live there." Of course, I didn't want her to know my parents could afford a place like that. Erin turned her goggled face to me.

"Tell your friends they should move out as soon as possible."

When she said that, my old fears came to life again: is she connected to some Muslim extremists involved in something nasty? To camouflage my discomfort, I said, rather nonchalantly: "Why should my friends move out when they have just moved in?"

"The soil is giving. The tower is tilting."

"Erin, this toy cost $350 million to build. Seven thousand tones of reinforced steel. It's going to withstand the earthquake, if that's what you mean."

"Tell you friends to move out as soon as possible," she repeated pressing her left hand to her chest. She was visibly suffocating, painfully struggling for air.

"What's the matter, Erin? What is it I said? You want to sit a minute?" I hustled her to the bench.

"Erin, stop it! Stop your stupid games!" I shook her listless body. Her head was on my shoulder and I was just about to remove the cloth covering her mouth to see if she breathed, when she came to.

"Forgive me. It'll go away. A dizzy spell."

"Do you know what caused it?"

"A sudden glimpse of the future. It's called erythania."

When ten minutes later we were returning to the car, I realized I hadn't even mentioned my theatre project. But now I didn't have the slightest desire to.

# 9

It sometimes happens to me after I've thought long and hard about somebody that my thoughts will seem to come to life, taking a material shape. I imagined seeing her in various places. Usually those projections or images (rather than visions or hallucinations) occurred at night, but sometimes they happened in broad daylight. One Saturday morning, for example, as I was driving down Oak Street, I thought I saw Erin on the steps of a synagogue. Startled, I turned into a side street and parked the car to get a better look at that "apparition." But then after I got out of the car, I realized that this time it really was Erin. She was wearing a dark cardigan and a black kerchief. But what was she doing at a synagogue? Two men in yarmulkes intercepted her at the entrance and blocked her path. I saw her open her bag, obviously at their request. They must have asked her to remove her scarf and uncover her face too, since she did so. I didn't see her face, only her back, and was shocked by the straight blond hair that fell down almost to her waist after she took off her scarf. Finally they let her in. I quickly followed. It was a Reform synagogue and packed, with the men and women all sitting together. The only unoccupied seat was some ten rows behind Erin. When I got to my feet with the rest of the congregation during the prayers, I would lose sight of her. But then after we sat down, I would see her again. She was leafing through a prayer book. A Muslim praying in a synagogue? It didn't make any sense.

Another incident added to the mystery. On Sundays, Erin usually left home early, but I had no idea where she went. This time, after she had been back for a while and I heard the basement door being locked, I got in my car and followed her at a distance. I saw her get on a bus at 10th Avenue. She got off again at Broadway and Ash, where up the street I saw the bulky, thick-set dome of the Ukrainian Catholic Church. She opened its heavy front door and went inside, without anybody stopping her this time. I followed. The church was almost empty, since it was still too early for the service. Erin was wearing her sunglasses, as usual, but the white scarf she had on matched those of the two or three other women present. They didn't pay her any heed. She prayed ardently, kneeling in front of an icon of some dark-faced saint. Then she took a candle from her bag, lit it from another, and added it to those already burning in the stand in front of the icon. I left at once, afraid she might see me. Who was my tenant? A Muslim, a Jew, a Ukrainian Catholic?

## 10

I had finally found a location for my theatre: an abandoned industrial building downtown that could easily be converted. Now I had to find money for the lease. I made a list of potential investors, about eight, all of them connected to my parents. The first person I spoke to listened amicably (my name had at least got me that). Yes, a very interesting idea. Vancouver certainly could use more culture. But did I have a business plan? For my second meeting with him, I came armed with documents and a prospectus that had cost me a few hundred dollars to produce. He said that he would look at the material and get back to me. Instead, a couple of days later, my father called me. "Do you need cash? I'll give it to you, only stop bothering serious people with silly ideas."

After trying all the others on my list, I reached Monsieur Leblanc, my last hope. I had known him since I was a child and he had believed in my artistic talent when I was five. I suspected that he had been my mother's lover. As I mentioned before, he had once owned a small theatre in Paris, but now he was retired on Salt Spring Island in the Georgia Strait, a place mostly occupied by potters, writers, and sculptors, along with various llama breeders, green enthusiasts, yoga practitioners, and lesbian tangoists. Twice a month Mr. Leblanc would fly over to Vancouver for a pre-mière, a vernissage, an opera, or one of my mother's soirées. It would take me, however, two long ferry rides to get to his island. He kindly offered to let me stay overnight. I told Erin that I would be gone for two or three days.

"For that long?"

"You'll survive, won't you?"

"I don't know," she said with quiet seriousness.

"Oh, come on, Erin!" I drew her close to me and kissed her concealed cheek, feeling a bit foolish as I did so. "By the way, the collection day had been changed. Please don't for-get to put the trash cans out on Wednesday this time."

I suddenly became keenly aware how much I would miss her.

## 11

Monsieur Leblanc smiled in his vague way while smoothing his hair with both hands. It took me awhile to steer the conversation to money. "My dear, you're making a great mistake!" he said in his thick French accent. "You're only thinking about money? But it's not only about money! Give me ideas too! You're going to recreate the interiors of the great opera houses? Do you have any idea how much that would cost? You'd need an orchestra pit and an orchestra too. The addition of a pit requires a particular kind of interior structure, electrical wiring, and a good deal else besides. And, my God, how could one and the same building simultaneously contain La Scala and the Bolshoi and all the others? Or maybe you mean to change the architecture of your theatre every year? And you want to reproduce the original productions? But that's impossible! To properly research, never mind replicate them? To duplicate the original costumes and sets? It's just impossible." He rubbed his thumb and index finger together in my face. "Where would you ever find the money for all that?" He stepped over to his front window with its view of the ocean, boats, and a lighthouse.

"But let's say that you got whatever you needed. Two million? Five million? Who would your audience be? Young people? Older folks? Chinese seniors with money who are just dying to see historically accurate productions of European opera?" He broke into a long, dry cackle. I said nothing.

"Did you ever consider staging Chinese classical opera?"

"I don't know anything about it. Besides, how many Chinese living in Vancouver would want to see a Chinese opera performed in English?"

"Those are the kinds of questions I want you to answer before you start."

"I have a business plan ..."

He made a sour face. "Documents, plans — not for me. You want my advice? Forget about opera. Start with something small. A theatre with 30 or 40 seats, no more. Contemporary plays that will appeal to a younger audience. There are plenty of good actors in Vancouver, and most of them are unemployed. You could hire them for a whole season for a fraction of what you would have to pay some diva for a single run."

I left Monsieur Leblanc without staying over. I knew I wouldn't see a cent from the old bore even if I downscaled to a one-man performance. Yet, watching the gulls dipping into the white foam of the ferry's wake, I suddenly felt relieved. I needed Leblanc's frank response to free myself from my absurd dream, from the strange nostalgia for a past I had never experienced. The snow-capped peaks east of the city glowed with the last light of the day. As darkness fell, they seemed more assertive, as if they were advancing on the little ferry taking me back home.

Who else could help? Monsieur Leblanc had been the last on my list of possible sponsors. There was my father, of course. I knew he loved me, even admired me, believing my nature to be superior to his. I could mimic people, recite poetry, draw, play musical instruments. That somebody like me could come from his seed — a man with dirt under his fingernails, with no more imagination than a carp (my mother's cruel word, which he loved to repeat while roaring with laughter) — he could never fathom. But would his admiration translate into a million dollars? He would give me something, of course, but not that much.

## 12

I got home late that night. As I was pulling into the carport my headlights caught what looked like leaping, darting figures in the backyard. When I went to investigate, I found a long line of women, a human serpent whose tail reached the backyard fence and whose head seemed to swell around the alder. They were holding identical plastic shopping bags, which a strong gust of wind (a storm was coming) did its best to rip from their hands. I went back to the car to get a flashlight. When I returned, the women nearest to the alder were jumping into the air, screaming and howling, and even rolling on the ground. There was some bizarre, incomprehensible pantomime going on at the base of the alder tree, which the powerful wind seemed to be tearing apart, sending cascades of leaves in every direction. Competing for the leaves, the women jostled each other as they caught them in the air or bent over to pick them up and stuff them in their bags before departing without a word into the night.

I pointed the flashlight up into the tree, where I made out the figure of another woman in a loose white gown perched on one of its lower branches, her blond hair streaming in the wind. She was taking still more leaves from the lawn bag she was holding and throwing them down to the women below. My flashlight blinded her for a moment.

"Who are you?" I asked.

"Don't you recognize me? It's Erythia."

"Erin?" I took a closer look. "Is that really you?"

What I saw horrified me — a grotesquely deformed face with a tiny, misshapen jaw, enormous asymmetrical eyes with drooping eyelids that slanted downward at the outer edge, as if there were no cheeks to support them, and a gaping orifice for a mouth. Stripped of what I had taken to be a Muslim veil, my tender girl with the ethereal name was a monstrous freak.

"It's me," she said. "My real face."

"But ... but ... it's impossible ..." Then I collected myself: "What are you doing up there? And who were those women?"

"Twice a year after the equinoxes they come to me to learn their fates."

And then, suddenly, as if descending along the thread of her own words, she jumped down from the branch. I had barely reached her when she collapsed in a faint. The lawn bag half-filled with leaves fell to the ground beside her.

"Erin! Get up, get up!" I shouted, but it made no difference. "Erin!" When she still didn't respond, I lifted her up, taking care not to look at her face, and carried her to the basement, pushing open the unlocked door with my foot. I found her captain's bed and laid her down on it. It was no warmer in the basement than it had been outside. I turned on the space heater and tried the light switches, but nothing worked. The power seemed to be off. Since I still had my flashlight, I checked the fuses, which were all fine. But still there was no electricity. I looked out the window. There weren't any lights to be seen outside either. Apparently there had been a power outage from the strong wind. It was unlikely they would be able to repair it during the night, so what was I going to do with Erin in the meantime? It was already October and chilly at night. At least upstairs I had two fireplaces. If I made fires at once, the upstairs rooms would be warm in half an hour. I moved towards the staircase. My feet made a rustling sound as I did so. I pointed the flashlight around and saw leaves everywhere: on the floor, on her desk, on the chairs.

# 13

Ten minutes later, I returned to the basement, flashlight still in hand. I found Erin where I had left her on her captain's bed. But her face was now covered again with the piece of triangular cloth I recognized, the wider part of it held in place with a string stretched across her face over the bridge of her nose. Only her eyes, now closed, were visible. Had she been able to get up and then fainted again? I leaned over her, listening to her breathing. The wind had started to die down and pale moonlight illuminated the room through the white muslin curtains drawn over its windows. The rhododendrons outside seemed to be coated with a milky film, and the shiny dark-green leaves of the Portuguese Laurel emitted a spectral glow.

A bird called from inside the alder and then was silent. I sensed that Erin was watching me. I went over to her again. She held out her pale hand to me. It was ice-cold.

"Can you get up? I've made fires upstairs. We'll have some tea and you'll feel better."

"Wait till my erythania passes."

"Oh … that again."

"It's a sort of sickness of compassion I get. We disclose secret knowledge and are overcome with erythania."

"Listen, I'm not going to leave you down here to freeze. There's been an outage and I doubt they'll be able to restore the power tonight."

She was too weak to walk. I picked her up into my arms, amazed once more at the lightness of her body. She pressed her head against my chest, and weakly wrapped her arms around my neck. I tactfully averted my face from hers.

My fingers felt the silk of her loose garment. Very likely she had been freezing up in the tree.

"What a beautiful place," she sighed as I carried her upstairs and lowered her into the leather recliner, inherited from my maternal grandfather.

I got an afghan and wrapped it around her. I lit some candles on the mantel and a chest under my collection of Noh masks. The heat of the fire and the soft light from the candles revived her.

"What kind of tea would you like?"

I found some crackers in the cupboard and some honey. I made the tea and put everything on a tray table next to her. But she wouldn't touch any of it.

"I saw your face, Erin. I can look away, if you want, but you need to drink something hot."

"You won't love me any more. I know that," she said in a barely audible voice.

"How do you know that? And what if you're wrong?" I tried to keep my irritation in check. But she had sensed the truth. When I saw her face, my desire for her vanished. Call me a low creature, a moral coward, but I couldn't love a woman with an ugly face, even if she should have a heart of gold and the most brilliant gifts of imagination. I just couldn't, and I don't apologize for it. The sudden revelation of her face was so shocking that I resented it.

"Don't be hard on yourself," she said, as if reading my mind. "You're not the only one. My face is repulsive to most people."

She lifted the bottom of the triangle and drank some tea, while I gazed into the fire in distress and listened to the tapping sound her spoon made as she stirred the honey into her tea. The sound's peaceful repetition brought with it another revelation. She had deceived me from the start and had been doing so for seven months, and I was her willing victim.

"I feel better. Thank you for the tea." There was another tap of the cup as she returned it to its saucer on the tray table.

"What you saw is an untreated case of Treacher-Collins syndrome," she said. "I was born with it. I have no cheek bones, and poor hearing too. I get by reading lips mostly."

Ah, so that's what it was, her curious way of talking, both odd and charming; a hidden question mark at the end of each sentence, as if she were never sure of what had been said ... A veil was a deception forced on her by something beyond her control. The wretched girl was hiding her misery.

"I'm very sorry." I paused for a moment, not knowing what else to say. "Couldn't your parents ... Well, maybe, you know ... while you were still little? Couldn't they try to treat it with plastic surgery?"

I knew nothing about the plastic surgery, of course. I was just trying to say something positive that would hide my aversion.

"My parents abandoned me soon after I was born," Erin said in a matter-of-fact tone.

"I didn't realize that."

"Of course you didn't! How could you?" she replied, now sounding almost cheerful, as if I had in fact said something nice to her.

"So that's the only reason why you've been wearing a veil. That is, you're not a Muslim, are you? And didn't the veil make things more difficult for you in another way?"

She sighed and pulled the afghan more tightly around

herself. She was still shivering, even though the room was already quite warm.

"Occasionally people would make snide comments, but usually they would just glance in my direction and then quickly look away, as if they hadn't seen anything unusual. Some of the customers at the thrift shop complained about it, which eventually got me fired."

"So they did fire you."

"I thought you knew that."

"Not really. You told me you had lost your job. Remember?"

"All the same, the veil was better than walking around with ... with a face like mine. It frightens people, children especially. I was always bullied and teased at school."

"You never saw your parents after they'd abandoned you?"

"Only once, two years ago. I finally found them. You know Selkirk in Manitoba? That's where they live. A beautiful house right on the river, a dog, two healthy kids. They turned out to be of Ukrainian descent."

"Is that why you went to the Ukrainian Catholic Church?"

"How do you know that, Matthew?"

"I saw you on 16th and Ash."

"Were you spying on me?" I could tell by the tone of her voice that she wasn't angry. "Yes, I go around my birthday to pray for Helena and Paul Vashuk, my real parents. My birthday must be hard for them, especially my mother. Remembering how she gave birth to a deformed little girl and then abandoned her. I pray for her suffering to end."

"But how do you know they've been thinking about you all this time?"

"I don't know. But if she's trying to forget all those years, it would be even harder on her, wouldn't it?"

Erin stuck her hand out from under the afghan and pointed to the black and white photograph above the mantel, her wide sleeve falling back she did so.

"Who's that?"

"Samuel Beckett, a writer. Do you know him?"

"No. And what's that?"

"It's Kafka's house in Prague. Where he was born. You've heard of Kafka?"

She shook her head.

"All these masks you have and pictures of different theatres. They must be old."

"They're lithographs that belonged to my great-uncle, who helped to restore some of the theatres."

"That's so beautiful!" The familiar naïveté in her voice made my heart sink again.

"Your parents must have been happy to see you after so many years." I was instinctively looking for something good in her life that might match the comfort and ease of my own. But I was obviously looking in the wrong place.

"Oh no!" she exclaimed lightly. "As soon as they realized who I was, they didn't want to have anything to do with me. They made me leave right away."

"Rejected you for a second time?"

"I don't really blame them. They have a good life. Two other children, both beautiful. I was an unpleasant reminder of what they did once. Nobody likes that."

Her selflessness amazed me. "I wouldn't be able to forgive them, let alone pray for them," I said.

"It wasn't their fault they gave me away. They had no choice."

"We all have choices. Even if it's a difficult one, it's still a choice." I heard my mother's voice say through me.

"Like Abraham, they couldn't have disobeyed. They followed the order and rule. I pity them just as I do Abraham."

I felt the same vague unease somewhere in the pit of my stomach. "What rule, Erin?"

"No sibyl may be raised at home. A sibyl has to be turned over to the world, and as soon as possible."

"A sibyl?"

"Yes, I'm a sibyl of the Erythean line in the 30th generation. My real name, as I told you, is Erythia. The first generations of sibyls were beautiful young women, just as Michelangelo painted them. That was before we asked the gods for immortality but forgot to ask for eternal youth too. Though I myself don't think that's what actually happened. I think that's just a beautiful myth. Already by the fifth generation, deformity had become the mark of our calling. Our destiny is to foretell the future, but when misfortune strikes, people blame us, the oracles. Revenge and fear guided their hands when they threw stones at us. Gradually, over the centuries, every stone thrown, every scratch inflicted, was embedded forever in our faces as a memento. We've paid dearly for our prophecies."

# 14

I listened to her melodious voice speaking those words devoid of any intelligible meaning, and was overcome with panic. My little tenant, my ethereal, mutilated angel was clearly insane.

"When did you find out that you had this gift, Erin?" I asked.

"I don't remember exactly. Somewhere around twelve, I think. Until then I was a miserable child from all the bullying and teasing. I would save money from my breakfasts to buy presents for the kids who were the most hateful, but it never worked. Adults can hide their emotions, but children are naturally cruel, so they don't bother to pretend. There was a little girl named Amy who was the only exception. For some reason she wasn't repulsed by me and didn't mind playing with me. So I said to her once: 'I'm going to do something nice for you since you're being so nice to me. Tell your father to reschedule his flight to New York for a later one. The plane's going to crash.' Her father was a businessman and travelled a lot. After I said that I fell ill with erythania for the first time. I had no idea what it was then. It's like dying together with the people whose deaths we have foreseen. Erythania seals the truth of our predictions."

The Punchinello puppet she had given me, on a settee next to the fireplace, seemed to be listening to her ravings, his pointed hat tipped over onto one shoulder and his crudely painted mouth stretched wide in a smirk.

*I wish they'd turn the damn power back on*, I thought. *Or else what am I going to do with this fruitcake?* I was dreading the prospect on a long night filled with her babble, since I certainly couldn't send her back down to the freezing basement.

"What happened to Amy's father?" I asked in desperation.

"After he was killed in the crash, Amy told her mother what I'd said to her. The mother suspected me of some evil and called the school. I was called to the principal's office. He said he would investigate. That's what he said, *investigate*. He looked strange. I couldn't grasp it right away; something was intruding, blocking me, some shapeless mass shifting all the time. And then I sensed what it was: cancer had spread from his stomach to his liver. I said to him: 'You shouldn't be worrying about any investigations right now. You have only six months to live. If you can, it would be better for you to avoid anything unpleasant.'"

"Did the principal die?"

"He expelled me from the school, so I never saw him again. But our prophecies always come true. Later I learned that they had a new principal, so I think, yes, the old one must have died. How could it have been otherwise?"

Should I have turned it into a joke or have pretended that I took it all at face value? I went over to the window and then turned around, putting my hands on the back of her chair.

"Well, my dear, tell me how you're able to do all this! Your prophesies, that it."

"You don't believe me, Matthew?"

"Of course I do!"

"I knew you would!" She sighed like a little child and reached up to caress my cheek. "Do you mind? You're the first person in my whole life to say that. I'll tell you how it's done. We, Erytheans, take a leaf, and on each one we write a word."

"What word exactly?" Did I insist on precision to show that I completely accepted her nonsense?

"Sickness, Betrayal, Financial Ruin, Poverty, Death, Slavery of all kinds. Or sometimes, Good Luck, Love, Mercy. I sit in the tree with my bag of leaves. When the wind starts to blow, I let the leaves out. The seekers of hidden knowledge catch them. What's written on the leaves comes to pass."

"But how do you know who gets what?"

"I don't know."

"But what if they, those ... um ... seekers, make a mistake? The one who's going to go bankrupt might, for example, catch a death sentence instead. Is the poor wretch still going to die?"

"Whoever's going to lose his fortune will lose it. And whoever's going to die will do so."

"Can you prevent the disasters you foretell?"

"No, that isn't within our powers."

"Let me ask you another question," I said, feeling a strong urge to change the subject. "I saw you once in a synagogue praying. Are you a Jew or a Ukrainian Catholic? I'm pretty sure you're not a Muslim."

"You won't laugh at me, will you?"

"Have I ever?"

As it turned out, Erin had as a child been passed among several foster parents, all of whom, according to her, had treated her with kindness. One couple were religious Jews and took her to a synagogue on high holidays and taught her some of the Torah. She made it a rule to pray in a synagogue for them several times a year. There were also two Jehovah's Witnesses, a husband and wife, who travelled from province to province with a trailer, delivering God's word from door to door. She enjoyed the sight of the highway slicing through fields of golden wheat all the way to the horizon. And then after that there were atheists, another husband and wife, owners of a small restaurant, where Erin worked as a waitress until ... I never found out what happened after that. The events of the evening had worn out my Scheherazade, and she fell asleep in the armchair in mid-sentence.

I lifted her almost weightless body and carried her to the small guest bedroom next to my own. I lit a candle on a chest of drawers in case she needed to get up at night and also left the door ajar.

# 15

I couldn't sleep that night. I got myself a beer but it was warm and I put it back in a non-working fridge. The night confirmed in its concentrated stillness what I had already concluded: Erin was seriously ill. Inventing stories is one thing, but acting them out is quite another. Was it well-entrenched schizophrenia or a temporary psychosis? Knowing very little about such things, I certainly couldn't tell which. But that she suffered from a dangerous self-delusion was obvious. Suffered? Suffering implies a certain passivity, a condition imposed and accepted. But doesn't part of us always want to be deluded, always want to negate the world, spitting in the face of the obvious? Erin's case seemed to have taken that impulse to the extreme. And yet for all the incoherence of her beliefs, there was great courage in her.

She had been born with a deformed face. Her parents had rejected her at birth. She was tossed from one foster family to another. Her classmates hated her, and as she grew up society kept rejecting her. But she was defiant. She invented a new identity. The deformed face would now be hidden behind a veil. But, as it turned out, the veil didn't provide the hoped-for shelter, and she remained an outcast. A fake Muslim trying to sit down between two chairs, someone who belonged nowhere. And still she didn't give up.

With amazing ingenuity she created another, unique identity, at last reversing roles with the world. She wasn't striving to belong anymore. She had found her place: she was an oracle. Now people sought her out. Her success gave her power. With that power came confidence and freedom from humiliation. But the stakes were high. She had to be able to deliver something for her daring. And she did. From time to time her prophesies came true and she believed them herself. Her faith convinced others. People have always been credulous. What did it take to convince Julius Caesar to embark on or avoid a battle? The entrails of slaughtered chickens! Have things changed very much since then? Not really. Under a veneer of science, there's the same fear of the unknown.

To my surprise, the explanation I concocted didn't help at all. What I really needed was to regain my state of innocence when her face had been a mystery and I could invent and love my own vision of her — even if I had now forgotten how uneasy and anxious that love was! I felt deeply sorry for myself and for her. I wanted to find a way, somehow, to salvage my fantasies. *Well, then, do something for her!* a voice inside me said. *Something simple but real, as if you were still in love.* But I couldn't pretend. I didn't love her any more. Yet she needed medical help. Perhaps I could find a good psychiatrist for her? What did they charge? $150 a session? How many sessions would it take? It didn't matter. I would simply have to come up with the money. But would she be cured? *Don't question, just act,* the voice within me said. *Your future theatre might be a creative outlet for the sick girl!* There was no doubt she was talented (the mentally ill often are). To maintain that persona took imagination,

thought, and courage. And the things she invented as easily as breathing: God writing on leaves, seekers deciphering
their futures. Where had she picked up those bits and pieces
of Greek mythology? Waiting on tables in an atheists' restaurant? She had a higher calling than sewing costumes.
She could be a fine actress who would make her name in
the new play I would write for her. In my new theatre, with
its contemporary fare. A re-enactment of her own life, for
example. All its doubts and struggles, and then, in an in-
credible denouement, a triumph of will and a cure! And
then, who knows? If she became famous, I would bring her
parents from their Selkirk sanctuary and make them watch
her and repent! Oh, wouldn't they regret, bitterly regret,
what they did to her!

I was breathing heavily from that foretaste of revenge.
But wait! Was that all I could imagine for Erin? Revenge?
No, there had to be something more. I had to grab the lost
time by its tail and finally right all the wrongs. I could start
with her face. I would fix her looks and her hearing. And
return her to the world, and the world to her.

For a moment I felt an upsurge of energy. Nothing was
impossible! It was only a question of money. Now I needed
it more than ever: for her and for my theatre, the two things
now interwoven. But where to get it? My father? A million
would put hardly a dent in his fortune. Didn't he say he
would help me whenever I needed it?

Excited, I jumped up from the chair, shook off my
shoes, and tiptoed into Erin's room. Her blanket had slipped
half-way down onto the floor, and the light silky gown she
had on exposed her birdlike collarbone. Her body was slender and of exquisite proportions. I touched a mole near her

cleavage, then traced my finger down. Her skin felt smooth, and of uneven temperature: cooler near her neck, warmer down below.

Erin's head was turned towards the window. To my relief, blond strands almost totally covered her face, leaving only her left ear exposed. To let her breathe better, I parted her hair around her nose, but leaving her eyes and cheeks covered. Then, obeying a sudden impulse, I got onto bed with her. The bed was narrow and I lay on its edge. I lay there for a long time, afraid to move. Then, gently, so it wouldn't press down on her, I put my arm around her. I became aware of the fragrance of her body, a touch of lavender, the familiar aroma of forest shadows and moss wet with rain. She murmured something in her sleep, then pressed her body against mine, putting her leg over my hip. I stiffened. She must have done it unconsciously, without waking. We lay together and I gently caressed her hair, then her back and her thigh. Her breath didn't change, but she pressed her body even closer, nestling her head against my chest.

I'll never know if she was aware of my presence or had just moved unconsciously in her sleep, but I would love to think that somehow she did, and that we did have one night together, the night of my acceptance and love free of expectation and fear.

I awoke quite suddenly. The blackness beyond the window had turned a milky hue. I blew out the candles and tiptoed out of the room. I lay down in my own bed and immediately fell into a dreamless slumber.

When several hours later I got up, the sun was already blazing in the window and Erin had left. On the coffee table

I found a strange note: "Save our alder. If it dies, I'll die too, and the city will disappear. I love you, Erythia."

# 16

I spent the rest of the day in the foulest of moods. To shake off my unhappiness I made a point of meeting with several theatre people, occupying myself with that until late afternoon. Then I invited myself to a family gathering at the Shangri-La penthouse. I suppose I was looking for vague support from relatives with whom I no longer had very much in common. Nobody had even expected me to show up for my nephew Bobby's fourth birthday party. While my sister and my mother were having a visit, their backs erect against the sterile white-leather sofa facing the strait in the distance, I went over the unpleasant task of asking my father for a million dollars to finance my dream. Since I wouldn't be doing it only for myself now, a voice inside me chirped, but for a cause, my chances should be good. (Oh, the logic of the needy!). And then my gaze fell on a tennis ball, one of Bobby's toys left by him under a chair. As I watched it, it began a slow, deliberate, accelerating movement across the expanse of the parquet floor towards the grey, convex wilderness of ocean beyond the glass wall. Perplexed, I looked around. Nobody else had seen the ball's odd movement. I picked it up and went to another room to see it if would do it again. Twice the ball repeated the movement, gaining momentum as it approached the western wall. And then I remembered something Erin had said, even though it was just too preposterous to believe at the time, about the tower's starting to tilt and that it would collapse.

As I was sitting down with my family in the three-star restaurant on the building's ground floor (my mother never touched anything in her space-age kitchen), I thought about the two things I wanted to say: the strange behaviour of the tennis ball, though they probably wouldn't pay it much heed, and, most important for me, the money I needed to ask for. Which one should I mention first? I stared at the two pork medallions with grilled asparagus on my plate and decided it would be the money.

"There's no way she'll ever approve, no way," my father whispered in my ear while looking across the table at my mother.

He patted the beads of sweat on his bald pate with his napkin. "You're already working at a theatre, right? I don't know anything about it, but who goes to the theatre nowadays? It will be too easy to lose it all. Keep your job, son, and if you're short on cash, I can always help you out. But let's not upset your mother. Promise me you won't mention it to her."

# 17

At what point did I realize that I would have to sell my house, my forest gnome? Initially, I rejected the idea, but the harder I fought against it, the more deeply rooted it became, until I knew unequivocally that there was no other option but to sell. Money for Erin's treatment was my new priority, and the theatre was no longer just a private dream but Erin's pass to a new life: her new spiritual as well as a physical home, at least temporarily — a place to live (two storage rooms in the building could be used for the purpose) until things sorted themselves out.

But how would I break the news to her? That we were going to leave the house: the alder, the swing, the bushes, the flowers, the birds? That it was necessary, but that she didn't need to worry, that she wouldn't be abandoned, and that we would eventually find something even better? Hmm ... What if she found out that I was the real owner of the house? What would she think of me then? She wouldn't have to find out: I could sell it quietly. Only that wasn't the point. The point was ... I watched a spider drop from the ceiling onto my shoe. Brushing it away, I suddenly had an idea. Why not look for a buyer who would purchase the house as an investment? Forty percent of the real estate in Vancouver is owned by buyers in China. They rent it while remaining in China. Erin and I wouldn't even have to move. In that scenario, she wouldn't need to know about the sale. And when my little theatre became a big success (and I had no doubt that it would), I could buy my gnome back!

In hindsight I marvel at the depth of my naïveté. How did I manage to convince myself of anything so foolish? To take a wish for a reality just because I so badly wanted it? Almost a week passed before I saw Erin again. After the night of her revelation, we had instinctively avoided each other. "I wonder if she knows that I was in bed with her?" was my first thought when she knocked on the kitchen door one early morning.

"Matthew, have you seen?" she said in obvious agitation. "There's a sign in the front yard. It says the house is for sale."

Oh, nothing to worry about, I assured her, while attempting a hug that she gently avoided. "It's just a change of the ownership. That's why I didn't mention it. Because it won't really matter ... For you, or I mean for us as tenants. They're apparently looking for a buyer interested in keeping the place as a rental property. At least that's what the owner told me." And as I said that, I firmly decided I would only sell the house to someone who would in fact allow us to stay there.

The Vancouver real estate market is the hottest in Canada. Eight Mercedes arrived at my gnome, vying for space at the curb. The owner of one, Mr. Yui, a man in his early thirties, offered the highest bid: $1.7 million, cash, with no conditions. He took little interest in the house itself, although he did carefully examine the back and front yards.

"I pay now, tomorrow go China," he said. "I have business China."

"I'm only interested in a buyer who wants to keep the tenants," I explained. Mr. Yui didn't seem to understand. After his realtor translated for him, he nodded several times. We shook hands. The deal was closed.

I signed a two year-lease on the theatre building and began renovation of its interior. Delighted with my progress, I hired actors, an artistic director, a set designer, and a crew of stage technicians. I also started to look for a plastic surgeon for Erin, even though I decided that it would be most prudent for her to see a psychiatrist first, and only then go ahead with any surgeries.

It was in the midst of the theatre renovations that I received a letter from Mr. Yui's attorney instructing me to vacate the house in three months. In keeping with the law, the last month would be rent free. "Clearly, there's been some misunderstanding," I said to the attorney over the phone while barely controlling my anger. "Our agreement was that I'd be able to stay on as a tenant."

"I don't know anything about that," the attorney's suddenly indifferent voice replied, "but I'll ask Mr. Yui."

The next day, the realtor informed me that Mr. Yui knew nothing about any such agreement, and that nothing could be done, since the property now belonged to him and those were his instructions.

"I don't care!" I shouted. "He made a promise!"

"But there's nothing in writing," the attorney said.

"Is Mr. Yui going to move in?"

"Move in? Are you serious? He's going to tear the house down, build a new one, and put the property back on the market."

"Is that what he told you?"

"Not in so many words, but isn't it obvious?"

"Then why didn't he say so in the first place?!"

"It takes months to get a permit to build a new house. My guess is that he just wanted the rental income in the meantime. But didn't you sell the place for the price you wanted?"

Rage, helpless rage, gripped me. I ran out the back door and almost stumbled over a raccoon that had got in the habit of coming to the backyard from the woods nearby. I shooed it away and watched it disappear through the ivy-covered back fence. Beside the fence, I noticed a wooden surveyor's stake in the ground. I looked around. There were four, each marking a corner of the property — a sure sign of impending demolition.

# 18

When I told Erin we had to move, she listened to me in silence, then took off her headscarf and veil and sunglasses. "Look at my face, Matthew," she said calmly. "I have nothing to hide from you. Why are you hiding the truth from me?"

"They tricked me, Erin ... The buyer told me ... I mean, he told the owner of the house that he was going to let us stay."

"They're going to tear down the house, then?"

"What makes you think that?"

"And chop down the alder? Tell me the truth."

"Of course not. Nobody would touch such a spectacular tree."

"Matthew!" She grabbed my hand, and brought her face close to mine. Her large asymmetrical eyes like those of some deep-sea creature expressed such raw, undiluted terror that I instinctively pulled my face back.

"Promise that you'll protect our alder!"

*What makes her think I have that power to do that*, I thought. *No, she doesn't realize that I was the owner, she just doesn't.*

"I'll do my best, Chickadee, I promise. The alder's unique. A perfect air conditioner right in their back yard. They're not stupid, these people. They know its value. You can build any house you like, but you can't just grow a tree like that. It would take 80 years!"

That night I couldn't sleep. You don't sleep easily on empty promises. I gazed at my books, at my Japanese masks, looking menacing in the dark, and at my lithographs. There was La Scala at the beginning of its construction, and there was the Staatsoper in Vienna in the process of rebuilding after the Allied bombardment of 1945 set it on fire. That world of mine would be gone, replaced in an instant by a "grey mausoleum" or a "pink crematorium," as an architect friend of mine called the new Chinese developments. And while they were at it, they would remove from the property every tree, bush, and blade of grass. Pavement instead of a front lawn. A three-car garage instead of my unruly tulips, peonies, trilliums, rhododendrons, and roses. A cinder-block wall instead of a living hedge. But why such disrespect for everything that lives and breathes? I got out of bed and took down a little book called *Feng Shui in Ten Simple Lessons*, a cheap, do-it-yourself paperback I had picked up at a garage sale out of sheer curiosity.

"A basement full of junk," it said, "interferes with spiritual growth. It will cause you to suffer a loss of power personally and professionally."

A promising beginning! I continued to leaf through the book. The front of a house, called the "Mouth of Chi," should have a vast imposing entrance, with wide doors to let the energy of Chi in. The Phoenix, the energy of fire, lives in the entrance. So as not to impede its flow, nothing should obstruct the facade: no bushes, no trees. If you have ivy, cut it down. Ivy represents clinging, stagnate energy. The space behind the house is dominated by Tortoise energy, which provides protection and support for the home's residents. A tall brick wall enclosing the backyard is best, but another building shielding the rear of the house is also good. The house retains the spirits even after its inhabitants are gone. To move into such a house is a bad omen.

I put the book down. How much of it was already being

put to use? And how did I know that Mr. Yui was even a follower of Feng Shui?

Feeling even more distressed than before, I got dressed and went out to look at the alder. The tree stood powerfully alive against the moonlit sky. I felt its dark brooding strength. There was no breeze, but its leaves seemed to gently move, as if responding to imperceptible currents in the dark air. The light from the house illuminated its lower branches but left its top in darkness. If the tree had been rooted half a meter or so to the side, it would have belonged to the city and been in no danger. By law, owners are allowed to cut down one large tree per year on their property (small trees don't count). I looked around. Mr. Yui could get rid of every tree on the property in two years if he wished. And if anyone objected, the worst that could happen would be a $200 fine. Would a man who had just bought a property for almost two million be intimidated by a $200 fine? I walked over to the alder and put my arms around it, as if trying to measure its girth. It would take two more men linking their hands together to completely encircle its trunk. As I patted the smooth, cool bark, it occurred to me that I had just given it a last, farewell embrace.

# 19

Erin moved into a small room in the back of the theatre. I took a storage room next to hers. During the day our plywood walls shook from the hammering and construction for the stage, and at night sirens and other street noises filled the air. We were in the downtown centre surrounded by thousands of people in high-rise office and apartment buildings, their opaque glass cubicles suspended high above our heads.

Erin had changed. She seemed frozen, defeated. Despair had taken the silver from her voice. Day in and day out she wore the same jeans, black top, and black head cover and veil. I noticed that she had stopped eating. I brought her groceries from Choices, a fancy glass and steel organic store across the street from us, but she didn't touch any of it.

She rebuffed all my attempts to talk to her. Once I saw her standing in the middle of the sidewalk two blocks from our building. She didn't seem to be going anywhere. Doing my best to seem cheerful, I went up to her and put my arm around her shoulder. "What's up, Chickadee?"

"They have hardened their hearts and withheld the tithe. The earth will be a shadow and I who toil will toil no more," she said, both scaring and annoying me with her old nonsense in the dull monotone that had became her voice. "Leave me alone, let me be."

I did as she asked. I left her alone in her room. I came to regret that bitterly in the days to come.

I read about what happened next in the newspaper. She somehow managed to chain herself to the trunk. The workers pleaded with the girl to get out of the way, but she refused. Finally, they called the police. When the police tried to cut the chain, the girl (it was Erin, of course) resisted. They managed to remove the chain, however, but in doing so injured her wrists. Although the injuries weren't serious, she was hospitalized. And that's where I found her, at St. Paul's downtown.

On my first visit Erin was slightly delirious and didn't know who had put the chrysanthemums in a glass on her bed table. The doctor was helpless to explain the delirium as certainly the light wrist wounds couldn't have caused it. The nurse put fresh dressing on her wrists in my presence but the blood continued to seep through the bandages.

I tried to get a diagnosis from the young female psychiatrist, who turned out to be in charge of Erin's case, but she was unresponsive. "That's confidential information. We can disclose it only to relatives. Are you a member of her family?"

"Well, I'm as close as anyone. There's no one closer."

At that moment Erin opened her eyes. "This is my fiancé. We're going to be married when I get better," she said softly before nodding off again.

The psychiatrist asked me to follow her to her office. I wasn't especially worried about Erin just then, since I'd already seen enough odd behaviour from her, including the so-called erythania that left her unconscious. Although I had no intention of sharing any of that with the doctor.

"What's wrong with her?" I asked directly. "She doesn't appear to have any serious injuries, but she seems to be withering away."

"Her injuries aren't physical but mental," the woman said while staring at the computer screen in front of her. She didn't turn in my direction even once. She wore long artificial nails with shiny polish. One of the nails was broken.

"Your fiancée went through a psychological shock caused by a feeling of guilt. After all, she was breaking the law, trespassing on private property and resisting any reasoning. Very erratic behaviour, you'd agree. Police had to be called as the last resort ... And now of course, she doesn't want to confront her own behaviour; hence the spells of unconsciousness."

When I came back the next day, I found Erin paler but more alert.

"I'm going to die," she whispered, looking not at me but over her shoulder, as if somebody might overhear and rebuke her. I touched her uncovered forehead. She was burning with fever.

"Don't say that. Remember, you and I have things to do. I'm going to write a play for you, and you'll be telling your stories from the stage. The kind you write on leaves. Remember?"

Why on earth had I mentioned the damn leaves?

She grabbed my wrist with unusual strength, pulled herself up, and brought her face level with mine.

"Have they cut down the alder already? Tell me the truth."

I winced at the sight of fresh red stains on her bandages.

"They're not going to. I told you that, Chickadee."

"You've seen it? Seen it yourself?"

"If you want me to, I'll go look."

"Come back quickly! Maybe there's still a chance for me." Her voice was flat, without any inflection at all.

I couldn't lie to Erin anymore, so I went.

## 20

I was just going to drive by the house. But as I approached it, I slowed down. Nothing had changed. My gnome was still there. Only the windowpanes of my study facing the street seemed to be shivering, as if they too had a fever. Astonished,

I got out of the car. The windowpanes obliquely reflected the sunlight, and the air was still. The shivering was coming from within, or, judging by the noise, from behind. I went around to the rear. A backhoe was at work. What I had taken for a standing house was nothing more than a façade like a theatrical set, with the back and the left walls already demolished. What chance had brought me to my house just moments before it was reduced to rubble? From the side I could see one of the fireplaces with its chimney sticking up from where the living room had been, now no longer connected to anything except my memories of sitting beside it with Erin. The backhoe paused briefly, took aim, and then sank the sharp teeth of its shovel into what was left of the roof, pushing it sideways until the shakes slid off and it sagged and exploded, crashing down and covering the fireplace and producing an enormous cloud of dust, which was immediately hosed down by one of the workers. The backhoe then took another run, rolling over a tall rhododendron and crushing it. Soon there was nothing left of the yard. The hedges and shrubs that had marked the boundaries were gone. The butchered cypresses were stacked in what looked like funereal pyres. Where the alder had proudly stood there was now a void on the other side of which utility poles were visible, along with the neighbour's garage and his garbage cans and a broken tricycle. What had once filled the air with robust life now lay on the ground in a tangled mass. The limbs that had already been sawn off were piled separately a few feet away. Tears of resin were visible on the exposed yellowish wood.

I turned and went back to my car. Perhaps the alder didn't know, didn't have time to know what was happening to it. It was the end of November and it was already asleep. Anesthetized by the cold, it didn't go mad with fear, didn't choke in an agony of pain from the chainsaw's teeth. And if it didn't know that it would never wake up the next spring to call upon the wind to help it clear away its dry twigs before displaying the furry caterpillars of catkins on each branch — if it didn't know any of that, then perhaps its death didn't matter. For isn't to be unaware of one's own dying to achieve a kind of immortality? If the alder missed its own execution, then perhaps it never happened. But then its life never happened either. The alder neither lived nor died. Chickadees never built their nests high up in its crown and never sang their hearts out to greet the first rays of the morning sun.

Whether the crocuses survived wouldn't be known until spring. In March, their pale-ivory bulbs would soften inside and push up shoots too small to break through the pavement laid over their heads. How many times would they try before realizing that they were trapped, were entombed alive beneath the cement?

It had started to rain. I felt cold stabs on my cheeks through my three-day stubble. I got back into my car intending to return to the hospital. Soon it began to rain in earnest. Great sheets of water flowed across the road, curling up and back like ocean surf and narrowing the surface to a strip of glistening grey.

At the crest of the hill near the house the road opens onto a spectacular panorama of the city framed by mountain peaks. By the time I reached that elevated point, the streets were already swollen with water and the houses and trees dissolved in greenish haze. Here and there fires were blazing like torches and running from one house to another with what seemed like merry winks. The flames were oddly beautiful and enlivened the bleakness of the city under the torrents of rain. Directly ahead in my line of sight the spiked dome of BC Place was burning. And then, silently, it exploded into a ball of fire before collapsing before my eyes. Horrified yet strangely fascinated, I drove down to the Burrard Bridge and across it to the city centre. The small fires behind me had fortunately failed to reach the bridge. But the heavy rain made it more and more difficult to drive as the high water resisted the wheels and made a hissing sound. It felt as if I were driving through a mass of seaweed. And then I realized that the water was coming not only from above but also from below. The bay was rising. The cars ahead of me had slowed and then come to a stop as the water submerged their wheels as they exited the bridge. I still wasn't as alarmed as I might have been: in the intervals between the sweeps of the windshield wiper, I saw the usual crowd of pedestrians strung out along the sea wall, even if in some places already knee-high in water. Strangely, they didn't seem to be concerned either, nor were their dogs, which happily jumped around in the water and then caught up with their masters. Yet it was obvious that the water was rapidly rising. I couldn't understand why it was higher near the bridge than it seemed to be at the beaches to the west. But there was no time to think about that. Two or three cars in front of me had slid off the bridge, breaking though its railing and disappearing into the surging water below. A nearby boat came over to help, but its mast suddenly snapped and then it too disappeared into the abyss. Trying not to panic, I hit the accelerator of my little Prius and was momentarily airborne. Half-flying, half-gliding over the rising waters, I reached the middle of the bridge. There the water level was lower, and I was relieved to hear the whisper of the tires on asphalt again. I slowed down and looked toward the sky. Outlined against the blackness of the mountains, the needle of the Harbour Centre Tower, one of the tallest buildings in the city, was rocking back and forth. The ring near its top with a rotating restaurant had tipped sideways. Immediately to its left, I saw Living Shangri-La start to lean forward. I gasped but was unable to take my eyes off it. I had barely grasped what the movement meant when there was a tremendous explosion and the tower crashed down onto the buildings below.

When I reached the hospital, the vestibule was already flooded and the elevators had stopped working. I ran up the stairs to the third floor and Erin's room. She was lying on her bed, staring at the ceiling with her eyes wide open. Her wrists were free of their bandages and showed no traces at all of her injuries.

"The Shangri-La Tower just collapsed! My parents lived there!" I shouted and then started to sob while kneeling beside her bed. "Erythia, I beg you! Make the waters recede! Save the city! Do it for me, do it just once!"

But there was no response. I stood up and embraced her body. It was cold. I looked at her face and was struck by its perfect alabaster beauty. There was no deformation at all. The hint of a smile was fixed on her lips, and her green eyes stared at the ceiling. *No, she can't be dead!* I thought. *She must have fainted or had one of her seizures, that disease she invented for herself! And what a beautiful, lovely face at last, at last!*

I heard the sound of hissing again: water was rushing into the room. I ran to the door and managed to close it and then went back to Erin's bed. But as I was about to lift her up and run with her to safety, wherever that might be, my hands touched a pile of rotted leaves. Horrified, I yanked them away. There was no body, just leaves. One of them stuck to my palm. On it were inscribed incomprehensible words: "... for now you see face to face."

Brushing the leaf from my hand, I ran out of the room.

# ~ THE HAND

*In my eyes there are no days. The shelves*
*stand very high, beyond the reach of my years ...*
*Who can keep me from dreaming that there was a time*
*when I deciphered wisdom*
*and lettered characters with a careful hand?*
  *— (From "The Keeper of the Books" by J. Borges)*

I'M LOOKING AT the photograph of Borges' hand. It is the hand of an old man, having absorbed time the way stone and cedar and earth absorb time. Its skin is fragile. Like an ancient papyrus it, too, holds the imprints of words.

There's nothing aristocratic about this hand. Joints bloated by arthritis, it looks too wide for the slender body of its owner. It has the roughness of a root. It's not photogenic, nor does it pose for the camera — it has always had other preoccupations.

Resting on a stone wall covered with hieroglyphs, it explores but doesn't reveal. The palm is probing the shapes of the carved inscriptions — perhaps a haiku — as if trying to read them, while itself eluding being read. Like the hidden side of the moon, the palm's deep channels are concealed from the observer. Does the Line of the Heart run its course through the mountain of Venus and Mars, crossing the paths of love, pain and loss? Or does it stop short, overtaken suddenly by the line of the Mind?

The back of the hand is traversed by wrinkles. They run vertically from the basis of the fingers in the North, all the way down to the South, stopping in the harbour of the wrist. Deep folds of skin resemble drooping sails that lost their breath on a windless day. Ulysses stands between them, his longing pointed in two opposite directions: towards his homeland and for the lands yet undiscovered. It is an old Ulysses on his last voyage: he has left Penelope for good to prowl the unknown. Together with a handful of men, like himself worn by age, Ulysses finally crosses the seas and reaches the mountain of Purgatory forbidden to mortals. At the foot of this mountain they all drown.

The hand is now immobile, its voyage cut short by a click. Yet, in its tired deepness, it holds all the memories of the three-faced time; all the pages it has written and the space it folded and unfolded and the voices of the dead it has resurrected, the voices softened and deepened by death.

But the time has come when writing is no more. The mystery of the world in which, Borges believed, there was nothing that was not mysterious, now eluded his earthly eyes. Only the hint of yellow was spared to him. Yellow, the colour of the sun; of gold; of harvested field; of sand; of maiden's hair.

The hand of a visionary became the hand of a blind man: oblivious to anything but touching.

Borges tells us an old Japanese legend of a haiku that once saved the world.

*In ancient times the Japanese Divinities got together to pronounce their judgement over Man. Seeing the evil of man, they decided to destroy him. Then one of the*

*Gods remembered that there was something fitting in
the space of seventeen syllables. He had intoned a
haiku. After that the world was saved.*

Borges also tells us about his friend Xul who had said to his
wife that he would not die so long as she was holding his
hand. At the end of the second day she had to leave him for
just one moment. When she returned, Xul was dead.

The eye of the camera holds Borges' hand forever.

# PART II

# BIRD'S MILK

THE SHINY RIVETS on the edge of the leather suitcase gleamed under the lamp through the irregular spaces between the crocheted snowflakes of the doily covering the lid. The suitcase belonged to the confined rooms of my childhood as solidly as did the old kitchen table, the rickety étagère, the bespectacled old television set with a glass filled with water in front of its screen.

With time, the suitcase itself became furniture: first a TV stand, then an end-table at my grandparents' bed sporting on top of a starched doily an assortment of disparate objects, most of which had nothing to do with going to bed or getting up: a darning mushroom, a sugar-bin, and a china ballerina on one gilded foot.

"When are they coming? We've run out of sugar," my grandmother said, inspecting the empty bowl on top of the suitcase. "You know Liza has a sweet tooth."

"Won't hurt them if they use sliced apples instead," my grandfather said. A severe diabetic, he had no use for sugar and was convinced that his own strange tea drinking ritual would suit everybody just fine.

My grandparents would fall into prolonged silences interrupted only by the sound of a spoon rattling in a glass. My grandfather never drank tea out of cups but preferred a glass in a simple metal holder. Why he needed to stir slices of apple into his tea was a mystery to me: perhaps he liked to watch them whirl in the water, a little chasing game, he created; or perhaps, the chime of the spoon reminded him of the morning tea trays rattling glass on metal, on the long-distance trains when he was the chief railways inspector before the war.

The Levins were an elderly couple, always dressed in dark baggy coats. They would remove the galoshes from their felt boots and put them side by side — one pair small, another big — in the hallway, leaving two muddy puddles of melting snow on a thread-bare mat. The knock of their knuckles on my grandparents' door was purely symbolic: hardly a sound emerged. They were strangely quiet, these two guests. Sitting, they never changed their postures, and no chairs ever cracked under their weightlessness. Auntie Liza, with her prominent Jewish nose and heavy half-closed eyelids, resembled a small tired bird. It was impossible to imagine this woman ever being young or vivacious. Her husband, whom everybody, including his wife, called simply Levin, was tall and emaciated, with a mass of black hair that sharply contrasted with his crumpled face and pale lifeless lips. Levin rarely spoke, but when he did it was always the same monotonous note: "Joseph, if Vladimir goes to Minsk to get the papers, I'll wait in Moscow till he returns. You know it's my last chance."

"Where are you going to stay in the meantime?" my grandfather said.

"Why do you ask?" my grandmother said, grumbling. "As if they had a place to go ..." She looked hesitatingly around the room. "They could stay with us while waiting."

"Oh no, we won't inconvenience you," Aunt Liza, eyes downcast, said. "Levin has already got six orders from Ryazan. I'm sure there will be more, once we arrive and people hear about us. We were planning to leave tomorrow."

"Going without a passport? Ryazan is not a small place."

"I'm telling Levin, small villages are much better: out of sight, out of mind," Aunt Liza said without lifting her eyes. "But he won't listen to me."

"I'll take a risk, it's only three or four days, right? I'll make a good buck and pay Gromov for the passport."

"I wouldn't count on three days," my grandfather said while stirring his tea again. "It can be a week, two weeks, you never know. As for Vladimir ... you know my son. He doesn't always knock at the right door. I can't go ... people might recognize me ..."

"You? Well, that's out the question, Joseph, that's understood." Levin sighed. "But I don't want to put your son at risk either, not on my account. Though, I think it's safe. I was told by people I trust."

"You think so? What if it's a trap?"

"Look," said Levin. "Gromov knows the guy. He is Kazimir's relative, completely reliable."

"And where is Kazimir?" my grandfather asked, moving his glass away and putting both hands on the table. "You tell me, where is Kazimir?" He pointed to the suitcase in the corner. "This has been waiting for him for eight years."

"He will return," Levin said quietly. "You'll see. But you should have opened the suitcase and looked inside."

"If he returns, why would I open it? It's your brother's. You should take it."

"Where would I put it, Joseph? I have no home. Besides, it was entrusted to you. You should keep it till he returns."

My grandfather bent towards Levin: "He will not return. Don't fool yourself."

There was silence.

"There is a difference between fooling oneself and having hope," Levin said finally. "Without hope, where would I be now, Joseph?"

Again there was a pause. My grandmother brought out two more glasses in metal sleeves. She put a plain saucer with a small heap of round cracknels on the table. The tea she poured into both glasses was pale. Auntie Liza took one cracknel, soaked it into her tea, and bit on it with her few remaining front teeth. Levin held the glass without drinking, warming his transparent fingers with its heat. I was afraid to look at his mutilated right hand. His thumb and an index were missing.

It was only recently that the Levins found each other after 12 years of labour camps. In 1936, Levin, a biologist and the Director of a Research Institute, had confessed that he was a paid Trotskyite agent, a tool of the German-Japanese-American intelligence services assigned to drown the conquests of the Socialist Revolution in its own blood by growing a deadly virus in his Institute's lab. The virus killed 1470 horses, 3304 pigs, and 1900 cows in one district alone. His wife Liza confessed that, as her husband's accomplice, she dreamt up a "smoke tax" and personally collected it from all the peasants who had chimneys in the nearby villages to finance the subversive activities of her man.

Miraculously, the Levins had survived the camps: Levin felling trees in Solovki, 150 km off the Arctic Circle, and Liza in Siberia, half a continent across, near Turukhansk. Liza turned out to be a fine calligrapher and painter, and instead of building the Salekhard railway road — the "Death Road" as women in the camp nicknamed it — she painted murals for the "Red Corners," the official rooms outfitted with Lenin's busts and red banners. She also designed *Lightnings,* Gulag propaganda bulletins.

The two beat the odds again when they reunited — only to discover that the miracle of their reunion was marred: their son Leonid was nowhere to be found.

The day after his parents' arrest, men in civilian clothes took the five-year-old into an orphanage, where both his first and last name were changed. That was, no doubt, the manifestation of justice but also mercy, aimed at removing the shameful stains from the boy's biography by a simple act of severing any links with his parents, the accursed enemies of people. As Comrade Stalin had pointed out, no sons should be held responsible for the crimes of their fathers.

When all their efforts to find Leonid lead to nothing, Auntie Liza gently but firmly slipped into another world. She would tilt her bird's head to one side listening intently to God's divine lisp which she alone could discern. Aunt Liza never questioned God's benevolent intercession into her family's affairs: it was only a question of time, and of all people, Liza knew everything there was to know about time.

She also knew that God, in his infinite mercy, after munching some sounds in his ancient mouth, would dictate to her the initial letter, then the first and the second syllables of her child's assumed name, and finally, reveal all: first, patronymic, and the last name. None of it would be as sweet as the boy's real name: "Leonid Lvovich Levin." No, it would be a rough name, in itself a guarantor of survival of its bearer. Something like Boris Petrovich Stepin, or Petr Andreevich Drozdov, a name with sharp corners, more palatable in this world.

The moment would always come when Aunt Liza would quietly move her tea glass to the side, get a pencil stub and scrap of paper out of her old purse and make some quick notes in her elegant tiny writing. She anticipated the revelation of the secret with humility, that moment when she'd see the name appear on paper, the right one, and then fill her mouth with its new sounds, savour them, sing them quietly to herself, and finally carry them to the Central Information Bureau in her open palm, so that in a month, at most two or three, her little boy now grown up, still pale and scraggy but all right, would run into her arms out of piles of stamped and signed papers, the jumble of metal orphanage beds, lice-infested shaven heads, steel mugs and plates, railway stations guarded with dogs, forlorn locomotive hoots, abandoned construction sites, entangled wire, fallen electrical poles, frozen dirt, coal piles soiling virgin snow across the immeasurable indifferent white expanses of her land: "Mama, mamoshka, I'm here! I knew you would find me!"

"Sonia," my grandfather said, turning to me. "Go out and play. Go."

"Leave her alone," my grandmother said, closing the curtains. "Where will the child go? It's late."

"Come, come over here, then," my grandfather said. "What's today, Sonia, Monday? Check if the candies in my pocket grew all right. Give me your hand, right there, see? Now, which one you want? A Bear of the North or a Golden Rooster?"

"Bird's Milk," I said firmly. "I want Bird's Milk."

"No, that one doesn't grow on Mondays ..."

"Tuesdays, then?"

"I'm afraid not."

"How about Thursdays?"

"Well ... maybe. But Friday is more likely."

"Ah, you're cheating! Candies don't grow in the pockets. You buy them in the store."

"Who told you that? Have you ever seen any candies in the store?"

My grandfather was right. In 1948, there were no candies or apples to be bought, but as a former secretary of the regional party committee and a War Hero, he was entitled to a special food ration from the party's internal food distribution centre.

"Look," my grandfather said, "here is Bear of the North. Did you see it yesterday? No. So what happened overnight? It just grew ..." He pointed to his pocket again.

"I want Bird's Milk."

"But birds don't make milk, didn't you know?"

"Yes, they do. If you say candies grow in your pocket, then birds make milk too. And besides, I just had Bird's Milk yesterday. They are the best candies in the world!"

"Where did you get them?" Aunt Liza asked, suddenly awakening from her trance. She scooped the scraps of paper into her purse and gazed into my face.

"Tanya gave me," I said.

"Tanya ... who is Tanya? And where did Tanya get them from?" Aunt Liza's eyes seemed alight. "Up North that's what I craved for most, candies ..."

"Her father brings Bird's Milk from the 'organs,'" I said quietly, looking away.

Tanya's father was a prosecutor at Lubyanka. He called Lubyanka the "organs."

I felt guilty having tasted Bird's Milk while Aunt Liza had not and now wanted it as badly as only a little girl would.

"Aren't there lots and lots of candies, up North, Aunt Liza?" I asked. "Don't bears from the North live there?"

"No, my sweetheart, there were no candies at all. But what does Bird's Milk taste like, tell me?"

"Like ... like ... like chocolate waffles."

"Chocolate waffles ..." Aunt Liza mumbled and looked away. She turned back to me. "If Tanya ever gives you another candy, will you treat me to one?"

I felt sorry for Aunt Liza. He eyelids looked so heavy. I wanted to hold them open with my fingers. "When I grow up and earn a lot of money, I'll buy you a whole box of Bird's Milk!" I said.

"Joseph, let's open Kazimir's suitcase, and see what's inside," Levin said. "Maybe there are some papers, or some clothing Vladimir can use if he goes to Minsk. Wouldn't it be good if ..."

"Now go and play with your dolls, Sonia," my grandfather said.

"I don't want dolls," I said. "I want to see what's in the suitcase."

Without the doily, the suitcase looked naked, ominous as if a stranger had suddenly appeared in the room. It wasn't new. Cuts and scars traced diagonals across the black leather. My grandfather pressed hard on the metal buttons. The two clasps popped up. The women held their breath. The lid fell open. The papers inside were faded, a disappearing print in an unfamiliar script. My grandfather removed the newspaper. I could smell tobacco and a faint odour of eau-de-cologne. My grandmother stared at the clothes: canvas tennis shoes, striped, foreign-looking shirts, a belt with a bright-golden buckle, turtleneck sweaters the likes of which none of us had ever seen. But none of it seemed to interest my grandfather. He rummaged. He was looking for papers about the fate of his vanished friend Kazimir Levin.

There were none. Instead, from underneath the heap of clothes a piece of fabric emerged, a print, shimmering tiny pink and purple flowers on a pale-blue meadow. It was a woman's scarf that must have somehow lost its way on the road of war before finding its unlikely shelter. My grandfather stepped back. My grandmother tentatively stroked the scarf, then handed it to Aunt Liza who suddenly with a small whimpering pressed it to her face, then returned the scarf to the heap of alien clothing.

The scarf was only a prelude. My grandfather's excavation had unearthed from the bottom of the suitcase the photograph of a woman. She was beautiful, a face framed with thick black curls, exotic, not Russian. Her lips were parted slightly with a hint of mischief as if she was gazing at a marvel no one else saw. I wondered whether the girl owned the scarf.

"I didn't know he had a woman in Spain ..." my grandfather said, examining the picture.

"Kazimir's fiancée," Levin replied. "They met in 1939 in

Barcelona, shortly before it fell to the Nationalists. He was going to bring her to Moscow and marry her here."

My grandfather looked at Levin and said nothing. Then, in reverse order, he started putting clothing back in the suitcase: the photograph on the bottom, sweaters, shirts, tennis shoes, and finally, the newspaper. He locked the suitcase and carried it back to the bed.

"I hope Kazimir will return," he said without looking at any of us.

Kazimir was born in Lithuania. Together with his elder brother, Lev Levin, he came to Moscow to make the revolution. That's where the two brothers met my grandfather, then an aspiring Komsomol leader. The three friends became inseparable. But the revolution was soon over, replaced by the Civil War. These were exciting times. "All men are Brothers! Down with the Rotting Corpse of the Bourgeoisie! Labour will Rule the World!" You could feel the air crackling with euphoria. Kazimir was good with horses and with sabre in hand he galloped from the Western to the Eastern Fronts, cleansing capitalist filth from the world, protecting the oppressed, summarily executing the enemy, all in the name of comrade Lenin, the World Revolution and International Proletariat. But when the Civil War came to an end leaving in its wake the Heroic Collectivization, Heroic First Five-Year-Plan, Heroic Construction of the First Metropolitan in the world, Heroic Conquest of the Arctic, Heroic Stakhanovism Movement, Heroic Three-Months-on-the-Ice-Floe-from-Pacific-to-Antarctic-without-Food; Heroic Soviet Woman-the-Mother-of-ten, also the World's First Parachute Jumper, Kazimir yearned for another revolution. He found it in Spain's International Brigades. When the

Republic failed, he fled to Russia, stopping at my grandfather's. He was trying to arrange the papers to get his fiancée across the border. One sunny morning he went to the post-office to send her a telegram. Nobody saw him again.

"Now at least we know what's in the suitcase," Levin said. "You keep it, Joseph. Keep it."

"I will," my grandfather said. "But I won't send my son to Minsk, Levin. This is a frame-up, don't you see? You have a 'wolf's' passport, that's true. You can't live in Moscow, or in any other city, but at least you're alive ..."

"Alive! You call this a life?" my grandmother said, interrupting. "Nobody would even register them! They tried Tver, they tried Ryazan, they tried every damn pin on the map. No place would have them!"

"Sh-sh!" my grandfather said, putting his index to his lips.

"Don't you worry, Anna," Liza said. She seemed to be looking sideways, her gaze avoiding the others'. "People are kind. They give us everything we need: food, shelter, place to keep our equipment. Sometimes money too."

Only years later, when nobody sitting around that table in that remote, dimly lit room was alive, I found out what she meant.

After 12 years in the camps, denied residence and the right to work, the two of them once again found a way to hoodwink fate. For several years after the war they walked from village to village, magnifying passport-size photographs of the dead. The pattern was always the same: people met them with suspicion and saw them off with grateful farewells. In many villages after the war, the names of the dead outnumbered the living and the Levins never lacked for work. Levin learned that it was easier to look into the eyes of the dead on a piece of a photo paper, than into the eyes of their widows and mothers, as they opened the door to him.

He proved to be good at his new trade. The men on the tiny photographs he was given were stern, solemnly closed into themselves, with a generic, often vacant expression. But when he enlarged and retouched them, they became benevolent, soft, even mildly romantic. Under Levin's skilful hands, these slightly out-of-focus faces would come to peace with their destiny. Mounted on the wall, or placed on a chiffonier next to a small cluster of artificial flowers, they finally achieved immortality. A certain safety was theirs at last.

The Levins were doing so well that they even managed to put away some money, the investment in the illusive dream of freedom.

My grandfather was as good as his word: he kept his son from travelling to Minsk. It must have been the old man's sixth sense, his insider's knowledge of the manhunter's lore that saved my father's life. But it didn't save Levin's. He was arrested again, charged this time with poisoning the wells in a city he'd never visited. He died in a labour camp the year before Stalin's death.

What happened to his brother's suitcase? I never saw it again. I vaguely remember my grandfather wearing colourful turtle necks and gaudy short-sleeved shirts that looked strange on this taciturn and sombre man.

After Levin's arrest, Auntie Liza went into hiding. A moving target, she rode the freights, slept in the railway stations latrines, shipping containers, or abandoned sheds. The blind chance that had destroyed her son and husband at the end let Liza off the hook. When I saw her again in much milder, 'vegetarian' times she was toothless, all skin and bones, her hair gone completely white; more than ever she seemed to belong to the weightless feathered tribe, the only one that could go where it pleased in her homeland.

I visited her in her six square meter 'corner' in a communal apartment shared by eight other families. There was almost no furniture in her room. Aunt Liza sat at the window looking vacantly into the street. Since her husband's death, she had time on her hands: she wasn't scribbling names on scraps of paper any longer. God had forsaken this land — she now knew it.

In late May of 1964, Auntie Liza received a summons. As a victim of Stalin's 'purges' she was now entitled to her own apartment, a small studio with a separate kitchenette and a bathroom. Coincidentally, she was supposed to view it on her 65th birthday. To our surprise, Aunt Liza refused to even look at the new place, never mind move in.

It is then that my brother Sergey and I came up with a plan. We bought a bouquet of flowers, a biscuit cake, a box of chocolate and even champagne intending to invite all Liza's neighbours to her birthday party. But first, we wanted to talk her into getting into Sergey's new car for a 30-minute drive to her new apartment. How exciting! The first housing projects in 20 years since the war! Fresh air, sunshine! Young mothers with prams moving into the building!

"The second floor would be perfect, just perfect for you!" I kept saying. "The first is unsafe because of breaks-in; the third, too high without an elevator, but the second? It was really the luck of the draw!"

"You'll have your own bathroom, too!" my brother said, egging Aunt Liza on. "When was the last time you had your own tub with running water? Your own kitchen?" Aunt Liza raised her eyes to Sergey but said nothing. I started setting the table for the guests who would be there when we returned. Then I opened a box of chocolate and handed it over to Aunt Liza. "Have some," I said, "before we go ..."

She was hesitant and looked away. But finally her fingers took tentative aim at one accordion-pleated pink rosette and suddenly her face brightened up.

"Do you remember?" she said. "Right after the war, you were eight or nine then, and you promised when you grew up, you'd buy me a whole box of Bird's Milk? Is that what it is, Bird's Milk?"

"It is!" I laughed, hugging her.

"Come on, let's go, Aunt Liza," my brother said, impatiently. "We'll take chocolates with us. You can eat all you want on the way there ..."

The new apartment smelled of paint and thinner. The newspapers were scattered on the floor bordered by piles of plaster in the corners. We propped Aunt Liza on a stool, the only chair left by the construction workers in the middle of an empty room.

In the kitchen the pipes under the sink were sloppily connected. Water dripped on the floor. While Sergey was looking for a bucket, I looked out of the kitchen window. Construction leftovers littered the landscape, competing with tree stumps and mud puddles dotting the bare earth. But one bush of white lilac survived, overlooked by the bulldozers. It stood alone, intact, tall and in full bloom. I wanted to let the scent of lilac into the flat and tugged at the window: "Aunt Liza! Look!" The window was painted shut. Sergey found a knife, poked here and there. Just when the window seemed to yield we heard a thud and a weak cry. In the living room Aunt Liza lay on the floor next to the stool. Her hands clutched her chest and she gasped in whistling gulps.

There was no telephone in the apartment. Sergey ran outside to look for the public phone. I sat on the floor next to Aunt Liza helplessly watching her jerk her head from side to side. Beads of sweat collected on her forehead. She was still alive when they carried her through the narrow door and twisted the stretcher awkwardly.

It was in the ambulance that God, whom Liza believed had abandoned her forever, finally returned to her side, gently took her by hand and led her into the golden glow of spring. She floated free on the fragrance of lilacs above her longed-for city, over the young girls in school uniform skirts and bare thighs playing hopscotch on the asphalt, over crowds still in winter coats queuing for food in great dark zigzag lines; over the street-cars cutting quick arpeggio on their celestial cords, smudging every turn with sheaves of fire. By the time the ambulance stopped in front of the Corinthian columns of the Sklifosovsky Hospital, Aunt Liza had already joined her husband and son. She joined them in that radiant, shimmering land that alone had given her a shelter and a permanent home, a land she would never again — never — need to escape.

# THE SQUALOR OF IRRESPONSIBILITY

## 1. LIP READING

INNA WAS A naïve young woman. She believed whatever people told her. When her husband whispered in her ear on their first conjugal night that the banging and gurgling coming from the radiator was only mice making u-turns in the pipes, her eyes grew wide.

"Really?"

He liked to feel the little parachute of her surprise drifting down past his stubble. "Hear that tip-tap-tip?" he had said as he nibbled on her ear. "That's the mice knocking their tails against the inside the pipes. Every fall the plumbers put them in one end to see if they'll come out the other. To check for blockages before turning on the hot water, you see."

When King Hammurabi, the founder and director of a residential school for the deaf and hearing impaired where Inna worked — a tyrant, intriguer and provocateur — told her that he was firing her because of her naïveté, for how could she possibly have followed his instructions so literally as to present him with such a transcript, she believed him without hesitation and burst into tears in front of his vastly entertained secretary.

"Here, mop up that deluge," Hammurabi said, taking the starched handkerchief from his breast pocket and holding it out to Inna between two expertly manicured fingers. And then he broke into a wide grin. "I'll spare you this time, young lady, but next time, watch out!"

Hammurabi, whose real name was Myrosyan, had founded his school for the deaf and hard of hearing after an event at Sheremetyevo International Airport. He had been a high-ranking career diplomat, possibly even a consul general or deputy ambassador, in some nice country, say England or France. But while boarding a plane to London or perhaps Paris one afternoon, he suddenly lost his hearing for no apparent reason. He returned from the airport and soon after founded his famous school. Of course, he had the right connections in high places to do that sort of thing. He was an Armenian and Armenians are handsome. They have soulful, almond eyes, aquiline noses, and dark, curly hair to die for. They carry themselves through the frost-bitten streets of Moscow with the proud bearing of an ancient, indomitable race. When a Myrosyan walks by, you notice. And now this pedigreed man was standing on the tarmac stone deaf, with the shards of his brilliant career scattered around him. *If I can learn to read lips, they'll let me stay*, he decided in the limousine on his way back home.

It's possible that, when they didn't let him stay, Myrosyan's skin burned. For the first time in his life he could see what it was like to be a pariah. And he didn't care for the insight. There must have been a moment when his proud soul shuddered in confusion, fear, misery, and self-pity. And a moment, too, when he was moved with compassion for those who had been deaf from birth and living out their lives apart from others — innocents who had been unjustly banished by the hearing world. Or maybe there wasn't any such a moment. Maybe none of that entered Myrosyan's mind at all. Maybe he just clenched his fists in his pockets and murmured to himself: "I'll show them! I'll prove to these scoundrels that you can be both deaf and intelligent. Every time one of my kids is accepted at a good university, I'll let them know about it."

Yet whatever it was that motivated Myrosyan in the end, in little more than a year, he had created his superbly equipped residential school, with innovative teaching based on a single principle: sign language was prohibited, with lip reading enforced as the only path, however difficult, to a happy, productive future. And year after year, the kids under his tutelage did indeed get into the best universities, find good jobs, and marry beautiful people. Soon Myrosyan's school was the pride of the country. Many a foreigner came to learn the secret of his success, fame chasing him like his shadow.

It was not for nothing that Myrosyan had been nicknamed Hammurabi after the ancient Babylonian king and lawgiver. The only difference between them was that the real king had a spade-shaped beard with curls like rows of tiny sheep running down his chest, while Myrosyan had only a moustache with erect waxed tips. Actually, there was yet another, more significant, difference. Unlike Hammurabi, who a legend says once ordered his youngest son burned alive for some minor offense, Myrosyan never so much as laid a finger on any of his charges. He actually loved his kids. He truly cared about them.

Other than that, both Hammurabis prized order, predictability, and punctuality. Myrosyan-Hammurabi personally made sure that the chef didn't pilfer bags of food from the kitchen, that the milk really was milk and not 50-percent added water, and that the sour cream really was sour cream and not 50-percent flour. Picture our director in his custom Dior suit and heavy gold cuff links sampling each pot with a ladle. Imagine him too in the dormitory, his suspicious fingers investigating every ledge, every headboard for dust. Whoever allowed even the smallest mote to sunbathe on a windowsill was in for it.

Hammurabi presided over the school from his distinguished oak-panelled office and a fancy swivel desk chair brought from Switzerland on a special diplomatic flight — the only chair of its particular kind to be found anywhere in our land of abundance. On it he slowly rotated in the direction of any deficient staff member called before him, twisting first the left tip of his moustache, then the right one.

"Well, Miss or Mr. So-and-So, it would appear that work is your life's greatest catastrophe. It would appear that you and honest labour do not share the same bed, if you'll excuse the intimate metaphor. Today you've given me unambiguous evidence of your desire to be released from that terrible burden. I have no choice but to respect your wish. You are free as wind. As of today."

At which point there were two options: panic or remain placidly calm. If you knew the ways of man and had managed to grasp the sinister involutions of Hammurabi's mind, you swallowed your pride and remained silent. He would then swivel his armchair 97 degrees, just enough for you to catch a glimpse of his noble profile, and observe in his velvety baritone, which he, unlike many deaf people, never raised above normal volume.

"I didn't invite you to Myrosyan's school to twiddle your thumbs, did I?" (He always referred to himself in the third person.)

"Forgive me, Comrade Director," you would squeak.

"I forgive you? For what? You didn't wrong me. You wronged our children. You endangered the health and the well-being of the future generation. It's they whose forgiveness you should be asking for, not mine."

"I'm not a vicious person! I'll prove it with renewed diligence. I'll correct my mistakes. Only please, sir, give me another chance!"

Hold on right there! That's far too wordy. You're bending your neck much too low. Hammurabi will start to wonder if your contrition is sincere or if you are just playing with him.

He would shoot a piercing glance at you and then swivel his chair another 83 degrees. The audience was over. Contrary to what many believed, he couldn't read your lips when his back was turned.

"My secretary will get the forms ready. You will receive your severance pay by five o'clock today. I want to be sure that the enjoyment of your freedom is not delayed for an hour."

Did you need to be brain surgeon with cordon-bleu culinary skills to know that your goose was cooked? Did you need to be a certified public accountant to appreciate that the double salary Hammurabi bestowed upon his courtiers was to be found in no other school in Moscow?

Of course, getting the boot like that was a worst case scenario. So, if you were a person of dignity and will, what kept you from working for a different outcome? You would say you're sorry, but you would stand proud and tall. There were worse disasters in life than a dusty windowsill. You would tell him that you fought in two wars, and will fight in a third if your country should call on you.

If Hammurabi then shook his head in dismay and said: "Look at the squalor all around you, the squalor of irresponsibility! Look at the cruel times we live in!", it meant there was a chance! That he was throwing you a lifeline, slender and frayed though it might be. Grab hold of it! Pull yourself from the muddy water of your errors back onto to the dry shore of your pitiful life as fast as you can. It could be your last chance!

## 2. TEN PACES

Inna had known nothing about Myrosyan-Hammurabi when her phone rang. It was her friend Olga pleading for help the next morning at 8:30 sharp. Olga's Hedgehog (as she called her three-year-old son) had a cold again, and if she missed work one more time, that could be the end for her. Inna pictured her friend slashing her throat with the blade of her hand at the other end of the line and said: "Sure. What do you want me to teach?"

"Pushkin. Before his duel and after it."

As a recent graduate of a teacher training college, Inna

had been scraping by with work, substituting here and there but finding nothing permanent. "Do whatever you like with Pushkin," Olga had told her, "only make sure that the director, Myrosyan, doesn't find out. If he does, it will be curtains for me."

Olga hung up. But no sooner had Inna run to the kitchen to rescue her burning potatoes than the phone rang again. "Listen, there's one more thing. Don't shout! The kids won't hear you anyway. They only read lips. And make sure you don't write on the blackboard and talk at the same time with your back to them. Okay?"

---

"During his brief life," Inna declared, facing grade eight at exactly 8:30 the next morning, "Pushkin challenged men to duel 22 times. The 23rd time was fatal. I mean Pushkin was killed. At the age of 37. So who had dared to raise his hand against our great poet? It was d'Anthès, a blond French playboy. By the way, Pushkin had always been afraid of blond men, superstition on his part. But that's beside the point. So d'Anthès came to St. Petersburg in search of a fortune. And wiggled his way into high society, where he met Pushkin's wife at a ball and flirted with her shamelessly. Needless to say, his behaviour was an insult to Pushkin. He challenged that good-for-nothing French fop to a duel."

Inna paused for a moment to catch her breath.

"Pushkin's wife, Natalie, was very beautiful. 'The first beauty of Russia married to the first poet of Russia,' as people used to say. D'Anthès was an unprincipled rascal, upstart, and coward, and he got cold feet!"

Inna's voice trailed off. She looked around the class-room. Twenty pairs of eyes were fixed on her face in total silence.

"So," she said, after taking another deep breath, "to save his skin, this coward, I mean, d'Anthès, married Nat-alie's sister. If d'Anthès was going to become a relative, he reasoned, Pushkin would have to call off the duel. But none of that stopped the wicked and corrupt d'Anthès from con-tinuing his ways! His marriage to Natalie's sister was just a trick! It made access to Natalie even easier. And D'Anthès kept wooing her and making fun of Pushkin. As you all know, Pushkin was a genius and the court hated him. Tal-ented and brilliant people are often envied. So the court was gleefully watching the intrigue and circulating vicious rumours to pour oil on the fire. Pushkin received libellous ... I mean really bad, mocking letters calling him a cuckold. Now Pushkin had to fight for his honour. He would have to challenge d'Anthès once again!"

"What's a cuckold?" a timid voice asked from the back row.

"A cuckold? Well ... Well, when a husband didn't know that his wife was unfaithful to him and nasty people want to make fun of him in the old days, that's what they called him. Any other questions? No? Let's continue then. Accord-ing to the conditions of the duel, the distance between Pushkin and d'Anthès was to be only ten paces. For all in-tents and purposes, the result would be murder."

A girl in the first row raised her hand: "How many me-ters are ten paces?"

Inna hesitated. "I'm not really sure, but it's very close."

"Five or six meters," a boy by the window said.

"Come on, for sure it's less," another boy sitting near him said, smirking.

"Why don't we all get up and count off ten paces? That way we'll know," Inna cheerfully suggested.

The class just stared at her. The school had never allowed such a lapse in discipline. But this teacher was new and young! Barely older than her class. The girl who had asked the first question nudged a short freckled boy sitting next to her. He jumped up and stood in the aisle between the desks, looking a little lost. But almost immediately, the other students were on their feet dashing around, waving their arms, signing to each other in excitement.

It was at that very moment that the door opened and Myrosyan walked in.

The kids all froze and then hurried back to their seats.

"Where's your teacher?" His voice was gentle, almost caressing.

There was no reply as he strode to an empty chair in the back of the room.

Inna returned to her desk in front and stood facing the director. "We were trying to ... to understand the conditions of Pushkin's duel ... and the distance is important."

"Crucial, I would say," Hammurabi said with a gently mocking glint in his eyes. "Well, why did you stop? Keep going."

"The only reason we're going into these details," Inna said after finding her voice again, "is that they led to the greatest tragedy in the history of Russian literature. To the death of our beloved poet. The 'sun of our poetry has fallen into the abyss,' one of his friends wrote in his obituary."

A bumble bee flew in through the open window. Inna

seemed to be the only one in the classroom who noticed. All the kids' eyes were fixed on her.

"We should remember," she said, "that duels were illegal. Participants were severely punished, sometimes even sentenced to death. But Pushkin's personal honour was more important to him than his own life. You can't live with humiliation. But there was no disgrace in dying. That's what our poet thought. And you know why he didn't complain about the unfair conditions of the duel? Because he despised his enemies! Negotiating with them would have shown them respect, and he refused to do that." Inna sighed in relief as if she had finally been able to put down a heavy bucket of water.

"Wasn't that irresponsible?" the same girl in the first row asked, raising her hand. "Why didn't Pushkin think of his motherland, that if he got killed, his country would lose its greatest son! Why didn't he realize that? I think he acted selfishly!"

Inna glanced at Myrosyan. His face expressed detached curiosity.

"Well," she said, "It's not like that in real life ... Pushkin wasn't a ... How shall I put it? He wasn't a monument. The way we see him in our squares today. For himself he was a living person, just like you and me. In his mind, the fact that he wrote beautiful poetry didn't excuse him, I mean, it didn't release him from the principles of honour accepted in his society." She paused again. "Perhaps, if he'd been a coward, he wouldn't have been a great poet."

After the class was over, Myrosyan patted the last child to leave on the head and then quietly shut the door behind him. Then he turned to Inna with an intent gaze. A practiced Hammurabi gaze.

"I'm very honoured, Madame, to meet someone who knows exactly what was going on in Pushkin's mind! A great privilege, indeed!"

Supporting himself with the heels of his hands on the desk, he leaned toward Inna.

"Who are you, young lady, and what are you doing in my school?"

"I'm Inna. Inna Borisovna Tesemkina. But it was a misunderstanding. I never said that I knew ... that I knew what was going on in Pushkin's mind."

"On the contrary, Comrade Tesemkina! That's exactly what you said. That art didn't relieve the poet from the duty of either murder or suicide, which is ultimately what a duel was. You had to commit either one or the other."

"I meant that the duel was unavoidable according to ... the rules of that society."

"If you were Pushkin, Inna Borisovna, would you, or rather should you, challenge somebody like d'Anthès to a duel? Knowing you have all those unfinished manuscripts sitting on your desk, not to mention a whole pile of new ideas?"

"No, I wouldn't. I mean I shouldn't."

"Are you sure?"

"Yes. I mean, no."

"Oh, that's too bad, Inna Borisovna."

Hammurabi stepped back. "That betrays a certain lack of principle on your part, not to say cowardice. If I were you, or rather Pushkin, I certainly would have challenged him.

Though of course, there wouldn't have been any duel in the first place, if Natalie had rebuffed the Frenchman's advances. But she didn't. I think they flattered her vanity. When d'Anthès married her sister, she was jealous."

"But Pushkin firmly believed in his wife's innocence!"

"How can you be so naïve, Inna Borisovna? What has that got to do with anything? Do you know what Prince Vyazemsky said? 'I avert my eyes from the sordidness of Pushkin's home.'"

Hammurabi went around to the other side of the desk.

"But you never answered my question, Inna Borisovna. How is it that I find you here in my school first thing in the morning talking about Pushkin?"

"I'm substituting for Olga Turina," Inna said, quavering.

"Why wasn't I informed?"

"It's not her fault, sir. I was hoping for an opportunity to teach at your famous school. She offered me a chance."

Hammurabi squeezed himself behind one of the student desks. He covered his eyes with fingers and rocked his head back and forth.

"You may be a good teacher, Comrade Tesemkina, but you are a bad liar. Nobody would offer you so much as a peek into one of Myrosyan's classrooms without Myrosyan's permission."

"I'm sorry ..." Inna said.

"As indeed you should be. I was going to hire you, but you spoiled everything."

"Hire me?"

"Yes!" Hammurabi got up, producing something like a groan. "I like people with spunk, so to speak. People who dare to think differently. People like you! Even though you did lie to me ... I'm sure you had noble intentions. To cover up for your friend, for example. Am I right?"

Inna lowered her eyes.

"Let all that be between your conscience and your friend," Hammurabi said. "But here's a question for you, Comrade Tesemkina. Are you sure your friend will repay you in the same currency? That's often a problem between people. Who pays with what?" Hammurabi came over to her. She could smell his expensive cologne.

"But tell me why Olga Ivanovna isn't here."

"Her son got sick."

"That happens, of course."

Inna sighed with relief.

"Are you married? Any kids? I suppose you're too young for that."

"Yes, I'm married, but no children."

"Planning on any?"

"Well, not right away."

"Hmm. That's a good sign. Prefers literature to procreation. By the way, did you know that the descendants of Pushkin and D'Anthès are related? A great irony of history. The murderer and the murdered."

"Of course. D'Anthès was married to Natalie's sister."

"And do you know what happened to d'Anthès after he killed our beloved poet?"

"No."

"I suppose that isn't part of teacher training curriculum. Well, I once met a descendant of d'Anthès, his great-great-granddaughter, in a café on the rue de Varenne in Paris. She told me about him. After the duel, he was expelled from Russia. Back in France he put together quite a career for himself and was even elected to the Senate. He died peacefully at 83, surrounded by his children and grandchildren. It seems unfair, doesn't it?"

"Yes, very."

"That's why in this country" — Hammurabi rapped his knuckles on the black desk top — "we defend fairness and the principles of justice. If evil can't always be punished, at least goodness can and should be rewarded. Would you like to come work at Myrosyan's school?"

"But ... but I don't have any training with special-needs children. I was just filling in ..."

Hammurabi waved his index finger back and forth in the air like a pendulum. "Remember this once and for all. My children do not have special needs. They have only one need, common to everybody: the need for love. They need teachers who will love them and love the subjects they teach. My intuition tells me you qualify." Myrosyan's mouth spread into a smile. His eyes, until then looking intently at Inna's face, moved down to her breasts and stopped there. Instinctively, Inna's fingers followed the direction of his gaze, and then struggled to repair the disaster around the third button on her white blouse, which had somehow come undone. She blushed to the very roots of her light hair. Noticing Hammurabi smile again, she blushed even more. "If I take you on, it will be on one condition. That you never violate the school's first principle!"

"What principle, Comrade Director?"

Myrosyan's hands moved in a rapid demonstration of sign language. Then he waved an admonitory finger at himself and slapped his wrist. "That isn't allowed here. No signing! Only articulate speech."

## 3. PAINTING WITH A DONKEY'S TAIL

And that's how it happened that Inna's life, purposeless before, expanded and took on meaning. Although on the surface not much had changed. There were the same lines for food, the same crowded, unheated buses, the same cooking and cleaning and washing for Vova, her husband, who had twice skipped sleeping at home and often turned up in the middle of the night. But none of that would derail Inna's life. It would now grow sinew and the strength it needed for selfless service in Hammurabi's great cause. Unpaid overtime, hours of decorating the literature classroom, staying after class with the students — none of it seemed a hardship.

Hammurabi came to trust Inna. After two years of devoted toil in the service of his educational establishment, she was invited for a chat to his oak-panelled office.

"How are you holding up, Inna Borisovna? So far so good?"

Inna nodded.

"Enjoying your work?"

Inna nodded again.

"Excellent! Not that I expected anything different from you! You're a very conscientious worker! Diligent, reliable ... Though sometimes scrupulous to a fault, ha-ha! But overall, you deserve some kind of a reward, don't you think?" He watched her closely. "Should I give you the honour of preparing a transcript, I asked myself. And I concluded that you would be the best candidate for the job by far."

"A transcript?"

"Yes, a transcript. The school has been assigned a very

special task." Hammurabi lifted his head and pointed toward the ceiling.

"It's not at all surprising, of course. We've earned the Party's trust through our hard work. In a word, they're going to show you some very important film footage. It needs to be lip read. Take the best kids from grade ten and let them do the job. The transcript should be on my desk no later than six tomorrow night."

⌁

The days had been getting longer and warmer. Even the most self-absorbed people completely indifferent to politics could feel the fresh currents in the air. At the Twentieth Party Congress, Nikita Khrushchev had acknowledged Stalin's blood-thirsty crimes, and the ice had not only started to melt. People were jubilant. They didn't know (and wouldn't have cared anyway) that that turning point in history had been partly precipitated by personal vengeance on Khrushchev's part for the humiliation he had endured for years behind the high fence of Stalin's dacha. Whenever Stalin got drunk, he would force Khrushchev to drink too and then dance Cossack-style, squatting and kicking his legs up. Khrushchev was short and fat and would topple over on his back. And Stalin would laugh. After his tormentor's death, Khrushchev officially unmasked Stalin's "cult of personality." It was a daring move that struck artistic people more intoxicatingly than any wine. Writers began to write, painters to paint, composers to compose, and filmmakers to spin their yarns with renewed energy. On the crest of that wave somebody had the idea of inviting

Nikita Sergeyevich to the first exhibition of Soviet avant-garde art. Which — as it turned out — was no less a folly than the leader's own campaign to grow three-meter-tall corn all over Russia, even in Siberia, to compete with America. Khrushchev arrived to the exhibition and looked right and then left and then straight ahead. And then he pointed his finger. His grim retinue watched it go up and down like a broken railroad semaphore. "This is what? This is who? Where is her second eye? Are you all morphine addicts or pederasts or what? My grandson can paint better than this!"

And he summoned all those so-called painters and sculptors, and writers too, to the Palace of Congresses for a "cordial conversation." Like all events of that kind, the "conversation" was to be filmed. But when the sound man heard what the First Secretary of the Communist Party of the Soviet Union had to say, he turned off the microphone, since the way he said it was not for public ears. The decision created havoc. Snippets of the footage had to be included in the newsreel shown before every movie in every theatre of the vast country. You would see the Chairman pounding his fists but hear no words. Myrosyan got a special assignment from the Party to decipher the missing parts of Khrushchev's philippics. Inna instructed the five best students to lip read the Chairman very carefully and to write down every word he said.

"Inna Borisovna, there's this word I don't understand, something beginning with a 'f'," Petya, a winner of the Mathematics Olympics, reverently whispered in her ear, though nobody could hear them in the dark room.

"What is he saying?" Inna turned off her voice, trying to articulate clearly in the semi-darkness.

"He's saying: 'How can you paint like this? This is dog shit, not art! A donkey could paint better with his tail!'" Petya giggled. "And then there is ... this f-word. He's asking: are you real men or faggots that you paint like this?"

"Well," Inna covered her mouth to muffle the giggle, "you go ahead and write down exactly what you think his actual words are! What else have you got there?"

"He's saying: 'Ten years in prison, that's what faggots like you will get in our country! All of you, all of you! To the camps — to fell trees!'"

"Anything else?"

Petya spoke rapidly with surprising accuracy. "'You've sold your souls to the stinking capitalists! Good riddance! Go then! There's no room in our country for capitalist asslickers! The people doesn't need your art. Go, we'll give you free tickets as far as our borders!'"

In her office, next to Hammurabi's, Inna stared at the transcript on her desk the way one might stare at a tarantula, hoping it will eventually crawl away on its own. But the transcript wasn't about to crawl anywhere, and at ten to six she knocked on Hammurabi's door.

He leafed through the document, looked up at Inna, and then leafed through the document again.

"I always took you for an intelligent woman, Inna Borisovna. You don't actually suppose that I could hand this over to *them*, do you?" And he pointed at the ceiling, his handsome brows coming into a triangular.

"But they're Comrade Khrushchev's own words. Transcribed verbatim, sir."

"Wonderful! And if I tell you to jump from the 15th floor, will you do that verbatim too? Give you enough rope and you would hang yourself." He tapped the middle of his forehead with his finger. And he swivelled his chair 180 degrees.

For the next three weeks she walked through the school corridors as if they were mine fields. If Hammurabi had turned away from her every time their paths crossed, she would have considered it fair punishment. But he stared through her as if she were made of air. Which was much worse. At the end of the month she was on the point of nervous collapse. That's when he called her into his office. Greeting her with a smile.

"Do you like my chair?" he asked, getting up.

"Yes, of course ..." Inna said, not knowing how else to reply.

"Would you like to try it out? Go ahead, don't be afraid."

Inna sat down on the edge of the chair. Hammurabi gently placed his hands on her shoulders.

"Don't be afraid. Make yourself comfortable." He rotated the chair several degrees.

"How does that feel?"

"Very nice," Inna said, trying not to tremble.

"Here's the situation, Inna Borisovna. Krapivina has applied for maternity leave. Which will obviously be no surprise to anybody. What is a surprise, however, is that she expects to return to her current position as deputy director for curriculum. A strange delusion on her part. She may come back as a rank-and-file teacher — that's possible — but as my deputy? I'm sure you would be a much better choice. And don't tell me this time that you don't have the necessary qualifications or skills." He raised his eyebrows. "Shall I order another swivel chair for you?"

"Thank you, sir."

"Needless to say, I'm not going to reduce your teaching load. What would you be without our kids, right? But I won't burden you with additional administrative duties. Instead, we'll try keep that sort of thing to a minimum. To begin with, I want you to focus on teacher evaluations. Try to sit in on every class a couple of times a week. And then tell me what you observe. Just drop by — no formalities. All right?"

"Yes, sir."

"By the way," Hammurabi said, already opening the door for her, "pay special attention to Turkina. I have very little faith in her." He grimaced. "Sometimes I get the impression that she doesn't care. How is that possible? But you never know with people, you just never know."

## 4. SUBJUNCTIVE MOOD ONE AND SUBJUNCTIVE MOOD TWO

Turkina, a buxom bottle-blond who preferred provocatively short skirts and, whatever the ensemble of the day, a cunning pink scarf, taught English, the director's favourite subject. Whether the posh inflections of Oxford had once signified better times and places to him, or he believed that the road to happiness might be paved with the cobblestones of English grammar, Hammurabi required that all his charges begin study of the language in grade two. Though they could by grade seven produce a semblance of the foreign speech they had never heard, the emphasis was not on oral communication, for which Hammurabi appreciated there could rarely be any call. Rather, his charges would learn to read and write the language, so that as cutting-edge scientists (his vision for them) they could read technical articles in English with perfect ease.

Inna herself had but a nodding acquaintance with Hammurabi's beloved language, but she could still tell at once that Turkina wasn't making much of an effort.

The first time Inna visited her class, the topic was something that Turkina called Subjunctive Mood One and Subjunctive Mood Two.

"'If your parents *earned* a thousand rubles a month, how much of it w*ould they give* to the people of Cuba, the shining island of freedom?' That's Subjunctive Mood One," Turkina explained after writing the sentence on the blackboard.

Her gaze then fell on at a skinny boy chewing on the end of his pen as he stared out the window. She waved at him to get his attention, and then after he had turned toward her and could read her lips, she said: "Proshin, give me a sentence using Subjunctive Mood One."

The boy slowly rubbed his chin and then offered: "My parents work in a factory. They earn a hundred rubles a month. If they will earn a little more, they will be able to buy me winter boots."

"If they *earned*, and not *will earn*. And *would be able*, and not *will be able*," Turkina said.

"But my parents won't earn a thousand rubles in the future. They aren't some kind of bourgeoisie," the boy replied. "Besides, if it's all in the future, how come I need to use the past tense?"

Exasperated, Turkina instinctively raised her voice. "I've already explained that! You should have been paying attention instead of counting the crows in the yard. You have to *pretend* that it's possible in the future. Use your imagination. In Subjunctive Mood One, you imagine the future by using the past tense. But on the other hand, if there isn't the slightest chance of their earning a thousand rubles, then you use Subjunctive Mood Two instead. Like this." And on the blackboard she wrote: "*Had my parents earned* a thousand rubles last year, they *would have given* five hundred to the children of Cuba or Angola."

"Had my parents earned a thousand rubles," repeated Proshin slowly, carefully enunciating each word, "my parents will buy shoes to me and winter coat to Masha, my sister."

The students sitting near him who could see his face and read his lips laughed. Before turning to the blackboard again, Turkina said: "That will do! We'll now have a quiz on Subjunctive Mood One and Subjunctive Mood Two." And she quickly covered the blackboard with 20 sentences to be translated into English.

"I don't understand," Proshin said in a characteristic monotone. "You didn't give us any warning."

Inna had to pinch herself to believe what happened next. After the class had settled down to write, Turkina took a bottle of bright-red nail polish from her cosmetics bag, and, starting with her left pinkie, applied loving strokes to each of her fingernails.

After finishing her left hand, Turkina blew on it and waved it in the air. When she moved on to her right hand, Inna couldn't take it anymore. She rushed out of the classroom, ran to the teachers' lavatory, and splashed cold water on her burning face. There was no doubt that Turkina had done it on purpose to flout Inna's new authority, to humiliate her. "But why?" Inna wondered in bewilderment. "What did I ever do to her? She's married to a general, and I'm married to ... a man who sees other women. I'm younger than she is. Maybe she resents it."

That night Inna didn't sleep a wink. She listened to her husband's breathing and stared at the ceiling as if the answers to all the questions tormenting her were written on its rough plaster surface. To report the nail-polish incident would mean Turkina's immediate termination. Not to report it would be to collude in her wrongdoing.

When the first birds announced the dawn, Inna got up intending to follow the voice of her conscience. In the oak-panelled gloom of Hammurabi's office, she reported Turkina's transgressions as if they were her own. "The whole lesson was conducted in Russian and the pedagogical method left much to be desired. And not only that, but ..."

"But what?" Hammurabi said, narrowing his eyes.

"Nothing, really. I just wanted to say that Turkina had a hard time explaining some aspects of grammar."

"You've already told me that. Concrete examples?"

Inna glanced through her notes.

"The difference between two types of subjunctive mood was vaguely presented."

"You don't say!" Hammurabi scoffed with a dismissive gesture.

"Unfortunately, it's true," Inna muttered in dismay.

"Hmm ... Just look what humanity is coming to, what degradation, what squalor, what irresponsibility! But let me ask you, Inna Borisovna, in complete confidentiality. What is the source of that indifference? Myrosyan is old, he won't notice, is that it? Or maybe Myrosyan is ignorant and no English word was ever uttered by him? Ha! Is that what they think? Tell me the truth!"

"How could you say that, sir?! Everybody knows that your were ... "

"Don't try to pull the wool over my eyes, comrade Tesemkina! I know what's on their minds. Myrosyan's a doddering old fool! Who cares that Churchill personally invited him to tea at his home? Or that the two of them spent hours discussing the fate of the world when the war was over? They don't give a damn about any of that, do they?"

Hammurabi sighed deeply and was silent for a moment.

"So, what does the woman think she's doing? This English instructor, so to speak."

"That's what I was wondering too," Inna said, now as pale as chalk.

Myrosyan swivelled in his chair.

"You wanted to tell me something else, didn't you?" he said with a mysterious smile.

Inna gazed pleadingly at him.

"Come on. Do your duty! Tell me!"

"Her fingernails." As soon as she said the word, it seemed strange, alien to the tongue.

"What about them?"

"Well, Turkina was ... Well, she was ... she was doing her nails in front of the class."

"No!" Myrosyan said with a moan. "Not her nails, Inna Borisovna, no!"

"But I saw it with my own eyes."

"How many students were in the class?"

"It was full. Twenty-two, I think."

"Twenty-two witnesses!" Hammurabi leaned back in his chair, his hand on his heart.

"And what measurements did you take? Did you immediately point out to your colleague the impropriety of her behaviour?"

"I didn't take any measurements."

"Don't fool with me! What I meant was *measures*. Did you take any *measures*?"

"I didn't take any measures. I wanted to tell you about it first. To get your advice."

"That was very prudent of you, Inna Borisovna," he said, drumming his fingers on his desk. "You couldn't have done better! Anything else?"

"No, that's all."

Hammurabi got up. "Thank you so much. I appreciate your insight!" And before she was even out of the room, he had sat down again and turned his chair 180 degrees away.

## 5. STOREROOM ANTICS

A week later, after the classes were over for the day, Inna noticed that she had run out of chalk. She ran downstairs to the storeroom next to the gymnasium where spare desks and chairs were piled up. There on its shelves in dusty cartons were chalk, pencils, and other school supplies. The door squeaked as she entered. The stifling smell of chalk and dust made it hard to breathe. In the semidarkness on the other side of the room (its single window near the ceiling provided little light), she glimpsed bobbed blond hair and a pink scarf in the embrace of a white shirt: Hammurabi's silver-gray head was buried in Turkina's unbuttoned blouse. Her kicked-off high heels lay on the floor next to her. Inna had never seen the director without his jacket before. The sight of his muscles working under his shirt struck her. Like a mole digging in his burrow, she thought with disgust.

Turkina moaned a few times and then suddenly stopped and looked in Inna's direction. Hammurabi dropped his arms. Inna hurried out of the room, slamming the door behind her.

That evening, after she got home, Inna spilled a cup of boiling-hot tea on her hand. The scald took a week to heal. The day after that accident she left her wallet behind at the bakery, and shortly after that, at the end of the term, she misplaced her grade-ten final essays. In the end, she just couldn't deal with it anymore and told Olga what she had seen in the storeroom.

Olga shot a startled glance at her friend.

"Have you just come from the moon? The whole school knows about Hammurabi and Turkina. It's been going on for over a year!"

"Isn't he married?"

"Sure he is. And so is Turkina, you silly goose."

"But how can that be?" Inna's lips quivered. She blinked helplessly. "What eats at me is that Hammurabi heard me."

"What do you mean?"

"When I opened the door to the storeroom, they were both startled."

"Hammurabi's deaf, silly."

"Anyway, I'm pretty sure Turkina saw me."

"So what if she did? She knows everybody knows. And is proud of it! She finally managed to push Nilina out! She wants everybody to know. Though some say that Myrosyan is screwing them both now."

"Nilina too?!"

"Inna, you never fail to surprise me. You're ... you're like a somnambulist. Walking around asleep."

Inna squeezed her temples with her fingers.

"Tell me one thing, then. Why did he sic me on her? 'Inna Borisovna, please pay special attention to Turkina. I have very little faith in her. I need a confidential report.' Why would he do that?"

"You're asking me? Ask Hammurabi. He'll give you a much better answer than I ever could." Olga glanced around. There was nobody else in the hallway. She leaned closer to Inna's ear. "He's a degenerate and a clown and enjoys manipulating people. It's his favourite pastime."


## 6. A MATTER OF BELIEF

Inna thought of the days of the year as thin and thick. Summer days were thin: the thin, luminous trunks of birch trees; the thin, limpid voices of brooks in the woods; the thin stalks of grass in the meadows; girls playing hopscotch, their pale thin legs freed of wool stockings. Winter days, on the other hand, were thick and increased everything in size: the snow-laden fences, railings, window ledges, and trees; people bundled in many layers of clothing. The thick days were duller, more hollow somehow, and if misfortune struck on one of those days, its blow was muffled.

When on one of those thick days Inna found a letter lying on her desk, she didn't immediately pay it any heed, and then when she did, it didn't particularly affect her, at least at first. It was from Hammurabi. He was, in the customary way of such things, advising her to resign from her job voluntarily. She put the letter in her pocket and went home. Vova was out. She peeled and fried some potatoes for supper and then reread the letter. It was then that it hit her. She locked herself in the bathroom and sobbed. The next morning she went to school as usual. Sitting in her new swivel chair, she wrote a brief reply to the director.

> *Dear Comrade Myrosyan:*
> *I worked hard for you, honestly doing my duty.*
> *Nevertheless you're firing me for reasons unknown.*
> *Since the decision to terminate me is your own, I*
> *cannot submit an application to "voluntarily" end*
> *my employment.*
>
> > *Respectfully yours,*
> > *Tesemkina, I. B.*

"What am I supposed to do with this?" Hammurabi's secretary asked, waving Inna's reply in front of her. "You're giving him no alternative. If you refuse to do as he asks, he'll be forced to put in your employment record, 'terminated for lack of professional qualifications,' or some such thing. Do you realize what that means? Nobody will ever hire you!"

"Do whatever you like with it," Inna said. And then she walked out the front door of Myrosyan's school for good.

Two or three decades passed. Out for a walk one warm spring evening, Inna came upon an old man feeding a squirrel from a bench in nearby Sokolniki Park. Her hair had turned gray and her complexion was an unhealthy yellow, but the blue forget-me-nots of her eyes still gazed at the world with the same startled wonder. And the old man on the bench recognized her.

"Inna Borisovna? How nice to see you! You haven't changed a bit, not a bit," he said with the ingratiating smile of an old lady's man, an old flatterer.

"Mr. Myrosyan, is that really you?" Inna gasped as she came to a stop in front of the nearly bald, shabbily dressed figure.

"What? Am I so unrecognizable?"

"Yes, almost."

Myrosyan chuckled. "Time has no power over you, Inna Borisovna. No power over the wonderful simplicity of your heart. How many years have passed? Twenty-five, 30? But you've remained the same." He looked at her almost tenderly. Then he sighed.

"I buried my wife last week. Half a century of cloudless marriage. Not a single quarrel, not a single angry word between us. And now she's gone."

Holding out a handful of crushed walnuts to the squirrel, he patiently waited for it to overcome its fear and approach.

"And you, Inna Borisovna? You must have grown-up children by now."

"No children. I've been divorced for many years."

"That's too bad!" It wasn't clear what Myrosyan was referring to: her divorce or the absence of children or both. "On the other hand, you and I gave our hearts and souls to the next generation. They were our children. We did a good job. We can be proud of that. You know, I have no regrets in my life at all. Except for one, perhaps. That I let you go. You were one of my best teachers. I found very few as good as you."

Twitchily, hesitantly, the squirrel moved closer, at once fearful and attracted.

"Now that so much water has gone over the dam, I have to make a confession. There was one little problem with you, Inna Borisovna. You were extraordinarily naïve and gullible. Charming, even endearing, but in a way also dangerous."

The squirrel looked at them both with the gleaming dark beads of its eyes, waved its tail, and scampered off.

"Well, I have to go," Myrosyan said. And leaning heavily on his cane, he slowly got to his feet.

*He won't last long*, Inna thought without looking at him directly.

"I may never see you again, Inna Borisovna," Myrosyan said, as if he had heard her thought. "So let me ask you one question. Why didn't you fight back then? Why didn't you try to stop me from doing what I did?"

"I don't remember, Mr. Myrosyan. It was a long time ago," Inna said, lowering her eyes.

"You were too proud, eh? You wouldn't beg?" Myrosyan paused and looked up at the trees covered with pale-green buds and at the sky, its early evening blue especially deep and clear.

"Perhaps, like Pushkin, you believed that there was no disgrace in dying?"

Inna looked directly at Myrosyan for the first time.

"Why did you fire me, then, Comrade Director?"

"I simply wanted to see if you would remain true to your beliefs."

# A ROOM BETWEEN THE TWO GOGOLS

## 1

GOGOL WAS A melancholy man, as befits a great satirist. But genius though he was, he couldn't write sitting, standing, or lying on his back or his belly, as ordinary writers can. Inspiration only came to him in a carriage hurtling somewhere. Which may account for the famous apostrophe in *Dead Souls*: "Oh Russia, troika-bird! Where are you flying? Answer! But no answer came."

Gogol had a long nose and a predilection for mysticism. He hated dank, miasmic St. Petersburg, and spent years in sunny Italy, begging his friends for truthful accounts from home, vivid vignettes of domestic goings-on. But since none of his friends was a Gogol, their dispatches were useless to his nostalgia. Defeated, he returned to the hated city. He hoped his great art would heal life, but when he realized that it hadn't left so much as a dent in human misery, he stopped eating and died.

Two sunbeams of boulevards, resplendent with linden blossoms, radiate from Arbat Square in the very centre of

Moscow. At the end of one beam, a bronze Gogol stands tall, with straight hair nearly touching his mighty wrestler's shoulders and the inevitable pigeon perched on his head. "To Gogol, from the Soviet Government," the inscription on the pedestal reads.

At the end of the other beam, near a row of the eighteenth-century townhouses, a different Gogol sits stooped in a chair, his little head withdrawn into the collar of his cloak, which is too large for his emaciated body. He's cold and shivering, and looks like he's just let a bronze drop fall from the tip of his runny bronze nose and is embarrassed about it.

This is the Gogol who consorted with no mortal woman during his sad, brief life, the Gogol who burned the second part of his great novel in the townhouse behind his seat, where several decades before that the incandescent Natasha Rostova had danced at her first ball in *War and Peace.*

Stop, turn around, and retrace your steps along the second boulevard beam. In 15 minutes you'll come to the Kremlin and Red Square. South of the territory between the two Gogols is the famous Arbat district, where writers, artists, and anybody who mattered used to live.

Andrey and his girl moved into the heart of the Arbat, into a garret room in one of the yellow but now ramshackle townhouses hunched between the two Gogols.

You might think there couldn't be a better place in the whole city for a young couple to feather their love nest. But that isn't what Andrey's girl thought, a dreamy, languid, moody 18-year-old.

What Andrey felt about the room between the two Gogols remains a mystery even for the author who, occupying the next room to the right, was not averse — let's admit it

—to occasional eavesdropping. But Andrey's whole demeanour, the way, for example, he sauntered to the toilet and back, implied that a real man shouldn't give a damn about his surroundings, least of all a garret.

Who knows why the glimmer of a useless pebble in moonlight will send a tingle down your spine, whereas a room of your own in a communal apartment that instead of the usual 40 residents along its dreary hallway has only 14 will leave you indifferent?

The abiding mystery of the human heart!

Communal apartments, that shrewd contrivance of the Russian Revolution, have been so brilliantly and exhaustively described by so many gifted writers that you'd think Lenin and his confederates had brought them into existence just for the sake of Russian literature.

Your ordinary, garden-variety writer would have had to twist the plot's arm to arrange encounters among characters whose paths wouldn't have had the slightest chance of crossing in normal circumstances. But not your Soviet Writer! He didn't have to pull any such fantasy from his magician's hat. Life, dancing to its Leninist choreography, had brought all the characters together for him on a single, miniature stage, four square-meters per person, and —ready, set, go!—raised the curtain.

In the blue haze of the communal kitchen, machinists, violinists, construction workers, accountants, doctors, petty thieves, and KGB informers were brought together, quickly producing in the chafing of unshaved cheek and jowl a tumult of savage accusation and squabbling against a shabby background of zinc wash basins, boiling bed sheets, and seething kettles of borscht.

The sole bulb hanging from a braided cord in the hall-way throws pale shadows on the warren of scheming. The infernal poison of intrigue and blackmail seeps into the tiny rooms, each one further subdivided with cardboard: a nook for granny, a cranny for her daughter, a third, slightly larger space for her son, his wife, and their infant. The attic cavity is crammed with communal junk: dusty, yellowed stacks of newspaper, a jumbled heap of broken chairs, a rusty tricycle with a missing wheel, for nothing may be thrown away in the land of dialectical materialism that has almost managed to eliminate everything material.

The poetry of early morning washing! An erratic stream of water issues in turn from a spigot in the wall onto 14 pairs of impatiently waiting hands. The continuous gurgle of the solitary toilet, the urgent destination of all 14 people at six am when they all awake with the rest of their great nation to fulfil its daily round.

The night imparts to the falling snow a blue-green tint. The toiling residents have returned to their warren, their crannies, their lairs, their bedbug-infested dens. They take refuge in front of their televisions, the flickering images on their tiny screens magnified by water poured between double lens of convex glass.

A telephone rings on a rickety, scribbled over shelf in the hallway. Ears prick up behind each door. A woman with an apron tied over her robe and paper rollers in her hair opens her door a crack and then slips out.

The heavy black phone is, for her, a treasure trove. Cupping her hand over the mouthpiece, she whispers in mono-syllables, speaks in coded phrases, and chuckles seductive-ly. Take care! The rocky vessel of communal patience may capsize at any moment. As if by command, all the doors will be thrown open, heads will peer out, and fingers will reach for the phone, pulling it away from the woman. "Have you no shame? Making it out over the phone with your hick! Tying up our line! Get off or we'll lodge a complaint!"

Where else could you get comedy and drama tied up into farce for the same low price?

Alas, Andrey's girl was immune to all of those art genres. No sooner had she stepped into the room between the two Gogols and Andrey closed the door behind them than she got pregnant, the implacable truth of which declared itself in bouts of morning sickness and a morbid fear of cockroaches.

Cockroaches! At night their mighty hordes would storm the little table in the room. Turning on the light dispersed them only for a moment. Brazen, impudent, they would return in ranks again, resuming their search for food.

Imagining the rustling of their feelers, Andrey's girl was sure she could hear them talking to each other in menacing whispers as they lurked behind the floor moulding or between the furniture and wall, waiting for her to fall asleep. Closing her eyes, she could see them peeking into every crack of the broken cupboard by the door, then moving over to her bed and feeling her blanket and pillow with the long quivering antennae that extended from the gleaming shells of their bodies: dark brown, black, and sometimes a translucent red, with their insides showing through.

Tooth powder and brush in hand and as pale as the terry-cloth towel over her shoulder, the girl would join the morning line at the kitchen tap. In a daze, she would try to remember her neighbours' names. Olga, a single mother, lived in the same room with her 20-year-old son, Misha. Whenever one of her string of lovers visited, Misha would retreat behind the buffet and strum his guitar, drawing sad, broken sounds from it.

Vova, a young alcoholic who worked as a cop between binges, shared a room with his divorced wife and new girlfriend. Both hated Vova even more than they did each other. When the ex-wife's anger reached the boiling point, she would curse him in a special way: "May dicks grow on your grave instead of weeds!" With that imprecation, Vova would collapse like a punctured balloon and cover his head with his hands in fear. He came from a village where the women claimed prophetic powers.

The room at the very end of the hallway, the only room with a balcony, was occupied by an elderly widow, her daughter, crippled from polio, and an empty fishbowl with dry coral. By a caprice of fate, the widow was from the same region, perhaps even the same village, as Vova. Years of urban life had not touched her, and each spring she would secretly try to raise chickens among the clutter of her balcony. At the sound of their clucking, Vova would fly into a rage and threaten to beat the two "bumpkins," the two "yokels," and kick them black and blue out into the street to die a dog's death.

"I'll take care of them! I'll break that fucking cripple's legs," he would rant, while his two women grabbed him by his arms and pulled him back into their room. The next morning a plucked and headless sacrificial chicken would be placed on the table in Vova's room. The offering accepted, Vova and the women would share a feast and declare a truce.

The room to the left of the widow's belonged to two elderly women, Mina and Zina. In some ungraspable past, perhaps even before the war, they had been mother and daughter, but time had long since erased any difference in the grey sag of their faces.

In the long history of the floor's communal life, nobody had ever entered their room, which was guarded by two lap dogs not much bigger than rats and both incessant, ferocious yappers. Even while cooking in the kitchen, Mina-Zina would carry the dogs under their arms. The rest of us were sure that behind their closed door, they subjected the little beasts to feeble punishment with branches pilfered at night from the birch that filled the patch sky in our courtyard.

Andrey's girl contemplated the barren landscape of our world with sad almond eyes. Whether Mina-Zina didn't like eyes of that shape or merely envied the newcomer's youth, they couldn't bear the sight of her. If it was the second reason, then it may be fair to say that they were determined to help their enemy onto the fast track of aging.

One time they sneaked into the kitchen at night, held the dogs over the girl's lidless coffee pot, and let them pee in it.

Unable to hold down any food or drink in the morning, it wasn't the girl who sipped coffee in the morning. "What did you bring me? Just smell it!" Andrey chortled. Oh, my, she had had no idea, it wasn't her fault, but she wasn't ever going to leave her coffee pot on the kitchen table again.

Luckily for her, the Soviet government came up to her rescue: Soon after the incident, coffee disappeared from all the stores for the next two decades. But Mina-Zina, veterans of communal life, found a way to hoodwink even the Soviet economy.

It was after the girl had made some borscht, the only thing she knew how to do. Since there wasn't any place in their tiny room for it, she left the saucepan on the kitchen table again. That night, Mina-Zina added a large piece of brown soap to it. By morning the meat in the soup had acquired a nasty stink, leaving Andrey with no food. He called the girl stupid, a lame brain, for her carelessness.

Was it after that second episode that he stopped using the girl's name? Or had he avoided it even before that? She tried to catch him out, to make him use it. How else could he call her if he needed something? But all she noticed was that empty place, that void affixed to her being. It preceded her into the room before and remained, wrapping itself around her wherever she sat.

Frightened, she decided to retrace the steps of her life. She would be free again, an unladen vessel. She would harden her heart and not tell him what she was going to do to punish them both. But she was too weak to carry it through and too broken-hearted. She wept every night, reaching out to him with her tears.

"Stop sobbing for God's sake! Look, I'm not forcing you to do anything. If you really want it, go ahead." He moved away, so as not to touch her.

"But how? How?" she kept sobbing "We have no income and barely a place to live." She resigned to his aloofness by pulling her knees to her belly like a child, and all he could hear was her muted snivelling. "I'm afraid," she whimpered.

"If you still think we can have it, then go ahead."

"I'm not thinking anything."

"Well, don't be angry at me then. It takes two to tango, right?"

He reached for her, putting his arm under her hot dishevelled head.

"Sh-sh. Enough already. You're agreeing with me that it's not a good idea right now, a baby in our room ..."

"There is nothing wrong with the room. Yes, it's tiny, but the baby will be small too ... we can disinfect the cockroaches ... and by the time the baby grows up, who knows ... If we get on a waiting list now, in five or seven years ... we can get something, like the Chernovs did."

"Chernov's father is a big fish in the Union of Architects. But right now — right now — how am I going to solve The Hodge Problem with a baby in the same room, you tell me."

"What problem?"

"Oh, never mind."

"The problem of our life, you mean? It's unsolvable."


## 2


Auntie Shura and her husband, Uncle Petya, a cobbler, came from Old Believer stock. Old but trim and tidy, they smelled of cleanliness, as if somebody had washed them in a cool brook and rinsed each wrinkle separately. Auntie Shura liked the girl, perhaps for the same reason that Zina-Mina hated her — her youth, her innocence, her lost, brooding look.

Once, Auntie Shura invited the girl to their room. The bright, festive arrangement astonished her: the icons decorated with paper flowers, the neat little altars with their doilies, the incense and votive candles.

Sitting on a stool beside an altar, Petya was repairing a shoe. Shura kept her wisdom under a white kerchief tied beneath her chin with a double knot. Though usually taciturn in the evening, she liked to chat with the girl whenever they were in the kitchen by themselves. She would lift one of her feet up onto a bare wooden stool, revealing from under the wide fan of her skirt a surprisingly robust calf in a homespun wool stocking, and then lean over and say: "You, my girl, don't know how to cook! Your husband comes home and what have you got to show for your day? Take this" — indicating a plate containing sour cabbage with two meatballs resting on top — "My Petya loves it. I bet your man will too."

Scratching a bedbug bite on her forearm, the girl thanked her benefactor. She didn't want to say out loud what the old woman already knew anyway: that Andrey didn't need to come home because he had never left in the first place. He had dropped out of the math department at the university, then quit four jobs in succession, and now, finally free of all obligations, he would lie in bed for days at a time, enlarging an indent in the wall with his finger, waking the dormant bedbugs living behind the wallpaper.

Shura shook her head. "You were caught, my girl, caught just like a chicken in a plucker's clutches."

Somehow the old woman knew.

# 3

Andrey was a large man: six-foot-five, big-boned, broad-shouldered, with a massive, well-shaped head, a reddish crew cut, and a spattering of freckles on his muscular neck and shoulders and his forearms lightly covered with ginger hair. What spoiled the look were his narrow, off-kilter eyes, vaguely like those of an ostrich.

He must have fallen in love with his girl by accident. Actually, it hadn't really mattered to him whom he fell in love with, that not being something that a real man should worry about.

But the timing had been right. The girl was young and pretty, and her eyes changed colour: hazel-green in the morning and chestnut- brown at night.

The first time he saw her she was wearing a tight-fitting, hand-knitted wine-red dress, proof of her female domestic skill, he decided.

How could he have taken her for a homemaker on the flimsy evidence of a dress? It was a mirage, an illusion. The girl, as it turned out, was neither an able amateur seamstress nor even a knitter. The dress had been produced on a knitting machine by a classmate of hers in trade for her long copper-coloured braid.

No, she certainly couldn't knit the way Andrey's mother could, with turrets of coiled yarn guarding every corner of her apartment. Though a mix of contradictions, like most people, Andrey didn't lose any sleep over them. He took no interest in his hearth, so long as others looked after it for him.

Nor did he have that much use for his mother, either, even though he hoped that his girl would have the same knitting skill. His mother was adept at making her dreams come true, the sort of dreams her son regarded with silent disdain. The way she rubbed shoulders with film stars in elite clubs that would otherwise have been closed to her as a mere knitter and dressmaker. The way she could make dresses with patterns from the German fashion magazine *Burda*, sewing onto them labels from Dior, Yves St. Laurent, and Valentino before selling them to the wives of movie directors or trading them for tickets to exclusive shows.

So, before anybody had even had a chance to blink, it looked like the whole thing was quickly moving to a wedding. Andrey brought the girl a bunch of dry, artificially coloured flowers whose stems released poisonous purple ink into the vase. He had just been discharged from the army. How could he have had any grasp of the subtleties of civilian life?

The girl paid no heed to such trifles. She desperately wanted a wedding ring on her dainty finger. It was the prerequisite for a happy life.

Andrey had a rucksack among his possessions. The girl was delighted. They could camp in the woods and loll in the meadows and drink milk and honey. Though no camper herself, she assumed that Andrey could pack a neat, orderly universe that she would carry up and down the flowering hills on her shoulders. But he took any effort as a personal affront. In the end they didn't go anywhere, cuddling instead on the narrow sofa in her parents' little apartment, while the latter loudly talked on the other side of the wall, pretending they didn't hear or were even aware of the activity on the sofa.

Andrey and the girl would lie very quietly, pressing their bodies against each other ever closer, as he tried to remove her tight-fitting wool turtleneck, while she resisted, before burying her face in his chest and going soft and limp as a sign of her consent. And he would continue to undress her, determinedly pulling the sleeve off her left arm and then off her right one and pressing her now naked body hard against his own, feeling her long slender smoothness against his skin, hungry for her, for all of her. As his desire for her grew, he tried to restrain himself, to conceal his excitement so he wouldn't frighten her — for as she had told him during their previous session on the sofa, she knew very little about male anatomy. Yet at the same time she herself wanted to excite him even more, as he could deduct from her moans, something he couldn't help responding to. He silenced her with the greed of his kisses, and then once more she would fight free, breaking into tears. That confused him, but he decided to ignore it and remove her sweater from around her neck. Now their caressing had become a struggle: the sweater at first wouldn't cooperate. So that when he pulled it hard over her head, she shrieked: "You're choking me!" That strangled cry chilled his ardour, wrapping it in a sudden, cold cloud of fatigue. Suddenly indifferent, he got up from the sofa and went across the room to look out the window at the lights of night-time Moscow.

# 4

It was only when the girl's mother had had enough that things finally got under way. She scratched her head, tapped the tip of her pencil against her desk, and then, by an obscure subterfuge, obtained room between the two Gogols. A relative had been killed in the war, his widow had disappeared into the camps, and so there it was, that tiny room, waiting to be occupied.

Its window looked out onto the courtyard, where home-
less men retrieved bottles left under its two benches, and
pigeons cooed around the birch tree.

Even if you couldn't see the Kremlin or either of the
Gogols, for that matter, you still knew they were nearby, a
consolation for anybody who might have yearned for a more
rarified space.

And the Grauerman Maternity Hospital was little more
than a block away, just in case.

Later a mattress would be found, but on their first
night in the room, Andrey spread newspapers on the floor,
undressed the girl and put her down on the newspapers
next to himself. She cried from the sharp pain. It hurt to
know that her Andrey could do such monstrous things to
her right off the bat. He lit two candles next to the newspapers so he could see his young girl better. That meant he
must love her, after all, she thought. And maybe he did.
Most likely he did, and why wouldn't he? Deep in his heart
he considered himself a romantic, and expected the world
to hold up its end of the bargain.

While serving in the army in far northern Archangelsk
and assigned to guard duty, with hoarfrost gathering on his
eyebrows and Kalashnikov, Andrey would imagine some
vague, tender womanly presence hovering, twirling around
him. In the solitude of the black subarctic air, the creature's
soft, gentle laugh would seem to caress his ears, muffling
the angry barking of the dogs. That womanly presence was
always sweet and forgiving, the woman happy of her own
accord. Her laugh and hands were magical, little hands
weaving a domestic cosiness all around him, protecting
him from the cruelty and pettiness of life. And when the

horror of his service was over and he was discharged, he would step back into the world again and find that angel of the night. Only this time she would be real.

But what he got in fact was quite different. The girl was brittle and vaguely dissatisfied. And he sensed behind her brooding melancholy a stubborn, unquenched yearning. He wanted her to be for him, for him alone, while he continued to pick at the hole in the wall and think about taking a stab at one or another of the great mathematical problems in history, exactly which he hadn't decided yet. Perhaps the Hodge Conjecture, or Fermat's Last Theorem, if that one hadn't already been proved, or the Riemann Hypothesis, or … whatever would make him famous.

"And while I'm doing that, just be here for me, girl."

But she wasn't. She was somewhere else, in a mute world of vague longing. She wanted something but didn't know what it was and she cried and stared at him in bewilderment for doing nothing to provide it. He could see the deep unhappiness and reproach in her almond eyes, and resented it.

# 5

On that first real night together, instead of crying, the girl did her best to hold back her tears. That was a mistake. Had her lashes been moist with tears, their ends wouldn't have scorched so easily — with a light crackling — when one of the candles tipped over. The girl's auburn curls were burned too. Andrey smelled what he thought was burning flesh (that's how burning hair smells) and grabbed the blanket and waved it several times over her, both of them rigid with terror.

"Something's shaking. Is it an earthquake?" the girl said.

"In the centre of Moscow? Don't be silly. It's the Metro. A line goes under the building."

"Feel how it's shaking!"

"Yeah, it really is."

"It's all right about my hair. Don't worry. It's just the two strands in front."

"I'm not worried. You can trim them later."

The girl fell silent. Then she whispered: "Let's play a game. Do you know this one?"

"Which?"

"Where you don't say *yes* or *no*, or *black* or *white*."

"What?"

"It's simple. I might ask: 'Are you going to the ball?' And you say 'Maybe.' Or: 'I don't know.' Or something like that. Only don't say: 'yes' or 'no.' And then I might say: 'What kind of a pretty dress are you going to wear?'"

"A dress? But I'm not a girl!"

"I know, but just pretend your are. It's like two aristocratic ladies talking in the past. So then I might ask: 'What kind of dress, black or white?' since I want to trick you. And you say, 'pink' or 'purple,' or whatever, only not 'black' or 'white,' or else you lose. Or I could say, for example: 'Surely you're going to wear black lace at the ball. It looks so becoming on you.' And if you say, 'No,' then you lose. You have to come up with a different answer instead. See?"

"But that's silly."

"You have a tiny gnome hiding inside you, and he calls everything silly."

"Hold on! What have gnomes to do with 'Black and White'?"

Slowly, with a tip of her finger, she drew a line across his naked chest, from one shoulder to the other.

"See, you're so big, but your soul is tiny, like a gnome. And it's scared of having to live in such a big body. And that's the cause of our problems."

"Andrey caught her wandering hand and squeezed it.

"Ouch!" she cried. He let her hand go.

"Your mind works in crazy patterns, I can never quite follow it."

They both fell silent. He sat up in bed, then fumbled in his trousers hanging off the back of the chair, looking for a cigarette.

"And you, of course, you never have fear, right? A real Jeanne d'Arc," he said lighting the cigarette and taking a deep puff.

"Oh, sure I have. Give me a puff. Sure," she said sitting up in bed next to him and reaching for the cigarette he had just lit. In the pallid light coming from the sole lamp stand behind the window pane her naked shoulders and back looked childishly thin. She pulled a little smoke into her mouth and immediately choked.

"I told you not to smoke."

"Can't you just not interrupt me? I started telling you something important. You asked me about fear, didn't you? Today, for example. I'm walking down the street … The chestnut trees have already lit all their candles, kids plop through puddles. Everything is so beautiful because it's a bit strange. Even old toothless babushkas on the benches are beautiful, the way they squint their eyes at the reflection of the sun in the puddles and the windows panes, as if it were their first spring. And I'm scared. This beauty demands something from me, you understand? And all I have inside is void, void! Nothing within to stand up to this beauty, see? Something is trying to break through, yet it can't. I'm dumb, I have no voice and it's scary and painful."

"Good brains given to a fool, that's your case, my dear."

"It's as if I weren't worthy of this life, because I have no power to express its beauty. And so I'm afraid. We're both afraid. You're afraid of your things, I'm afraid of mine. That's why we fight."

When the girl woke the next morning, Andrey was gone. She remained lying on the floor. She was embarrassed to leave the room with her eyes so strangely exposed. She thought she might move to a chair by the window, but it hurt to sit, so she looked at the small patch of the grey sky visible from their marriage bed, the newspapers on the floor, all the time expecting Andrey to come back. He would kiss away the nakedness of her eyes and her pain down there.

But he didn't come back.

She watched the day die, night finally swallowing the streets and boulevards with houses and trees. Darkness stared back at her with the black eyes of a widow. Soon the cockroaches would come out. Then the girl heard soul-wrenching cries. It must be babies, she thought.

Naked babies cut with a dull knife. Or being boiled or skinned alive. But who would give up their children for such torture? She listened. Then she knew it was just the wailing of cats: lascivious, insatiable, hunting, pinning each other to the earth, violating each other in hatred and ecstasy. It frightened the girl. She began to pray. "Dear Andrusha, please come back! I'm scared! I'll never wrong you again! I promise!" She now loved him more than ever and would come to love him even more.

But still he didn't come.

After two days, the girl knew she'd been abandoned. She packed up her few belongings, meaning to return to her parents. But then the door opened. It was Andrey.

"A clandestine overnight operation," he said, chuckling with a sidelong glance. "My sister was getting divorced in Novgorod. I had to sneak all her furniture out before her husband could. My mother asked me to do it. I couldn't say no to my mama, could I?"

"Why didn't you leave me a note or something? It was our first night, after all. I woke up and ... and you were gone."

Needing air, she opened the window half way and was struck in the face by a flurry of snowflakes. Where had they come from? It was April.

She closed the window again, and they went on with their lives in the little room between the two Gogols.

What embarrassed her the most with Auntie Shura was that Andrey wasn't her husband yet. They had planned to get married at once, but an unexpected circumstance had interfered: the marriage registrar, a buxom woman tucked into an official blue suit, had taken the official seal with her on a vacation to the Black Sea.

By the time the registrar returned from romping on the beach, the girl had put herself on a long waiting list for an abortion at the nearby maternity hospital. She lost sleep agonizing over what would happen if she passed the deadline before her turn came up and they would send her away. By early summer, her morning sickness had passed, and then at last the procedure was done and she was bereft. She fell into catatonic melancholy. How the wedding went, who was there, what was said and eaten, she had no idea. She came too only when the men shouted the customary "Bitter! Bitter!" and somebody's hard, dry lips for some reason pressed against her own. They were her husband's.

# 6

For the rest of the summer she remained weak and ailing, reluctant to go on living with her now empty self.

But in the fall the iron fingers of necessity seized her by the neck. She was a second-year student, and lectures began at 8 am. Missing even a few could result in expulsion. Her eyes were red from sleeplessness and tumultuous nights with her man. At the seminars, she covertly yawned into her fist.

The fall also brought some relief. She loved the remorseful sadness of the falling leaves. They softened the air, their rustling somehow filling it with the promise of forgiveness. Later, when the snow came, she found herself pregnant again. "A little boy is knocking at my heart," she whispered in Andrey's ear.

"How can you tell?"

She sat down in his lap and put her arm around his

close-cropped head. She felt small next to his large frame and loved the feeling. He had grown a massive red beard, which made him look even more imposing.

"The baby told me," she said, pointing to her flat belly. She felt a surge of tenderness for the boy and his father.

"And you're not going to ... ?"

"Oh, no! I'll never do that again."

"What's changed since the last time?"

"Nothing, really, but we'll manage somehow, won't we?"

"But how, exactly? You're a student."

"We both are."

"I'm not anymore."

"What do you mean?"

"I officially withdrew."

"You did? When?"

"What difference does it make? Last spring."

"Why didn't you tell me? Why didn't you say something? What have you been doing all these months, then?"

"I've been doing nothing. Absolutely nothing. Going to movies every matinee. Look: they'll certainly give you an anaesthetic."

"They didn't last time. But I ... I just can't believe what you said."

"Well, I'm sure that labour is worse."

"How would you know?"

She pulled back from him and thought that he looked ridiculous with so much hair on the bottom of his head, on his cheeks and chin, while on top there was almost nothing at all.

"You should let your hair grow," she said, standing up.

# 7

The baby's skin was milk white, and his head was covered with barely visible fluff. The girl gently touched his fontanel with her finger and for no reason began to laugh.

Back home, she swaddled her baby, and nursed, and washed, and rocked him to sleep, while looking out the window at some men doing work in the street. She washed and boiled the soiled sheets (as diapers have not been invented yet), until they were spotless and then hung them to dry on a cord stretched across the length of the communal kitchen. When Mina-Zina took the sheets down and stuck them under the girl's door, she said nothing and hung them out in the room instead.

Andrey seemed indifferent to his son. Afraid to approach, to hold him. "Now the creature will know everything about me, which is a scary thought," he once confessed.

"How so?"

"I mean, what if he turns out like me, God forbid, then he'll know. He'll feel the same, and there'll be no hiding from that. He'll figure me out, all right."

Then he left them alone, the mother and child, in their oneness of their being.

The bed bugs tormented them at night. The girl thought they should replace the old wallpaper, since they all lived in the same room and the bugs could crawl from their mattress to the baby's cradle. But she wasn't good enough with her hands to undertake such a venture alone. And Andrey seemed to move slower and slower, as if walking through fog.

He called the girl a birdbrain and a nothing for being

so naïve about life, for lacking domestic skills, for not erecting around him a fortress within which he could solve the Hodge Conjecture or maybe prove the Riemann Hypothesis.

But now she paid no attention to the noises he made. After putting a bowl of soup in front of him at dinner time, she resumed singing little songs to her baby.

Andrey threw the bowls at her. None of the conjectures or hypotheses could be solved or proved or even approached. When there were no more bowls to eat from, girl mockingly poured the lukewarm soup into Andrey's cupped hands. His hands were capable of holding a lot of soup, for he had inherited wide, strong hands, until then of little use to him.

Andrey said: "You bitch! The soup's cold. You can't even cook. You're a nothing! A zero!"

She covered her baby's face with a lace handkerchief and barked at Andrey as if she were a dog.

"Not funny, idiot!" he said.

Then she tried hooting like an owl, wailing like an angry tomcat, and bleating like an injured sheep.

"What was all that about?" he asked her in the evening when the baby was a sleep.

"You call me a bitch," she said in the evening exasperated from howling. "Don't dogs bark? I won't talk to you ever again, till you call me by my real name."

Andrey tried to remember her real name, Masha or Sasha or Tasha, yes, that's it: Natasha! But the name had long before withered as to become unusable.

With time the girl stopped using her human voice altogether. With time she came to understand the voices of beasts: howling and barking, mewing and growling.

One night she was climbing up their dark stairway. At the top, near the attic, a cat made its den. The girl was carrying her pink fluffy baby up to the sky, up to their room under the roof, when she heard the cat moaning. Not a moan of pleasure or desire. But of a wish for death. The girl listened carefully. Last year the cat's three kittens had been thrown in the river. This year all eight were drowned.

The cat was startled by the girl's pink baby and froze, its fur erect. But then it said: "Give me your baby for half a day to play with. It will comfort me and I'll stop mourning my kittens."

The girl felt sorry for the cat and handed over her clean white bundle.

"Play a little, while I go cook. Then I'll come back for my baby."

The girl made some borscht, took the pot back to her room safely out of Mina-Zina's reach, and returned to the stairway for her son. But he and the cat had vanished. She looked everywhere. She climbed up to the roof, she searched the attic, she peered into the nooks and crannies under the stairs and in every other dark place, but her son and the cat were gone, never to be found again.

Many years have passed since that time. Recently I was walking along the Arbat and turned into that familiar lane. The building between the two Gogols was still standing, although it was apparent from the boarded-up and broken windows that it wasn't long for this world. Its plaster was crumbling, its entranceway was falling apart, and soon the building itself would pass into oblivion. The noisy, abusive crew that had taken shelter in its warren had long since scattered. Auntie Shura and her husband had passed away and Mina-Zina had been relocated by the housing authority to a new apartment in Moscow's outskirts. Andrey never found the key to the mysterious mathematical door he had so desperately tried to unlock. But the door he did open was of a much more ordinary and kinder sort: a real apartment with a real woman good at sewing, knitting, and cooking, the very skills the adolescent wife of his youth had so sadly lacked.

And Vova, the policeman, had replaced his two women with a German shepherd and been promoted to lieutenant.

# IF A TREE FALLS IN A SOLITARY FOREST

**1**

December is dark with vague sorrows and fears.

Dasha never knew her father. But in December she missed him as if she had. January was better. The afterglow of Christmas gave some warmth and the days were longer. By the end of February you were almost there. The snow clung in moist clumps to the seat of your wool pants or dangled from them in silvery wisps. When you made a snow ball — pat-pat-pat — and the snow drenched your mittens, you knew that spring was sending it first wink. "Where shall I hang my icicles next month? The balcony? The eaves? The downspout?"

But December is dark and dreary.

When Dasha was little, she didn't notice her father's absence. But later at school the other kids teased her. Had she grown up in the thirties or forties, she would have been like everyone else. By the fifties children had started to have fathers again.

"Where's our father?" The seven-year-old had long held

back the question always in her eyes, until one New Year's Eve it suddenly tumbled out. It scared her, and she wanted to take it by the scruff of the neck the way she'd seen a stray cat grab its kittens to move them out of sight, but it was too late. The question was already staggering between Dasha and her mother. Her Mama glanced at her, lit a cigarette, and blew her hair off her forehead.

"Is our life so bad the way it is?"

No, it wasn't. Dasha had her own nook with a cot, a little bookshelf, and a doll. On the floor next to the doll was a rusty pair of *Eider* ice skates. Not the white figure skates that every little girl dreams of, but boys' hockey skates.

Dasha's Mama slept in another, larger nook, where besides her bed there was a desk with a typewriter on it, along with some dried flowers in a green *Borzhomi* mineral-water bottle and a figurine of the goddess Diana holding a javelin in one hand and touching the back of a deer with the other. Hanging from the deer's antlers were paper clips her Mama used in her work.

Boiled carrots for breakfast, boiled potatoes for dinner, and, for a Sunday treat, salt herring with sliced onion and sunflower oil. No, their life wasn't bad. Once a month, Mama brought home an apple, but since neither of them would touch it first, it sat on its blue saucer until it shrivelled up.

Their warped old kitchen table reminded Dasha of an abandoned skiff she had once seen in a village lying upside down in tall grass far from any water, its bottom bleached bone white by the sun. When she peeled back the oilcloth covering the table, she could see a round indentation in one of the table's corners.

"The previous owners must have had the bad habit of cracking walnuts there with a hammer," her Mama said. "Why don't you leave the oilcloth alone and finish your carrots?"

But the indentation intrigued Dasha. The fact that it was there even when she wasn't looking at it was strange. Or even alarming. What was it doing when she was at school? And what about the trees that spent the whole winter all by themselves in the frozen ground? Or the bugs that lay hidden in little cracks in the earth? Or the rivers that flowed in solitude across far-away plains? She wanted them all to be with her continuously, all the time, since she somehow felt responsible for them. At other times, she thought it was probably all right not to see every thing every minute, since you could just think about them and that would keep them going. For example, the two black floral-shaped spots in the bottom of her bowl where the enamel was chipped. They would reappear as soon as she finished her carrots. The smaller one looked like a lily of the valley, while the larger one was shaped like a tulip.

Mama typed in an office all day and cleaned in a hospital at night. The long lonely evenings by their icy window were Dasha's alone. The dead fly on the cotton wadding placed between the double panes for the winter would lie there on its back until April. Then Mama would untape the windows and remove the soot-blackened wadding, together with the fly.

Exactly at nine, Dasha would crawl into her mother's bed and turn on the night light. To keep her fear at bay, she would put on her mother's nightgown and then wait under the covers. From its depths the building would send up a friend, its ancient elevator. She and the elevator shared a secret language. Late into the night the elevator would speak to her with the clicks and clacks of its metal cage. As the elevator crept from floor to floor up to her own, the sounds naturally grew louder and more distinct. And then the elevator would play a cunning game with her as she held her breath: would it stop at her floor or continue on? The elevator had two doors, one that opened in halves to the inside, its shiny black surface covered with unintelligible graffiti, and another solid metal one that opened to the out-side on each floor. "Guess who's inside me?" Dasha would ask in a deep elevator voice. She could often tell who by the way her neighbours managed the elevator doors. The man who lived on the floor below threw them open with an im-patient bang. But Dasha's Mama passed through doors without a sound, as if somebody were watching. Dasha would count the up-and-down clicks, holding on to them as long as she could until she lost track and drifted off. And then she would scold herself in her sleep for having missed her Mama again.

The triple folded wool blanket Mama put under the East German *Erika* portable typewriter to muffle its tapping didn't keep Dasha from waking up. (Mama often brought her work home.) But soon the clicking, which sounded like hail striking the roof, would lull her back to sleep.

From time to time the steady routine of their mother-daughter happiness was interrupted by mother's mysterious ailments. Dasha drew the curtains, wrapped the hot-water bottle in a towel, and placed it on her mother's forehead. Then they would lie next to each other in the dark, while Dasha kept watch to make sure Mama didn't die in her sleep. When her Mama got better, Dasha would read her Pushkin's fairytale about Tsar Saltan. Believing outrageous slander, the tsar orders his young wife and son to be sealed in a barrel and hurled into the sea. Inside the barrel, the boy grows into a strong youth, knocks out the bottom of the barrel, and saves his Mama and himself.

On ordinary days, they got up before dawn. The clothing on the chair was stiff and cold. Without turning on the light, Dasha's Mama handed clean underwear to her in the warm cave of the bed, and then pulled Dasha's listless body out from under the covers, drew her sleepy arms through the shoulder loops of the garter belt, and buttoned the five buttons in the back. Then she attached the suspender clips to Dasha's stockings, two for each leg, one in back and the other in front. Dasha yelped at the sudden touch of the cold metal on her thighs. A splash of tap water in her face gave her a start, even though her Mama did hold it in the palm of her hand first to warm it. Dasha's last efforts to remain asleep were completely routed by the bite of the metal comb in her hair.

"Why is your hair all matted again? I just combed it out yesterday?"

Dasha stifled her tears. Crying wasn't allowed in their happy life.

Mother's job started at eight on the other side of the city. Dasha's school opened at nine. That meant they could leave no later than seven. Once they were on the trolley bus, her Mama stared out the window, her face impassive.

The schoolyard was dark and empty.

"Don't sit on the bench. Your bladder could catch cold. Walk around or jump up and down to keep warm."

Mama bent down, pressing her face so close that Dasha could see the dark specs in her grey irises with the yellowish rim around her pupils. Mama remained still for a moment, then deftly drew herself up and quickly left. Dasha wiped the moisture from her cheek with the back of her mitten and timidly looked around. The schoolyard was still dark and empty. There was a frozen puddle just beyond the metal fence that enclosed the playground. Noticing some twigs in an icy froth of ice, Dasha pushed her head through the railing and managed to get one leg through as well. A tap of her heel cracked the twigs' icy tomb, which Dasha immediately regretted. Set free, the twigs lost their magic.

To warm and cheer herself up, Dasha hopped first on her left foot, then on her right, but the effort steamed up her glasses, so she abandoned it. Bored, she picked up a fallen ice-coated branch and used it to brush away the pillows of snow covering each bench. The flurries amused her. Then she arranged her thick mittens on the freshly cleaned surface of the bench so her bladder "wouldn't catch cold" and sat down on them. The sky was getting lighter. When the first kids arrived, Dasha hid behind the Doric columns of the school portico. If they had seen that she had been waiting all alone in the schoolyard, she would have been a laughingstock: a neglected child, an outcast.

# 2

In March, when the shadows and days got longer, Mama said: "You're a big girl now and can take the trolley bus to school by yourself. Ten minutes and you're already there. You remember our stop?"

It was getting to the stop that was the tricky part. You had to cross a busy intersection with heavy trucks and streetcars making turns without slowing down. "It's dangerous even for adults," her Mama said. "You'll have to ask some nice lady to help you cross. Always ask an auntie, never an uncle."

To make sure Dasha followed her instructions, Mama took two days off and watched her after mingling with the crowd. Now they could leave home half an hour later, which meant an additional 15 minutes of sleep and no waiting in the schoolyard alone.

Dasha, however, had no intention of following her mother's instructions to the letter. Nor was she going to ask only aunties.

"Could you please take me across, kind uncle?" she said, looking up at a stranger and quickly slipping her hand into his, so there would be no time for him to think or ask questions. But usually the men didn't ask questions, nor did they change their quick gait or alter the sombre expression on their faces. Dasha instinctively tried to match her short stride to their long one, running and skipping by turns. She gave them a few minutes to get used to her, and though she was always ready with the most important question, she waited until they reached the streetcar track in the middle of the road.

"Do you have children, uncle?" If the answer was yes (by far the most frequent), Dasha would thank the stranger and run off to her stop.

But one man said no.

"Would you like to be my father? Please!"

The stranger looked searchingly at Dasha's face. Then he turned and ran after a streetcar.

# 3

With April came spring. The first rooks held rowdy meetings in the tops of the still bare poplars. As promised, icicle troves appeared on the downspouts and balcony railings. The afternoon sun, a merry percussionist, knocked them down with a delicious crash. Dasha was now allowed to put away her coat and go to school in just her uniform. How lovely! Although her uniform with its brown dress and black apron wouldn't attract anybody's attention, her white cuffs and collar would be noticed, she hoped. After all, she had only learned the month before how to sew them on by herself.

For her birthday at the end of March, Mama gave her a pair of second-hand figure skates. She hadn't been able to skate backwards on her old *Eiders*, but now she could learn all sorts of tricks on the elegantly curved wonder of the new blades. The ice in the yard had already become soft and porous, and gingerly attempting her first turn, she stumbled over a dry patch and fell hard on her back. Suddenly she didn't feel like moving, and lay there staring at the sky, watching the blue patches gradually disappear as the clouds sailed across them. Looking at the vanishing blue, she understood why nobody had agreed to be her father. It was because she had been selfish and asked only for herself.

The next morning on her way to school, Dasha let several waves of people pour off the curb until at last she noticed a young man in a light sports jacket with a bright yellow scarf around his neck and a soccer ball tucked under his arm. While the dark, dense crowd waited for the light to change, she quickly sidled over to the man. He was whistling under his breath.

"Could you please help me across? My Mama won't let me do it by myself." The whistling stopped.

He ignored Dasha's extended hand, but they crossed side by side. By the time they got to the tracks, Dasha had already calculated her chances as negligible, but she liked the man's athletic figure and bright scarf.

"Do you have any children, uncle?" Dasha asked, deciding to try her luck anyway, since they had already crossed the tracks and were close to the other side of the street. The man stared at her. "Suppose I don't. What business is that of yours?"

"My Mama and I need a father," Dasha firmly replied.

"Your mother? Terrific! How old is your mother?"

"Twenty-nine," Dasha said.

"Is your mother a blonde or a brunette?"

Dasha didn't know what a brunette was and hesitated.

"My Mama is beautiful," she finally said.

The man chuckled.

"Will your mama be home sometime tomorrow?" He took a tangerine out of his pocket. "Give this to your mama. Tell her I'll come by Saturday around noon. We'll take a look."

And then he was on the move again and about to dissolve into the crowd. Dasha ran after him.

"Uncle, you forgot to ask for our address!"

The man turned around. He looked at her with curiosity.

"Your address? All right, go ahead."

"Taganka 31, Apartment 6. It's right across from the bakery. Will you remember, uncle?"

"Oh, I'll remember, missy."

He shook his head and bounced the ball hard twice on the sidewalk before disappearing into the crowd.

That night Dasha didn't see her mother. She fell asleep with the tangerine in her hand and woke up late the next morning to an empty apartment. Her Mama worked the early morning shift at the hospital every second Saturday, which Dasha had forgotten. Now she feared the worst: that their Papa would arrive before her Mama got home. She climbed up on the windowsill, looked out into the street, got back down, fed the two goldfish in the bowl, and listened for her friend, the elevator, even if it mostly slept in the daytime and refused to speak, as if to ensure that the long dull day would drag on. Then she remembered the tangerine. She peeled it, meaning to leave half of it for her Mama but somehow popping the whole thing in her mouth, so that its tangy juice ran down her chin. And then the door bell rang.

Since her Mama always used her key, it sounded abrupt and alien. Dasha ran to the door, almost choking on the tangerine. Standing on a stool to look through the peephole, she saw yesterday's man waiting outside with a bunch of red tulips in his hand. And then, just as she was opening the door, the elevator doors opened too, revealing first a net bag of groceries and then the hem of her mother's coat.

"Are you looking for somebody?" Mama asked, coming over to their door and standing between it and the stranger.

"I'm looking for you," the man said in a gentle baritone.

"There must be some mistake," Dasha's Mama brusquely replied.

"Whether it's a mistake or not we'll soon find out. Though something tells me it isn't." He eyed her appraisingly: "Let me help you with your groceries."

Her Mama hesitated. The man looked straight into her eyes and smiled.

"How about a trade? I'll give you these flowers and you'll give me your bag. Fair?"

Mama blushed, blew her hair off her forehead, and finally took the tulips.

"But why? It's not a holiday or anything."

"Do I have to have an occasion to give a ravishing woman flowers? I'm Sergey, by the way. I teach phys. ed. What school does your daughter go to?" He nodded towards Dasha, who was watching from the doorway.

"No. 280."

"See, we're neighbours. I'm at No. 365, at the other end of Taganka."

"You don't say. But what I'd really like to know is how you got my address!"

"A little birdie whispered in my ear: 'Go you don't know where, and find you don't know what.'"

Sergey winked at Dasha, as if to say: "You didn't warn your mother, but I promise I won't tell."

"Well, don't trust your little birdie too much!" her Mama said playfully as she sniffed the flowers. "But why are we standing on the landing? Why don't you come in?"

"Do you know how to keep tulips from drooping?" Sergey asked as he stepped inside and glanced around their little entryway.

"Sure, everybody does. Trim the stems before you put them in the water. The groceries go in the kitchen."

"On the table?"

"Fine. Thanks."

"I'll give you a better one: put a copper coin in the water and your tulips will last all week."

"I never heard that before," Mama said, smiling for the first time as she sniffed the flowers.

"Here!" He took a coin from his pocket.

"Oh, please! I have my own," her Mama said, waving his hand away.

"I'm not offering you a diamond, am I? So take it."

He whistled lightly.

"You live here alone, just you and your daughter?"

"Yes, it's just us," her Mama said, sighing. "Go do your homework, Dasha."

From the kitchen, Dasha heard the water running from the tap into the kettle, the clatter of tea cups, and, later on, bursts of laughter. Left out of the fun, Dasha crept from the main room and hid in the hallway behind the frosted glass door to the kitchen. She didn't recognize her mother. She had let her long hair down, and her head was tossed back in a hearty laugh.

"Salami? Butter? Bratwurst? On a magic carpet? Stop it! Please stop it, Sergey, or I'll split in two!"

"Yes, exactly! On a carpet! You have the word of an intelligence agent!"

"I thought you said you were a teacher."

"Me? Did I say that? Take your pick! Whatever you like suits me fine, sugar! And I play for the national team too. Nothing to sneeze at."

Dasha had never heard anybody call her Mama "sugar" before.

"Here she is!" Papa shouted when Dasha, overcome with excitement, entered the doorway.

"So, what are your plans for tomorrow, young lady? Shall we all go skating? In Gorky Park? In their huge skating rink — music, skaters, the last weekend of the season!"

"How did you know, Sergey? You're a wizard! I got her skates for her birthday. She's dying to try them."

"A birthday? We'll have to celebrate!"

"I don't know how to skate on figure skates," Dasha said, sulking. She remembered her fall and now was afraid to tumble again in front of the stranger.

"Ah, it's very easy! If you're used to *Eiders*, figure skates will be a piece of cake. I'm training the Moscow figure-skating team, by the way, so I'll be able to show you a thing or two." "Tomorrow, then?"

Papa winked at her again, and then at her mother.

That evening, Mama and Papa went to a movie comedy called *The Carnival Night*.

Dasha listened to the elevator for a while, and then happily fell asleep. In the middle of the night, she was wakened by whispering and unusually heavy breathing. Peering into the darkness, she recognized in the vague shape lying next to her Mama her new Papa. She withdrew deeper under the covers, pretending to be asleep.

When Dasha woke the next morning the sun was already up and their Papa had left. Since it was Sunday, there wasn't any hurry, and she and her Mama had their customary breakfast of herring. Papa had something urgent he needed to attend to, but would be back by the time they were ready to leave, Mama said. Her face was smooth and radiant. Even so, she put a mask of sour cream on it for a few minutes, the smell of which Dasha has always detested. Humming to herself, she got out two red and white striped sweaters and matching white caps with red pom-poms. The sweaters, which they had only worn once before, were made from expensive Shetland wool and had been a gift from Mother's work. After they had put everything on and got Dasha's skates ready, they sat down to wait for Father. They jumped up when the doorbell finally rang.

But it was only their neighbour come to ask if Dasha could babysit. Mama said no, not today, today Dasha's busy, and after the neighbour left, they sat and waited until there was another knock at the door. This time it was a neighbour who had borrowed two rubles and was returning them, since she had got paid. After that nobody rang or knocked. They took off their warm sweaters but still kept waiting, just in case.

"Sergey played soccer for the national team when he was 18," Mama said.

"Did he win?" Dasha asked.

"His team, you mean? Probably, they did. Why wouldn't they? But it doesn't really matter. You have to be really dedicated and hard-working even to get on a team."

Dasha nodded. Mother appreciated hard purposeful work.

And soon the day was on its last legs, with dusk starting to fall. They exchanged furtive glances and avoided each other's eyes. Mama finally sat down at her typewriter, while Dasha got out her book bag to prepare her school things for the next day. Their Papa must have meant to go skating next Sunday, not this one, Dasha thought.

When next Sunday came and passed, Dasha removed another page from a tear-off calendar thinking that there are many Sundays in a year and that you can't always be sure which is the right one. Since Sundays often feel the same, the best thing will be just to wait. And so she waited for another month. And then she decided that it must be because their Papa had forgotten their address.

On the way to school every morning, Dasha would go to the busy intersection where she had met him. For two weeks she would wait at the corner, but he must have had a different teaching schedule now, for he never came in the morning. Then she changed her strategy and would come after school, around three, and waited till five.

She stood in the same place at the very edge of the sidewalk, holding onto a dusty streetlamp with her arm, lest the crowd, sullenly rolling away toward the opposite shore with the green light, sweep her into the roadway. When an outflux began, she, like an pebble forgotten by the wave, waited orphan-like on the shore now bereft of people until the signal blinked its command for a new influx.

She looked avidly then at the mournful, preoccupied faces rolling toward her in compact ranks: women weighed down with string bags and purses and wearing, out of season, knitted hats and warm coats; men with briefcases who were more often lightly dressed and empty-handed; a fat man with a garland of toilet paper rolls around his neck awkwardly waddling like a penguin with his belly stuck out. It was funny, and Dasha burst out laughing.

But the one person she needed, their Papa, so far wasn't among them. And even so she believed that he would finally come, lithe, his jacket fluttering as he moved, a ball in his hand, a carelessly tied yellow scarf round his neck. He would come, he would definitely come!

It was only for the time being that he was unseen, was hidden from her eyes, the way rivers are hidden beneath the ice in winter, or birds in a forest thicket, or any lost thing. But she would wait. For everything that is unseen remembers us and expects to meet us again and resume its life.

And only if we disavow or forget, only then will people and everything on the earth cease to exist.

# ～ A REQUIEM FOR DANDELION

THERE WAS NO way the newcomer would fit into our twelve-square-meter room. It just wasn't possible. He couldn't be put between my parents' bed and the wardrobe, since my cot already occupied that space. Nor could he be put behind my mother's desk with its two stacks of essays on top and my homework in the middle: the larger, uncorrected stack on the left, and the smaller one with the gashes of my mother's red pen on the right. And I wasn't going to share my only sanctum of privacy either — the bookcase's bottom shelf reserved for my toys, even if it was half-empty. (I was indifferent to stuffed animals and dolls and their frills.) The main pleasure of that shelf wasn't its toys, however, but the nylon pennant that hung from a nail inside the bookcase's glass door.

The pennant was studded with pins, badges, and medals that my father, a Greco-Roman wrestling champion, had brought back from tournaments abroad — odd triangles and squares and translucent disks with mysterious inscriptions on them that were our only proof of "abroad's" otherwise mythical existence. When I was alone, I would open the door wide and then slam it shut, producing a chorus of sound as the pennant slapped against the glass: the solemn bang of the medals won in East Germany, the fussy tap of the badges from Bulgaria, the diffident chink of the lily-shaped pins from Poland. So no, I wasn't going to share any of that with the boy which I was sure he would be, as I had no use for girls at all. Beyond our rime-embossed windows lay the building's courtyard. Veils of snow caressed the earth at night, and by morning the wooden slide, shaped like an inverted "y," awoke muffled to its neck. Holding big pieces of cardboard, we rushed up the slide's rickety ladder, elbowing each other aside as we struggled to be the first to swish down through the fresh snow covering the slide's surface. After a couple of rides, the now wet cardboard would fall apart, and then we would slide down without it, on our bottoms, risking salvos of scolding at home for our torn flannel pants.

How would I ever elbow my way to the top through all those boys if I had to drag him along too, holding his tiny hand in the cocoon of my mitten? The brisk, breathless liberty of snow and winter was mine alone. There was no place in it for anybody else.

Earlier that fall, I had imagined myself a mighty ship patrolling a sea of dead leaves, as I ploughed through their rustling heaps. There could be no question of taking him on board for that either. Leaves' whispering belonged to me alone.

But my greatest worry was that I would have to share my birthday if he was born the same day I was, on the 7th of

November, the *Day of the Great October Socialist Revolution*. Kneeling on a chair by our front window five stories above, I would watch the parade that seemed to have been organized every year just for me. Tanks and trucks with *Katyusha* rockets would rumble past on their way to Red Square, and then after an interval would come a tide of red flags and banners and artificial flowers, and, carried high above the human surge, portraits of Lenin and Stalin and a fierce-looking man with a black, shovel-shaped beard. The rippling white letters on red banners would gradually coalesce into words and then entire phrases: *Long Live Stalin, Father of Peoples! The Party is the Intellect, Honour, and Conscience of Our Era! Long Live the Great Soviet People, Immortal Builder of Communism!* And all of it, all of that exuberance, belonged to me by my birth date and eagle's aerie. To keep them safe from my brother, I wanted to take up those tanks and trucks and people in my arms and hide them. Let them celebrate every year for my sake alone.

There was of course no certainty that my brother would arrive on November 7th. But what was sure was that it would be ten years too late, an inexcusable miscalculation on his part that made him, even though he wouldn't be a girl, still quite useless to me. Being so young, how could he defend me from the wickedness of adults or the apprentice cruelty of other children? Obviously, he would be unable to take revenge on the boys who had tied my braids to the fence as I intently watched a caterpillar nibbling on a leaf.

But useless and still invisible though he was, he had already affected our lives. My mother, who was so quick and nimble in her management of the day's many tasks, had because of him been turned into a sluggard. And because of him she had put away all her jewellery and begun to wear a baggy, nondescript dark calico dress with the tiny, sad-looking polka-dots. One morning I suddenly saw that dress in a completely new light. I realized for the first time what it concealed: irrefutable evidence of the truth of the nasty jokes of the boys in the yard. The adults — and even worse, my own parents — must in fact have been doing *that* awful thing with each other out of my sight. My mother's bulging dress was proof that she and my father had done it at least once.

The landslide of that logic quickly gained momentum, overwhelming everything else. If they had done it once, then what would have kept them from doing it twice? Or ten times? Or all the time? And then came the logic's inevitable conclusion. If they had done it to bring my brother into being, then they must have done it to bring me into being too! No, my beginning couldn't have originated in that humiliation, that shame. I knew at once with perfect confidence that I had always been here, had always been uncreated, free, and independent of anyone's will. At least the idea of me was — the *necessity* of me.

Instantly losing all respect for my parents, I felt there was only one way to escape their treachery. I had to free myself totally from *their* life, *their* home.

There were throngs of Gypsies in every train station in the city, bands with fearless curly-haired children who begged in the nearby streets, and women in wide, brightly coloured skirts who went from door to door with infants on their hips. If I gave them money, they might take me to their camps. Thirty kopeks a day saved from school breakfasts would come to ten roubles in not much more than a month. To get ready, I sewed myself a little satchel for a change of clothing and some biscuits.

It was near the end of October when I finally had the sum in hand: ten roubles and twenty kopecks. The Gypsy women could come to our door any time now. Before falling asleep, I mentally said a bitter farewell to my betrayers, feeling little pity even for my mother.

Early the next morning, there was a knock on the door. Suddenly gripped with fear I managed somehow to get into the sleeves of my school uniform, and to open the door to my long-awaited rescuers.

"Did you call a cab?" a man with a crumpled early morning face asked when I finally got to the door. My father had already left for work, and I was supposed to go to school. Not even a Biblical deluge could have altered the regular routines of our universe. And so my mother left for the maternity hospital by herself, no less subject to the same immutable order in which she too was a staunch believer.

My brother was born several hours later, one month premature but luckily a week before my birthday.

Unlike me, he was the image of his mother. He had, as she would later remark with rueful regret, the same snub nose. And the same eye shape. And the delicate curve of his ears and his fingers and his nails were miniature replicas of hers. And instead of the usual old, wrinkled appearance, his skin was angelically pristine, as if the rough passage to this world had cost him no effort at all. Because of the white down on the crown of his head, my mother called him Dandelion. It was his name of first rapture, the name he received before any real one.

"When they brought him to me the first time," my mother said, "I gently blew on his face to test his reflexes. And his lips quivered in a little smile, as if he recognized me. He looked like a fluffy dandelion."

The next day she remarked to the nurse: "What an amazing baby he is! I haven't heard a peep out of him! Not like my first. She screamed non-stop."

"That's too bad ... That he hasn't cried," the nurse said, avoiding my mother's gaze. "The ones born two months prematurely usually survive. But a month early won't make it." Was it a folk's belief she had brought out as the excuse unwilling to tell my mother the true story?

Every time they brought Dandelion for feeding, he responded with that tiny smile which in itself was unusual: newborns don't smile. At what point did he decide to leave? Was this whiff of a smile a gentle apology for his departure?

I never saw my brother. He died a week later on my birthday. The hospital insisted that my mother leave the body to them.

Where is my brother buried? We'll never know.

For a long time after his death I thought that, if I had consented to give him a small place in my own life, he would have stayed. If I hadn't begrudged him the banging of the badges and medals, or the cardboard for the slide, or the leaves whispering farewell to the trees, or the tanks and trucks rumbling past on my birthday ...

It was at my silent request that he had spared himself the pain of being: the pain of acquiring a form, then losing it, then finding another of which we will know nothing. His tiny fingers left no traces on any surfaces. His tongue never tried any words. Every day he grows younger. First by ten years, then twenty, then thirty, and now he's nearly half a century younger than I am.

Because his was an in-between name, no one has used it in our family in the years to come. I couldn't give it to my sons, nor could they give it to their own. We never talk about Dandelion. There's nothing to recall. He was little more than a subjunctive, a might have done, a might have become …

In the beyond where souls are weighed, the scales with Dandelion's unblemished soul will be so light as to feel empty to the judge. He long ago yielded place in the sun to other souls. To me he granted what I wanted: the freedom of the solitary.

Sometimes, in a faraway city of rainy winters, I imagine Moscow's snow-shrouded boulevards and trees and street-lamps and monuments and cast-iron gates. I imagine dark winter waters of the river half-encased in ice, flowing out beyond the realm of the city into the wooded plains where Dandelion may lie, and I think of the quick moving through the snow to their final destinations and the dead pitying and forgiving the living.

# ~ THE MIRACLE WORKER

**1**

THERE WASN'T MUCH to say about Tanya's looks other than that they were plain. Hundreds of such Tanyas made their way through Moscow's crowds every day. Not that her face was unpleasant, especially in profile with its straight line extending from her guileless brow to the tip of her nose and then gently dropping to her lips and the tidy curve of her chin. And her figure was nicely put together too, even if she was on the short side. But there was a meek uncertainty in the tilt of her head, in the way she lowered her eyes, so light they seemed almost colourless. The Creator had apparently run out of pigment when he got to her irises, although he had skimped her other parts too, leaving her hair and skin a dull, ashen tone.

But Tanya was married to a dashing fellow, the spitting image of d'Artagnan on the cover of the book she had kept under her pillow as a girl. His cologne, the erect points of his moustache, the glint in his eyes, the cleft in his strong, well-shaped chin — Tanya was in love with every part of him.

Yet d'Artagnan didn't love Tanya back. He couldn't possibly love that mouse. Why then he had married her? It was a mystery to all who knew them. She was *such a good soul*, he had told her once in a moment of offhand, lukewarm affection. The phrase wounded her. Nobody ever falls in love with the goodness of somebody's soul. She was smart enough to know that.

While Tanya suffered in silence, d'Artagnan saw no reason to miss out on life. Apart from his own, many other wives and single women too took great pleasure in his company. Like the sun, he shared his warmth unstintingly. He had a generous heart. He enjoyed making women happy.

The proof of that Tanya found one day in a pocket of his pants before dropping them off at the cleaners. There were two notes, one in a childish, upright hand, the other in a hasty scrawl. Both had phone numbers, although Tanya wasn't tempted to call either one. To her husband she gave no hint at all of her discovery.

She couldn't tell what troubled her more: that he was sleeping with other women, or that he hadn't bothered to hide it. Was it deliberate carelessness? Did he hope that she, and not he, would set the awkward ball of their lives careening toward honesty until it had wrecked everything she held dear? That scenario would have undermined her stoic patience and threatened the perilous path she had taken to hold onto her man.

Nothing lasts, wisdom says, even the most exalted love. But time had been cruel to Tanya and left her own love intact.

She had no gift for words and had to borrow from others to fill the painful gap between the radiant landscapes in her soul and ways of expressing them. She grew fond of Central Asian poetry, its intricate laces beguiling her soul. One particular poem enthralled her. A young Tajik woman sends her beloved a pinch of tea, a blade of grass, some sugar, a pebble, an eagle's feather, and a palm nut. The gifts are accompanied by a letter: "I cannot drink tea anymore. Without your love I grow as sere as a blade of grass. You are as sweet as sugar but your heart must be made of stone. I would have come to you if I had wings, for I am to you like a palm nut to its tree." Tanya was just about to slip the poem into her husband's pocket, when she imagined his coldly quizzical gaze and thought better of the idea.

At the Aviation Institute where young men trained to be pilots, junior accountant Tatyana Perepelkina moved abacus beads back and forth all day long. Her diligence did not go unnoticed. At the end of each day, piles of new documents made their way to her desk. "Could you finish this report by tomorrow and check the figures for me? I'm not sure they add up." A son had got into trouble at school, a husband was drunk — women with children always had problems to deal with, whereas Tanya was unencumbered. She had no children, and most evenings she was free to work late, while her d'Artagnan was out fooling around, as everybody knew. And Tanya's help was certainly needed by her friend, Zoe. Zoe was clumsy with figures and had got her job through her connections. How could Tanya refuse to help her, somebody she confided in?

"I wasn't planning on staying late today, if I didn't have to. Can I take a look at your balance sheet tomorrow?"

"What's up?" Zoe asked. Tanya paused. She avoided looking at her friend.

"All I want is to go to bed. Sitting still hurts," she said covering her mouth with her hand.

"Yeah, you look like death today. You didn't have another one, did you?"

"Yes, three days ago ... They gave me nothing for the pain, as usual. I'll die if I have to go through that again."

Zoe quickly glanced up from her balance sheet.

"Good Lord! You have to be crazy to abuse yourself like that! Letting him enjoy himself at your expense!"

"But what else can I do, Zoe? Practically speaking?"

"Practically speaking, you can tell him that, if he gets you pregnant again, you're going to have the baby!"

"He doesn't want children. He sleeps on the couch now. He says there's no pleasure in it for him anymore, since I'm, you know, so paranoid about it."

Zoe leaned back in her chair, stretched out her feet in their high heels, and stuck a pencil into her pile of hair, scratching her scalp and fluffing her coif at the same time.

"Not smart, babe, letting him sleep on the couch! Men can't live without *it*. You know how that always ends up. He'll find himself a lover."

"What if he already has?" Tanya whispered.

"See? What did I tell you?"

It occurred to Tanya that her friend wasn't exactly unhappy about her misfortune, but she suppressed the thought.

"Listen, what are you getting out of the marriage, anyway?" Zoe sat bolt upright and moved her face close to Tanya. "Children he doesn't want. Money he won't provide. Why don't you divorce the rat?"

Tanya blinked and reached for her handkerchief. Zoe,

obviously, didn't believe in suffering. Unlike Tanya, she was a free spirit.

The two friends resembled each other in that nature's initial design for them was the same. But Zoe had bravely twisted nature's arm towards the exotic, her preferred look. Her naturally straight, light-coloured hair had become curly and black, her pale eyes were thickly outlined à la Nefertiti, and she stood taller, thanks to her spike heels.

"I have an idea. Why don't you get baptized?"

"You mean ... Like how?"

"Just like I said. And then you just go ahead and do it and see what happens."

"You think it might actually help? In my situation?"

"Your situation's pretty shitty any way you look at it. But miracles can happen."

"Isn't baptism only for newborns? I'm a little past that, don't you think?"

"Don't be silly. You won't have to get into a font naked. There are other ways." And Zoe gave Tanya an appraising look from head to toe.

"Let's go have a smoke," she said. "I'm dying for a cig."

Zoe took her first puff sitting herself on the marble windowsill in the ladies' room down the hall. Her tight mini skirt moved up baring her plump thighs. Zoe noticed a run on her stockinged left thigh. A toilet flushed in one of the stalls. They waited until the occupant had left the room.

"Somebody I know knows somebody who's friends with a dissident priest. The guy can baptize you at home. All you need is a white robe."

"A white robe? Where would I get a white robe?"

"Oh, don't be silly! Make something. Just like a night

gown, only with long sleeves. He'll sprinkle some water on your head and *voilà*! Then you'll wait and see. You never know what could happen!"

On her way to work every day, Tanya passed the Elokhov Cathedral of the Epiphany, a gorgeous mint-green, gold, and white empire-style edifice sitting on the corner like a queen upon her throne. But Tanya had never been inside the church, let alone talked to a priest. It was rumoured that they all collaborated with the KGB, anyway. Before baptizing people, they would ask to see their passport, the only identity document recognized by the state, write down the information, and then pass it on to the authorities.

Zoe flicked her cigarette ash onto the tiled floor.

"Somebody I know with a tumour in her head *this* big," she said, sticking her fist in Tanya's face, "got baptized, and — wham! — the tumour was gone in a day. You think that God couldn't keep your hubby from fooling around?"

Tanya promised to give it a try.

She took a half day off to give herself several hours before d'Artagnan came back from what he called work, since he had said he would be having supper at home. She got out two bed sheets and her ancient Singer sewing machine, which she hadn't used in years. She struggled with it for half an hour. First, it wouldn't start, and when it finally did, it spat out bits of oil-blackened thread before coming to a stop for good. Tanya panicked. Sew the robe by hand? It wouldn't look good. How did she ever get talked into the whole thing, anyway? A stupid and possibly dangerous idea! She was about to call Zoe to say that she'd changed her mind, when there was a knock on the door. Her heart sank. But it wasn't her husband, who she thought had perhaps forgotten his key, but a short little man holding a scuffed leather bag.

"Repairing old Singers, repairing old Singers," he said with a lilt just like the one knife-sharpeners used when she was a little girl. "Have you got an old Singer?"

"Me? Yes, but how did you ... I mean, how is it that ... ?"

"Don't worry. I know how to fix them. My grandfather fixed Singers, my father fixed Singers, and I can fix them too."

Astonished, Tanya invited him in.

The little man seemed to know right where to go. He crossed the living room to the tiny bedroom where the sewing machine sat on Tanya's dressing table. He opened his bag, took out some tools, did some tightening here and adjusting there, and then asked her to try out some stitches on an old oil-stained rag folded in two. The ancient Singer now ran with perfect smoothness.

"How much do I owe you?" she asked.

"Nothing."

The little man then quickly gathered up his tools, clicked shut the rusty clasp of his bag, and was gone as if Tanya had had just made him up.

After finishing the gown, Tanya went into the kitchen to make d'Artagnan's supper. Outside on the courtyard pavement wet from a recent rain, two little girls were playing hopscotch.

God had just bestowed his first, light-handed miracle on Tanya.

## 2

The next day the dissident priest, a mild, amiable man with a fatherly smile, baptized Tanya at home. She felt awkward in the white gown with only her bra and panties underneath in front of that robust, still handsome man with his neatly trimmed black beard and lively dark eyes. Zoe confidently played the role of Godmother. When the ceremony was over, Tanya felt greatly relieved. She offered to pay the priest, but he wouldn't hear of it.

Now Tanya lived very carefully. She made an effort to notice every little thing, so that she wouldn't miss the next miracle when it came. That another was on its way, she had no doubt. But just how or when it would grace her she had no way of knowing.

Zoe had brought some candy and champagne. Baptisms need to be celebrated, she winked at Tanya — it's the rule. In addition to being her friend, she was now Tanya's godmother, and that meant responsibilities.

"What's the occasion?" d'Artagnan asked the two giggling women when he got home and saw the champagne.

"Maybe I got a raise. Would that be a good enough reason?" Zoe said with a chuckle.

"It works for me! Are we sharing three ways?"

Tanya chuckled too while marvelling at her friend's instant ability to come up with a good fib.

"I'm hot! Do you mind if I take these off?" Zoe started tugging on her knee-high black patent leather boots. The tops collapsed like an accordion, but the boots wouldn't budge.

"Tolya, give me a hand!" She stuck out her feet to d'Artagnan.

He placed her leg on his knees and pulled the boot abruptly off exposing her pink, plump knees and thick ankles. There wasn't anything unusual about those ankles, but for some reason the sight of them made Tanya feel ashamed as if she did something awkward.

D'Artagnan was at his charming best with both ladies that evening. With his arms around their shoulders, he first kissed Tanya and made Zoe count the time, and then he kissed Zoe while Tanya counted. The three of them drank and laughed, and then Zoe suddenly buried her face in d'Artagnan's shoulder for some reason and started to sob.

"Have some more champagne, you silly goose," he said, patting her shoulder.

Zoe became a regular visitor at her friend's apartment, and that brought another benefit: instead of wandering off somewhere after work, Tolya now spent every evening at home. Only once did he revert to his old habit, coming in loaded and falling asleep on the couch with a lit cigarette in his mouth.

Tanya's new vigilance was unceasing — even in her sleep. She smelled the chemical odour of smouldering fabric in the other room and rushed to her husband's rescue. Sending her in time was God's second miracle.

Tanya now walked the earth with a firmer, more confident step. She felt herself to be under God's protection. And the proof of it was Tolya's new attention. Love may get a second wind, Tanya thought. It only needs patience.

But the silver belly couldn't camouflage the darkness of the cloud crawling over — this time — her work. Nothing was said directly, just malicious whispering in the corridors. As usual, Tanya was the last to learn what everybody else already knew: that one of the institute's students had just, only two months short of graduation, been exposed as a churchgoer. He was a widower, in his early 30s, who was raising his son alone after his young wife had succumbed to cancer. The rumours claimed that he had been baptized five years earlier, while (and this was the most outrageous part) still in his first year at the institute. The administration and his teachers would certainly be reprimanded for having failed to notice.

Tanya was alarmed by the coincidence and, bent over her abacus, wondered if she would be exposed too.

The accused was to be "dealt with" at a closed meeting of the Young Communist League. At 28, Tanya was in her last year of membership, and she asked permission to attend the meeting. Her zeal surprised the administration. It was out of character, but one more vote against the offender certainly wouldn't hurt, given the administration's plan to use the League to disgrace and expel him, while keeping its own hands clean.

The institute auditorium was full, and nobody paid attention to the small figure of the accountant pressed against the wall. The director of the institute gazed out over the throng, and then addressed the offender, who was standing in front of the dais.

"Student Markov, are you a Komsomol Member? Explain to us then where your political consciousness was when you got baptized? How have you combined the proud name of Soviet student with such ... such mumbo-jumbo?"

Complete silence descended on the auditorium.

"What's the matter with you, cat got your tongue?" said Tamara Semyonovna Titko, the chair of the union committee, slapping the table for emphasis. She got to her feet revealing to all her impressive bulk. "Give us your answer! The collective is waiting!"

"Politics and religion are separate in our country as a matter of law," the lean young man replied in a careful monotone. "I've neglected none of my social or academic duties."

"We all begin at our own altitude and then soar higher,

carried aloft by our own daring, and at some point we exchange our simple gliders for great aircraft," someone blurted out from the side of the room.

Everyone turned to look. It was the clown Zhorka, leader of the institute's amateur theatre group, paraphrasing a popular song of the 1930s.

"He's already made the exchange. He's flown so high that the next thing you know he'll grab old man God by the beard!" somebody in the back responded to widespread if nervous laughter.

"Cut your inappropriate quips!" the dean intoned in a base.

"Student Markov, did you not take Atheism in your first year?" asked a professor of Marxism-Leninism, which like Atheism was also a required course.

"Yes, just like everybody else."

"What was your grade?"

"I don't remember. *Good*, I think." He was tall, gangly and his right shoulder twitched as he spoke.

"You don't remember?" the Professor of Marxism-Leninism said. "Wasn't too important to remember, was it? Perhaps, it wasn't 'good' after all? Apparently, you change colours like a chameleon! You betrayed our institute, the mother that nurtured you from your first year."

"That isn't true," Vitaly Markov replied in the same deliberate monotone. "And I've also been working nights to support myself and my son."

"Haven't you been getting a stipend?"

"Yes, like all students. Twenty-eight roubles a month. Not nearly enough to feed my son and me."

The director shuffled through papers in front of him on the lectern.

"It states here that you participated in extra-curricular activities and volunteered. Further evidence of your duplicity."

"As a citizen of this country I respect its laws."

"A man who wears a cross can't be a Soviet student," the director replied.

"How do you know he's wearing a cross?" came a voice from the audience.

"Why did he want to become a pilot anyway?"

"Maybe he thought it would bring him closer to God!" somebody added to subdued laughter in the back.

The director rapped on the lectern with his knuckle, calling for order.

"Those who think this is a joke may leave the room. Let's put the matter to a vote. Vitaly Markov doesn't deserve the title of Soviet student and is thus to be expelled from the institute. All those in favour, raise your hands."

"Hold on, comrades! There's no legal ground for ... for such a vote ... It will be, that is, it might be unjust, comrades. Freedom of religion is guaranteed by the Soviet Constitution! You can check for yourselves ..."

It was a weak, high-pitched, girlish voice speaking haltingly from emotion. Nobody knew its owner. All heads turned toward the small woman standing next to the wall by one of the windows. She was pulling at the sides of her dress with her fists while thrusting her body forward from the effort of speaking.

"Anti-Soviet propaganda!" came a shout.

"But she's right! Respect our own Constitution, comrades!" somebody else yelled.

A student in the back jumped to his feet.

"I know Markov as a reliable friend. He has helped me when I needed it!"

"A father raising his son by himself!"

Soon many people were getting up from their seats and shouting.

"Markov got baptized five years ago! How did that become known? Isn't baptism supposed to be a private matter?"

"Stop the debating at once!" the director thundered, as if suddenly coming to his senses. "The picture is clear. Those in favour of the expulsion of Vitaly Markov from the institute, raise your hands!"

"I disagree. There's no basis for expulsion!" the same girlish voice cried out again.

"She's right! The woman is right!"

"Who is she? How did she get in here? Who allowed her?" shouted the director. "Ah, it's our accountant! Congratulations! You're encouraging anti-Soviet agitation and an attempted coup!"

Tanya wasn't really scared. The majority was holding to the right position. God, as always, was up there doing his job, while she was down here doing hers.

Still, she was dreading work next day. But she had to go. The best thing, she decided, would be to immerse herself in her balance sheets as if nothing had happened. And her colleagues in fact made it easier for her: nobody asked her of any favours anymore. Zoe didn't take her eyes off the papers. Hubbub that hovered over the room where only women worked, now ceased. Nobody stepped behind the cabinet crammed with file folders to try on a new jacket or blouse the way they usually did on Wednesdays when the black market dealer Zhanna came by with Finnish pantyhose,

French push-up bras, and other appealing items, and then, with a sniff of the air, left just as stealthily as she had come. In that new silence, the constant clicking of abacus beads was especially audible.

It wasn't long before Tanya was ordered to report to the administration. Waiting for her was the usual triumvirate: the party secretary, the dean, and Titko, the union chair.

"How long has she been ill? And why didn't she let the collective know? It could have helped her," the secretary said in a compassionate tone to nobody in particular.

Tanya assured them that everything was fine with her.

The party secretary nodded solicitously. He wanted to help, but Perepelkina hadn't cooperated. He had been about to go on a fishing trip, but she had served up this surprise. What good could it lead to? He sighed and took a crumpled handkerchief from his pocket, loudly blew his nose, wadded up the handkerchief again, and put it back in his pocket.

"Let her submit a notice in writing," Titko languidly suggested without looking at Tanya.

"What kind of notice?" the dean asked.

"The usual," she said. "That's she's leaving of her own accord."

Then she turned to Tanya and, flashing her eyes, suddenly started to shout: "We don't keep your sort on at the institute! You're cutting off your own nose! You're hatching a religious swamp here! You're trying to spread a religious microbe! You're defending Markov! What is he to you, or did he bribe you? Or are you in cahoots? Anointed with the same myrrh or something? Both baptized?"

For a moment Tanya lost the gift of speech.

"I can't give you a statement like that ... There's no way

I could do that," she mumbled, getting over her initial fright. "I have to feed my husband ..."

"Feed your husband?! What were you thinking about before?! And what were you thinking with?!" Titko yelled. "Submit your notice!"

The party secretary drummed his fingers on the table and loudly sighed.

"You've made a real mess of things, and now we have to clean it up ... Tamara Semyonovna is right. If we want to, we can get rid of workers like you any time. But" — and he drummed his fingers on the table again — "but it all depends on you. Write that you are remorseful about what you did, that you admit your mistake. And then say it in front of everyone at a meeting and we'll excuse you."

"What do you mean write?"

"Well, just that. Write it down. You're not illiterate."

He pushed a blank sheet of paper toward her and started to dictate. "Manifesting ideological spinelessness in regard to the student Markov, I thereby enabled ..."

"I couldn't ... How could I ..."

The party secretary was flummoxed. He loudly blew his nose again and, opening his eyes wide, looked hard at Titko. She leaned over to him and, without taking her eyes off Tanya, whispered something in his ear.

"Yes, quite right," he said to her. "We need an expert assessment, a psychiatric evaluation."

"You can go now, Comrade Perepelkina," Titko said. "We'll inform you of our decision in due course."

When after a time Tatyana was called back to the office, her face had grown sallow and somehow she had become even shorter.

"We're letting you off. You're free to go! You can thank Mikhail Timofeyevich for that," Titko said in an unexpectedly gentle tone, referring to the party secretary. "It was entirely his doing."

"So I can just go, right?"

Unable to believe her ears, Tanya shifted from one foot to the other and remained standing where she was. "Oh, thank you so much! Thank you! You see, I didn't want ... I just wanted ... it to be fair. It's true, I didn't want ..."

"We're going to limit it to a reprimand in your personal file. Only don't even think about asking for leave tomorrow! Show up for work! Understand?"

"Of course, I do, yes, of course."

And on unsteady legs by no means suitable for walking, Tanya finally turned around and left the office.

Almost a week passed. Tanya lived surrounded by the same wary silence. That no one had touched her even though she didn't write a statement she attributed to God. He had protected her on his own, without being asked. Only once when she came across a beggar with stumps for legs sitting by the metro, and was bending over him to toss a few coins into his greasy cap, she started to cry bitterly from pity, but not so much for him, she realized, as for herself. And then around the beginning of autumn when as usual she was hurrying to work, her way was suddenly blocked by an ambulance.

Two orderlies shoved her into a panel van with sealed windows. Twenty minutes later, she found herself in the reception room of the Sailors' Rest psychiatric hospital. In front of her, she saw a bolted steel door. One of the orderlies took a key from his pocket, unlocked the door, and led her down a long windowless corridor. At the other end was a room guarded by two attendants. One of them opened its door with his own key and pushed her into something like a low storage room, where a doctor was waiting. He quickly glanced over his new charge and said something in an undertone to another attendant standing beside him. Tanya was quickly undressed and injected in a buttock. Trembling, she attempted a protest: "What are you doing? Why did you inject me? I'm not sick!"

"If you don't cooperate, we'll put you on insulin!"

"Why insulin?" she asked, her voice already starting to sound like a remote echo of something with no connection to her. And then they dragged her, or rather her body, to another room, wrapped her in a sheet, and put her in a tub of ice water. Then they pulled her out again, tightened the wet sheets around her, and threatened to strap her to the bed if she resisted. The last thing she remembered was a cleaning woman watching nearby with a broom in her hand.

"Do you still think you're Jeanne d'Arc?" a young female doctor in high-heeled boots asked.

"But I never thought I was."

"We have it all written down, so there's no use denying it," she said and then fell silent for a moment. "Well, all right. Who is it that you think you are, then?"

"I don't think I'm anybody."

"Well, who are you, then? What are you?"

"I'm just Tatyana Perepelkina."

After five days of interviews and treatment, the doctor produced a diagnosis: "sluggish" or latent schizophrenia. Tanya spent her days lying on her back, staring at the ceiling, her face swollen like those of drowned children retrieved from the water a week later. She vomited something yellow in the mornings, which brought relief. She grew interested in a spot on the ceiling over her head. Sometimes it looked like a creeping fly, and sometimes it was much bigger than a fly, fuzzy around the edges, and motionless. Awake, she remained silent. After two weeks, since she wasn't violent, she was allowed to have visitors.

# 3

D'Artagnan was waiting for Tanya in the special room provided for the purpose, with a steel bolt on its door, a little observation window for the woman who supervised the visits, and no furniture except for two chairs. There was also an acrid smell that was instantly familiar to him from his childhood and his time in the army: the smell of urine and of lime scattered around the toilet holes in the latrine floor.

"What have you got there?" a voice in the observation window growled.

D'Artagnan opened his briefcase and took out something wrapped in newspaper.

"Just pajamas," he said as he pulled at the wrapping.

"What's the matter with you? Don't you know the rules? No clothes from home are permitted! Germs!"

D'Artagnan returned the pajamas to his briefcase and fastened its clasp.

"What is allowed in here? Things to eat, maybe?"

"That depends. Generally speaking, the lunatics have everything they need."

"Take me home," Tanya said to her husband when she finally came into the visiting room. The tie strings on her hospital gown had been ripped off, so she held the two halves of it together with her hands, trying to keep herself covered, and d'Artagnan saw the triangle of her flat chest under the flimsy prison-coloured garment.

"Take me home, I beg you. They're giving me insulin shots." She started to cry and he wanted to put his arms around her, but she smelled so bad that he couldn't bring himself to.

And then he didn't visit her again for two weeks. When he did reappear, a bar of chocolate in one hand and his briefcase in the other, he was stunned by how much she had changed.

It was as if the disease for which she had been confined had finally emerged, forcing the real Tanya out and enclosing in a greasy, gelatinous shell whatever slow, listless semblance of her was left.

D'Artagnan took some documents from his briefcase. He was filing for divorce on the grounds of Tanya's diagnosis of schizophrenia.

"By the way, Zoe's moving in with me next week. We packed all your stuff in some suitcases. It'll sit in the storeroom until you return. No need to worry about it."

Tanya didn't say a word or even glance through the documents. She took the pen d'Artagnan held out to her and with unbending fingers signed them.

"Here, press again, press harder. So they won't find fault with it," he said.

# 4

The student Vitaly Markov had in the meantime been expelled from the institute. Since the administration had been unable to engineer a unanimous Young Communist League vote for the purpose, he was given a failing grade on the final exam in Dialectical Materialism. This automatically terminated his enrolment without a degree. A valuable worker, he was still able to hold onto his part-time job for a while. The news of his expulsion and the reason for it hadn't got out yet.

Even when the first warning call did come from the institute, his boss hesitated. It took a second one to convince him. "I won't give you a bad reference, if you ever need one," he said as he stared out the window. "But it's the best I can do."

They didn't want to let Vitaly into the hospital. "It's not visiting hours, and it isn't permitted anyway!" the receptionist at the front desk cut him short.

"I'll only visit her a minute and then come right back."

"But I told you, it isn't permitted! What's your relationship to her?"

"She's my sister," Vitaly said, handing the receptionist an opened box of candy with a ten-ruble note placed between the tissue covering the candy and the lid with its picture of the Kremlin.

"Well, all right, go ahead, then," the receptionist said, quickly moving the candy out of sight behind her desk. "She won't last much longer, your sister."

For several days Tanya's temperature had been elevated. Dusk fell early now, and just before sunset she would grow anxious and toss and turn, moaning and whimpering.

And then through the barred window of her ward, she saw snow falling. It came unusually early this year, in September. Against the visible patch of clotted bluish sky, it looked like handfuls of pebbly grey flour had been hurled down. The old woman in the bed next to Tanya's howled and swore obscenely, then snivelled like a little child calling for its mama, while white-gowned shapes hovered over her. But then they left and everything grew quiet. And then in the stillness Tanya made out the outline of a man sitting on the edge of her bed. It was Vitaly.

"How did you get in here?" she asked, feeling the apparition's hand on hers.

"I told them you were my sister. I hope you don't mind. In spirit, you are." The apparition added softly: "It's nice to see you, Tanya!"

"You, too ... " she slurred but with a vaguely caressing gaze.

The extreme pallor of her swollen face struck him.

"You need some fresh air. Don't they take you for walks in the yard?"

"That isn't the reason ... It's from the injections, I think." He was surprised by how hoarse her voice had become. He remembered the high-pitched girlish one calling out to people to respect their own constitution.

"You'll get better, Tanya, you'll see." He picked up her hand. It was burning hot. The pulse was racing.

"You have quite a fever," he said, trying to hide his anguish.

"Yes, I always do in the evening. Soon it will all be over with."

"Oh, don't say that, Tanya! Sure, the situation here is harsh, and it isn't any wonder you have thoughts like that. But you'll certainly get better! I've brought you something to eat." And careful not to attract the attention of the other people in the ward, he took some mandarin oranges from his pocket.

"Mandarins! Where did you get them?" she said.

"Shall I peel one for you? You need the vitamin C to get your strength back."

She weakly nodded.

"Do you know that you have the most beautiful eyes?" he said. "I've never seen eyes like yours. Like lapis lazuli, only not as dark."

"Like what?"

"Actually, I'm not sure myself. Maybe I'm pronouncing it wrong. All I know is that it's a very beautiful blue. Once I was on a ship in the Baltic. And I went out on the deck just before dawn. It was completely quiet, and the sea was very, very calm, almost motionless, and silver-grey, just like the sky above it, so that you couldn't really tell where the water ended and the sky began. And then the sun came up and broke though the grey haze, and the water turned a soft light-blue. Your eyes are just like the mysterious blue of the sea that morning."

She pressed his hand in response and he fell silent from embarrassment.

"What made you come today, Vitaly?" she asked in her hoarse voice.

"They were selling the mandarins on the street today, so I bought some for my son and for you." He lightly stroked her fingers again. "But can I ask you something?"

"Of course."

"Why did you do it? That is, take my side? I'll never forget that you did."

"Oh, that..." She sighed and her lips formed something like a little smile. "When God stops working miracles, some-one has to do it for Him, don't you think?"

# ~ THE SECRET VERMONT LABS

A STITCH IN time saves nine, the proverb goes. But we paid no attention to folk's wisdom.

"But how were we supposed to know?"

"There were signs all over the place," the language department head said his right eyebrow twitching, a sure sign of his displeasure. "You should have noticed."

In hindsight, I have to agree. She left more than a few traces and clues. But we were people of good will and trusting by nature.

So we gave her the benefit of the doubt. Which was foolish, since something had seemed off to us from the moment she came through our office door. My own view was that she must have had a good connection — a hairy paw, as we call it — in some high place to saunter in like that. With hardly a nod, let alone a smile. With a severe profile and black hair hanging spade-like down her back. And bangs cut straight across her forehead. Sturdy looking, as if made of bristle. Clear, pale skin. Squinty feline eyes. Arrogant aquiline nose always tilted at a disdainful angle. Pencil-thin and flat-chested, an assortment of sharp angles: chin, collar bone, elbows. Wiggling her almost non-existent derrière in a sly, even arch way, that was embarrassing to see. Bangles, five or six of them on each arm, clicking as she moved, and the swishing of her flared skirt. Was she an Armenian? A Georgian? A Gypsy? We had no idea.

*Azelea Butikova-Armand.* What kind of name was that? How could you have such a name if it was not as camouflage? *Azelea*! What was it, a garden plant? A species of African antelope, perhaps? But certainly not an appropriate name for a Soviet instructor of French! Most definitely not! And then *Butikova* ... What did that mean? Booties of some kind that nobody ever wears? Or that idle ladies of the past pulled on over their fancy evening footwear to protect it from nasty weather when they went to the opera? Does that mean her ancestors were shoemakers? Or was the name just part of the deception? And Armand? It fell, after the hyphen, like brick on your head: *Armand*! Who hadn't heard of the French Communist Inessa Armand? Comrade Armand, the passionate Bolshevik and intimate of Lenin and his wife, Nadezhda Krupskaya. Was our Azelea a relation or just named for her? That's a question we racked our brains over. Half of us believed she was related, while the other half thought it was a hoax. In the end we couldn't be sure, and that dumped the apples from our cart and paralyzed our thought processes.

When Lenin arrived from Switzerland in a sealed train with a secret cache of German money to finance the Bolshevik revolution, Comrade Armand had been on the train with him. Where Nadezhda Krupskaya was is covered with a veil. Some say that she shared the car with the lovers, while others say that she was even in the same compartment with them. Wherever the three were located in the car, Lenin emerged alone at Finland Station in Petrograd to make his revolution. Because the women were true revolutionaries, they didn't quarrel in a petit-bourgeois way, with tufts of hair flying in every direction. They showed respect. When you're blazing with a desire to reshape the world (a desire they all shared), there is no room for jealousy left in your heart.

Having the busiest schedule on earth as the leader of the world proletariat, Lenin was nevertheless both very humane and a stickler for detail. He personally turned up at Armand's front door with galoshes wrapped in a newspaper under is arm. Well, perhaps he did sent the galoshes through the NKVD of the Russian Federation. I'll give you that. But it isn't the point! The point is that he *cared*! But could it be that he cared too much? Wasn't it overshooting the mark to personally write that woman 150 letters while the whole world was holding its breath for his next directive? In other words, did Comrade Armand deserve such thoughtful attention from the leader of the World Revolution?

The character of Armand also raises some questions. Was she contemptuous of convention as a matter of ideology? Was she indeed defending a woman's right to free love by her own personal example? Or was she merely a lady of easy virtue, an adventuress of the age-old species that has always clung to great historical figures, as, for example, Madame de Pompadour did?

One day history will pronounce its verdict, and give us the answers.

A penniless French girl arrives in Russia. She insinu-
ates herself as a governess and gains the trust of the filthy
rich Russified Armands. She marries the elder brother and
immediately sets up an illicit printing press in her father-
in-law's basement. Clandestine meetings, conspir-
acy — those are her passions. Among her various secret
activities, she manages to produce four babies and seduce
her brother-in-law. Then she abandons her children, ab-
sconds with the brother-in-law, 11 years her junior, and with
him has a fifth child. Does that make the fifth at once a
cousin and a sibling of the other four? But she doesn't stop
there. She ultimately finishes her second husband off by
getting herself arrested and exiled to Siberia, where he fol-
lows her, catches cold, and dies. A truly revolutionary life
and temperament!

Well, now you understand why we handled Azelea so
gingerly. What if she was related to Inessa? From time to
time our Azelea dropped hints to that effect, but mostly it
was her swagger — the way she flashed her eyes, swayed her
hips, prompting us to find similarities and invoke Armand's
biography. To make it even more suspicious, Azelea taught
French, as I've already said. Why not English or German or
Spanish, if the two women really did have nothing to do
with each other?

It was a mystery, a hall of mirrors.

No wonder we played it safe, mostly leaving Azelea
alone, especially when it came to staff meetings.

On average, there were ten hours of meetings a week:
early morning briefings for faculty, weekly political information sessions for the students led by the faculty, separate
sessions for faculty led by the head of the department dep-

uty, five-hour work evaluation sessions, and late evening Socialist Competition reviews.

In the six years we were acquainted with her, Azelea showed up for meetings only three times. The first one suggested Cleopatra disembarking from a gilded barge with royal sails unfurled. And it was an important meeting, too. Not only was the head of the department there, but so were the union people and the local Communist Party chair. So in she strolled well after the meeting had begun, announcing her entrance with the usual clicking of her bangles. The chairs in the main recital hall were all of the folding variety. Unabashed, she ambled to the front row, selected a chair, and sat down with enough fussing to let everybody know that the queen had arrived. Worse, she had nothing with her except a pencil and a notebook. Crossing her legs, she opened the notebook and started sketching various speakers with rapid glances back and forth between it. Looked like it wasn't she who had been summoned to the meeting, but we who had been brought there for her sketching pleasure taking our turns at the lectern so she could see us better, like animals in a zoo, a parade of macaques, say. One of the women furtively hinted with her eyebrows that Azelea try to be more discreet and conceal the notebook. To no avail.

After the meeting she went over to the members of the presiding panel and handed out caricatures of each of them: the First Secretary of the Communist Party, the Union Chairman, the language department chair. And then with a shake of her bangles, she took her skirts in her hands and was quickly out the door.

The second time wasn't a meeting but a professional development workshop just before the winter break. When everybody was ready to go home, spend time with their kids, and catch up on all the domestic chores left unattended during the semester. Blizzards, temperatures of minus 30, lines for groceries, whining kindergarten kids with runny noses. We women have always counted on the winter break for our survival. But no, the order came down that it was instead to be time to demonstrate our technological superiority to the West by switching over to computers! That was the early eighties, when none of us had ever seen a computer with our own eyes.

We had one typewriter at the foreign language department and a secretary to go with it (if everybody started typing whatever they needed, how would you keep track of it?). The rest of us, 50 female instructors, plus two lost male birds, used chalk and a blackboard. Mimeograph machines, let alone photocopiers, were not something we ever saw either. Old blackboards and textbooks were our only instruments of enlightenment.

So here's the question. If there were no computers anywhere to be seen, how could you teach a group of mostly middle-aged, worn-out women, instructors of foreign languages, to use the things? The answer is: you put them through a crash course in computer programming. You feed them FORTRAN, COBOL, PROLOG, and the rest of it. So there we all sat after being herded into a large amphitheatre, and diligently copied down the impenetrable hooks, ticks and strokes — the Egyptian hieroglyphs that some young guy was scribbling on the blackboard, after announcing that there would be a test at the end. Our pens squeaked, flies dropped out of the air from boredom, and then suddenly, in the middle of all that tedium, came the familiar sound of clicking bangles. It was our Cleopatra making her appearance 40 minutes into the ordeal.

This time instead of a note pad she had brought a wicker basket full of poisonously red yarn. Swinging her skirts as usual and crossing one knee over the other in her nonchalant way, she began to knit in full view of all. What made it so hard to stomach was that we knew that she was knitting just for the fun of it. There was no way she could be a good housewife. Besides, she was single at the time.

The test day arrived. We were all bent over our text booklets and struggling to make sense of the dreaded questions. Azelea, however, merely glanced over hers. Then she got to her feet and, knitting basket in hand and her heels clicking, descended the amphitheatre steps to the examiner's table. We lifted our heads to watch.

"You don't really expect me to answer this rubbish, do you?" she said with narrowed eyes to the young instructor. "You haven't once shown me a computer. Here, take this. It will protect your brain from further damage." The examiner stared at her like a young bull at a new gate. She pulled a red watch cap over his head. And then after a lilting "Ciao, mio caro!" she sailed from the room.

But it was after the third meeting she came to that the back of our patience finally broke. I, as a instructors' supervisor, was responsible for the students' political information sessions, which meant that I had to keep track of everything that went on which I did, partly with a couple of students who provided me with the details about who had said what and why.

It was around that time that the Americans succeeded in growing the AIDS virus in their secret labs. At the routine information sessions (each monitored by an instructor), the students took turns briefing each other about what had happened in the world over the past week.

One of Azelea's students was giving a report on a new network of underground labs in Vermont, personally financed by Alexander Solzhenitsyn, who had settled in the state expressly for that purpose. The CIA was planning to use the virus as a new biological weapon against the Soviet people, and Solzhenitsyn had contributed his Nobel Prize money to finance the enterprise.

As the student spoke, Azelea stared out the window with her chin resting on her palm, as if that vile imperialist plot were the least of her concerns. She was obviously off in some dreamland, the student later told me, contemplating peaches and lemons ripening somewhere in the Caucasus. According to a rumour that Azelea herself had spread, she was on the verge of eloping with a violinist lover, a romantic soul leaving his wife. But we knew for certain that that was just a smokescreen. No peaches or lemons and no love-sick violinist were waiting for her anywhere. At her own tiny one-bedroom apartment shared with her two sons, she was nothing more than a single mother. And if she wasn't hard up, why else would she teach both morning and night classes and also bring her badly behaved seven-year-old to work with her? No, Azelea didn't have any rivers flowing with milk or honey waiting for her, and so had no right to belittle her student the way she did. The Vermont Labs had brought her back from dreamland, apparently, for she abruptly turned away from the window and snapped at the student.

"You believe all that?"

"Believe what?" he asked.

"About the CIA, growing the AIDS viruses."

"It's in the paper," the student said, pointing to the front-page editorial. The class was as still as grass on the moon. "What about you? Are you saying you don't believe it?"

"If they write that fish use umbrellas when it rains, should I believe that too?" That's actually what she said, according to the student, who would never have made it up.

I sounded the alarm. I informed the head and got things rolling. Azelea was immediately called in for a good thrashing. She didn't show up, of course. We sent her another summons, this time also calling her around midnight as a warning. At the time we had a back-up plan in place to fire her, although there were some who objected. If she was a real Armand, there was a risk that it could backfire. In any case, it couldn't be done in absentia; we would need to have her signature.

We waited for her to show up, pretending that we had other important matters on our agenda. But she never came. Neither that day, nor any other. We were upset. She had pushed us to the limit of human patience and we wanted to take her apart piece by piece, so to speak. Our subsequent phone calls produced no result. She seemed to have vanished from the face of this earth. As always happens in such cases, the number of rumours increased, each one more absurd than the last. The violinist has finally divorced his wife and was now making out with Azelea on a sunny beach of the Gurzuf resort in Crimea. Or she had escaped abroad by marrying some filthy-rich foreigner and was now loafing about Biarritz or else somewhere on the Riviera. We expected anything from her, but not what really happened. That's why when our Head was summoned to the First

Department and informed that our Botikova had applied for the immigration visa to Israel, his reaction was stupor and disbelief. What have the relative of Inessa Armand to do with Zionists? the head asked. Azelia's real name was Armuller, the First Department explained dispassionately. Her father had managed to change his last name during the war by faking his own birth certificate. But Armuller or not, how could you have allowed this to happen, that's what we need to know. Where were you all looking?

I don't think the head was able to provide any answers to that.

The truth is that decent people don't put their colleagues in harm's way applying for an exit visa. They quit their job first. Azelia wanted to let us have it, and she did. Since technically she wasn't fired yet, we, administration, had to take all the blame for her betrayal of her country.

As expected, the heads — I mean, our heads — began to roll. The top administration was relieved of their positions, and I was sent to an early retirement.

In the hindsight, we should have got rid of her quietly, and soon.

But if wishes were horses, beggars would ride.

## ⌒ EXPULSION

**1**

OF THE 15 problems Alexandra was supposed to solve for math, she had done only three. It was already five o'clock, and at roughly 30 minutes per problem there was almost no chance, with time out for supper, that she would finish the set until well after midnight. She gazed at the muslin curtains billowing in the afternoon breeze and then down at her math text, where a train carrying neither passengers nor cargo was hurtling from Point A to Point B, while another, its identical twin, was hurtling in the opposite direction. What was the point of calculating the distance, velocity, and time if the trains were going to collide anyway?

A moth had got into the vase Alexandra's father brought back from a conference in Venice. She watched its dull thrusts against the red glass and then tilted the vase just enough for the moth to see a way out before she set it upright again and covered the opening with a piece of blotting paper.

Then she skipped ahead to the next problem, which

involved the flow of water from one pool into another. Five pages in the other direction two empty elevators were moving up and down their shafts. Inside the Venetian glass, the moth's wings glowed red. Under the table, Alexandra's dog, Kerry, shifted in his sleep. She'd had a fever the day before but was sent to school anyway, since she couldn't afford to miss math. This morning she had a pre-emptive attack of vomiting and was allowed to stay home. The trick was simple enough. All she had to do was stare for a while at the marks in her exercise book. *2*, despite its presumed superiority to the scrawny *1*, was really the lowest, a mother-infuriating failing mark. It sent a wave of nausea up her esophagus. *3*, just barely passing, played its own nasty part by aping the shape of *5*, the highest mark and forever beyond her reach.

Whose fault was it that she wasn't any good at math? Or at much else, for that matter? If fairies brought talents to newborns, they had arrived at her cradle nearly empty-handed, having already given their bounty to her bother, an athlete, chess-player, and champion of the USSR Math and Physics Olympics.

When Alexandra was born, her brother's name, with a slight adjustment, was given to her too in hopes of passing on with it the family's wunderkind gene. True, she was born a girl, but let her try anyway. And so she did, for ten years and more, disappointing everyone but her brother, who had long left such things behind.

Alexandra never got to meet him. She was born eight months after he dove off a cliff above the Istra River near their summer dacha and hit his head on a steel rod sticking out of the river's sandy bottom. Ever since, Alexandra's mother had begged her father to trade the ill-fated dacha for another uncontaminated by memory and, ideally, capable of being reached by a different rail line entirely. Her father's unvarying response was to take his Adam's apple between his thumb and forefinger as if he'd just swallowed a fish bone and then rapidly chew on his lower lip, something he did whenever faced with a situation he regarded as hopeless.

Alexandra's father, the esteemed Professor Bolt, was a leading specialist in neurophysiology and developmental psychology, a follower of the famous Lev Vygotsky and Alexander Luria, and a Corresponding Member of the Academy of Sciences. And for his outstanding achievements and service he had been assigned a choice dacha by the state. Not only was swapping it for another impossible under the circumstances, but its continued availability might even be at risk thanks to the wobbly architecture of the Bolt family history.

Along with other peasants skilled in wine making, his ancestors had been brought to Russia from Switzerland by Catherine the Great. For nearly two centuries they raised grapes on land they had been given near the city of Odessa. But when Germany invaded the Soviet Union in 1941, two of Alexandra's great-uncles had, like many others of Swiss colonist descent, fled the country for Switzerland. Even though all contact with them and their children had as a result been severed, whenever Professor Bolt was required to fill out an official form, his "no" to the question, "Do you (or your spouse) now have (or did you ever have) relatives living abroad?" would make his stomach churn. For a "yes" could have meant the instant collapse of his career and the loss of the family's apartment and dacha.

For three years after Alexander's death, the dacha remained unused and neglected, with rank weeds and rampant morning glories gradually obscuring all signs of the Bolts' former presence. Alexandra's mother refused to set foot in the place where he son's life had been taken, and so they spent their summers at a Black Sea resort for distinguished scientists instead. Occasionally, in the winter when the temperature dropped below freezing, her father would visit the dacha by himself to make sure the pipes hadn't burst or that the roof hadn't fallen in after a heavy snowfall.

Alexandra's mother had adored her talented son, and not least because he looked nothing at all like her or his father. They, like Alexandra, lived inside large, lazy, doughy bodies topped with oblong heads and pale pudgy faces. Alexander, however, had somehow come from different stock, with an olive complexion, dark eyes, and curly jet-black hair. "One of our peasant ancestors must have taken a Cossack bride," Professor Bolt liked to joke in his lighter moments.

In the sepia photograph on their parents' dresser, the gaze of Alexander's dark, sensual eyes fringed with long girlish lashes was bold and direct. A young man with a face like that could have charmed his way around just about any adversary, his sister thought whenever she stopped to examine his familiar features. He must have been fearless, since he wasn't looking down or off to the side the way the other family members did.

Alexander's birthday in December was always celebrated. He would have been 22 this year. Katya, the Bolts' housekeeper, passed back and forth between the dinner table and the oak sideboard, the sound of her steps muffled by the apartment's soft Bukhara carpets. A starched hand-embroidered cloth covered the table, set with their best silverware and crystal and a large vase of flowers in the centre. Savory pastries stuffed with cabbage, mushrooms, and sautéed onions, Alexander's favourites, lay on a blue plate at the head of the table before an empty chair. Alexandra's mother, her pinkie extended, spread red caviar on a slice of rye bread, just the way Alex liked it. Then she resumed her seat and, sitting upright, signalled with downcast eyes the start of a Minute of Silence. Inaudible before, the hissing of tires on the street outside was suddenly heard. A hiccup from the refrigerator helped fill the memorial interval, along with the sound of trash being dumped into the hallway chute by someone upstairs. Steam rose from the chicken broth with dumplings and fresh dill that had just been spooned into separate bowls. Alexandra's mother then broke the silence. She stood up with a goblet in her hand. "For our boy, our special boy ... Today he would have ..." Her voice trailed off and she began to sob.

"There, there, Ira," Alexandra's father murmured.

With a slight twist of her shoulder, her mother evaded his comforting hand. Didn't he realize that she was entitled to her suffering? And then the phone rang. "It's probably Kozlov from the committee," her father said, anxiously chewing on his lower lip.

"You're not going to answer it," Alexandra's mother said in a monotone. The phone went on ringing.

With each commemoration, Alexandra's unspoken resentment of her brother took deeper root. He had been dead for many years, and yet her mother still yearned for him, while Alexandra was alive and neglected. It's true she had none of his talents, and she looked too much like her mother had when she was a girl: the same chubby body and puffy face with high cheekbones leaving little space for her eyes, and the same mousy hair and slightly raised upper lip that left her teeth exposed, so that more than anything else she looked like a bewildered fish.

Alexandra's mother, however, had managed to compensate for her unremarkable looks and, with the help of makeup and lipstick and carefully cut and styled hair, she had made herself into a pleasingly plump and even impressive lady. Alexandra, on the other hand, still showed no signs of remission. But her father seemed to have an abstract, distant affection for her, even so.

As she lifted a tasty dumpling from her bowl of broth, Alexandra stole a glance at her parents. Yes, it was mean-spirited of her to envy her brother's talents. Especially since he couldn't use them anyway, being dead for so long. And it wasn't his fault that she didn't know what to do with the life given her to live day after day. Katya shopped for groceries and cooked, played cards with the maid of another family on the fifth floor, and secretly read a prayer book. Alexandra's father made his discoveries about the nature of the human psyche, while her Mother chaired the local committee of Soviet Women for Peace. Alexandra's schoolmates competed for high marks and after class worked on new issues of the school's wall newspaper. Everyone in the world knew some trick for a smooth and purposeful ride. Everyone but Alexandra, that is.

After her son's death, Alexandra's mother started to call her just Alex. She didn't feel like an Alex, let alone a boy, but the name stuck anyway.

## 2

The second disaster for her parents after the death of their son was Alex's looming expulsion from Special School No. 1. Not that the awful word was ever said out loud, since that could have backfired, but the idea skulked in the same corner of their minds where the Swiss defectors also lurked — two time bombs now instead of one. School No. 1 was the only one like it in all of Moscow, just as its name unequivocally attested. Established for the sons of diplomats and Politburo members, it had opened its doors to girls the same year that Alexandra took her entrance exams at the age of seven. Although she could read well by then and even recite Pushkin by heart, she fell down on her multiplication tables. But since they couldn't turn away the daughter of the famous Professor Bolt, they admitted her anyway.

The school was proud of its exclusivity. It employed native speakers of German to teach German until, after the war, that language was replaced by English. A special program exposed the students to English very early on. A third of all their subjects, including history, literature, and physics were taught in English. By grade seven, girls — with little white bows in their braids and frills on their starched white aprons of the kind that servants wear in respectable households — could recite *Beowulf* in Old English, Chaucer in Middle English, and Alexander Pope for astonished foreigners, mostly Communists from Great Britain and America.

But the school's ambition went far beyond even Alexander Pope. Advanced algebra and solid geometry was considered essential for the development of young minds. And to establish an experimental math class in those subjects, a new teacher was hired. Her name was Vera Ivanovna Popova, or "VIP," as the students immediately nicknamed her, combining her initials.

Coming as they did from privileged backgrounds, all the students at School No. 1 were gifted by definition. Even so, Alex's family found it hard to keep up with the bluebloods of the Politburo, whose children were driven to school in black Volga sedans, whereas Alex, until she was old enough to go by herself, was taken to school by Katya on the streetcar.

Intimate, home-style meals organized by the Parents' Council were another sign of social standing. Unlike ordinary children, the students of School No. 1 didn't have to gather in a crowded cafeteria for their lunch break. The wives of the Soviet elite, freed from responsibilities outside the home, took turns serving brioches on white napkins and pouring tea into mugs decorated with the happy faces of Snow White and the seven dwarves. The dignified confidence of her mother as she carried these trays before her ample bosom embarrassed Alex. Everybody on the Parent's Council knew that the new math teacher's arrival had put Alex's place at the school in jeopardy. In view of that, her mother's confidence seemed false.

Chewing on a buttered brioche, Alex stared at the dreamy face of Snow White on her tea mug. She vaguely envied the fairytale girl in her daisy-bedecked apron for her power over all those little men in pointed red caps and for their undisguised admiration of her. Even the dwarves' diminutive size was enviable. They could squeeze into any cranny and, if need be, disappear completely.

Before advanced math struck with full force, Alex's marks were still tolerable. She dragged her fragile *3*'s from class to class — upstairs to the zoology room with its stuffed crocodile, parrot, and bear, and then all the way back downstairs to the woodshop in the basement. The mediocre marks stood at the ready as Alex struggled with a coping saw over a piece of plywood that was supposed to be turned into a cutting board for her mother on March 8, International Women's Day. Alex's last woodshop assignment, a kitchen stool, still staggered on rickety legs like a newborn calf.

"How did you manage to make each leg a different length, Bolt?" the woodshop instructor asked her. He too gave her a mediocre *3* and advised her not to come back, since the materials were precious.

"The earth is full of hidden riches," said the geography teacher, Pyotr Petrovich Shugaev, a pot-bellied giant with a black beard bisecting his chest, as he walked between the rows of desks. Using his pointer, he made sure that coal, gas, iron, and diamond deposits were identified with appropriate symbols on the students' contour maps: triangles for iron ore, squares for diamond deposits, and so on. Ocean depths were represented in darker and lighter shades of blue, while tectonic plates wavered between a yellowish and dark brown.

But Pyotr Petrovich's real passion was meteorology. Twice a day, seven mornings and evenings a week, the students were expected to record meteorological phenomena in ruled notebooks. Clouds formations were to be identified by type, an anemometer was to be checked for wind direction and velocity, the air temperature was to be indicated, and, after dark, the movement of constellations across the night sky was to be noted.

"Suppose you get lost in the woods at night, Bolt. How will you find your way if you don't understand the night sky?"

·Alex's gaze fell on his baggy pants smudged with chalk around the fly. "He went to the lavatory during recess," she observed to herself, her fear of getting lost in the woods thereby considerably reduced.

When the technical-drawing teacher put an old internal combustion engine in the centre of the classroom, Alex closed her eyes until she felt the reassuring touch of her friend Nina's hand on her hip. In the lavatory, always safely empty during class, Alex placed Nina's drawing against the window pane and traced its contours onto her own paper.

At the start of her seventh year at School No. 1, Alex fell in love with the narrowed eyes of the technical translation teacher, a war veteran of about 35 with an empty sleeve tucked into his belt. She spent hours in front of the mirror stuffing cotton wool into her bra, for her a totally useless article at the time. But as hard as she would try, technical translation had no more appeal than three-legged stools or internal combustion engines. But the mixture of awe and adoration that gripped her whenever her idol entered the classroom forced her through the pages of their big technical dictionary. She expected another "swan," that is, a 2, at the end of the semester, but when she got a 4 instead, the generosity of her idol's heart shook her to the core and she was unable to sleep that night.

Alex was the only student in her year, and perhaps even in the whole school, who liked music class. The lanky teacher, nicknamed "Goop" for his slick black hair combed across a shiny pate, provoked almost uncontrollable mirth from the boys whenever the girlish bow of his mouth produced a high soprano tremolo. Goop was also infamous for his fear of germs, and at every interval between classes would run to the lavatory to wash his hands. His taste in opera was, from a Soviet point of view, highly unorthodox. He omitted such obligatory examples of national art as Mussorgsky's *Boris Godunov* and Tchaikovsky's *Eugene Onegin* in favour of Purcell's *Dido and Aeneas*, Mozart's *Don Giovanni*, and Beethoven's *Fidelio*. Attendance was not unlike Swiss cheese. There were on any given day pockets of empty seats as students were either out sick or about come down with the flu and gone after the first break. To be sure, students were a lower form of life and Goop treated them accordingly — with a patronizing aloofness. Alex, however, was the exception. Who would have guessed that living within her thick body was a voice of such power, vibrancy, and lushness? Goop had no doubt that Alex was destined for a great future in opera and, ignoring the rest of the students, he would accompany her on the piano, while coaching her in the phrasing of one sentimental ballad or another.

Once after class, Goop gave his favourite a rare recording of highlights from Purcell's Baroque *Dido and Aeneas*. "Keep it. It will help you, Alexandra. You have a rare and precious instrument — a dramatic soprano. Cherish it." His eyes were moist with awkward emotion. "By the way, I saw you in the schoolyard yesterday without a scarf. That was a grave mistake! Wear a warm scarf whenever it gets cold to protect your voice from the fluctuation of temperature. That's just a little piece of advice I can give you." He tapped the window pane, listening to the sound. "I can help you find a good voice teacher, if your parents agree. I'd love to teach you myself, but I can't, of course. When the time comes, you'll be taught proper breathing technique, along with many other things. But what no one can teach you is how to cultivate an inner ... shall we say... serenity, tranquillity, and thoughtfulness. How to live with joy. Those you will have to teach yourself. How shall I put it? Young girls your age are prone to emotional volatility, even outbursts, but if you're going to be serious about your art, you'll need to master that."

At the beginning of the following semester, in February, Alex started taking voice lessons after school with a close friend of Goop's, a retired professor from the famous Tchaikovsky State Conservatory.

# 3

VIP appeared for the first time toward the end of Alex's eighth year, two months after she had begun voice lessons. A brusque nod was all the students got by way of greeting when she entered the classroom. Then their new math teacher would immediately turn to the blackboard and proceed to cover its chalk-smudged surface with the hooks, signs, and strokes of complex equations. As she paced back and forth in front of the board, the boys scrutinized her body, which was as flat as a board both fore and aft, with nothing to catch their eyes (so the verdict went) except for a hairy wart on her chin, old-fashioned laced-up brown shoes, and brown cotton stockings that rippled in accordion-like folds on her thick calves. When, with her back to the class, VIP opened her mouth for the first time, somebody whistled in surprise at how low and raspy it was. For a moment it even seemed like a man had just come into the room. But then VIP suddenly turned around and faced the class, the severe cut of her short, straight hair in keeping with her sharp, angular movements.

"Who whistled?"

Silence.

VIP cleared her throat. "I'm not deaf. I heard somebody whistle. If you're brave enough to do something like that, then you'll also have the courage to acknowledge it."

A finger pointed at Bolt. It belonged to Max Nosov, the class clown.

"She did," he said in an ingratiating voice.

Silence again.

While Alex's first and by definition unrequited love was for the war veteran technical translation teacher, her second was for the amusing Max, and though it still remained undeclared, it enjoyed at least the possibility of being returned. Not for nothing had he sent spitballs flying her way during music class or thrown wet rags at her when they shared floor-mopping duty at the end of the school day. Those pranks were, as Alex regarded them, evidence of his unspoken affection for her.

"Was it you?" VIP said to Alex.

"No," she barely audibly replied.

"You, eh ... Nosov, you said you heard her whistle?" VIP asked, looking down at her seating chart.

"I did," the boy repeated.

VIP looked sternly at Alex.

"Bolt, is it? Stand up when a teacher is speaking to you."

Alex lifted the black top of her desk and clumsily stood

up, knocking her eraser, exercise book, and compass onto the floor. She awkwardly bent over to pick everything up as VIP watched her.

"Yes, I'm Bolt," she said when she stood up again and looked at the teacher.

"Did you say 'Bolt' or 'Nut'?" VIP asked as she looked down at the seating chart again. "'Ah, yes, Bolt, Alex Bolt. Is that a boy's or a girl's name?"

The class exploded in laughter. Surprisingly, the dry old stick did have a sense of humour. "Well, whoever she is, one thing is obvious," VIP continued. "She's bored stiff in my class. Clearly, she already knows everything I'm going to say. It's no wonder she whistled."

VIP's use of the third person detached Alex from the rest of the students as if she weren't there.

"But I didn't whistle," Alex protested, her lips and tongue moving as if her mouth were full of cement.

"Did everybody hear that? She didn't whistle. Her classmate has falsely accused her. So, your classmate is a liar?"

"It was her," Max said again. "I saw her whistling."

It was as that moment that Alex began to sob. She couldn't help it. She had been cursed with quick tears since early childhood.

"Nerves!" her father would say as he watched her cry at the least thing.

"Given the circumstances of my pregnancy, it's no wonder," her mother would answer in irritation. "You're a psychologist. Do something about it."

VIP looked hard at Alex.

"Where's your integrity, your dignity, Bolt? What kind of person are you? To gain sympathy, apparently anything goes with you, even tears! Mathematics is the queen of the sciences. It requires strong, pure souls. You're disgracing yourself with your behaviour. Come to my office immediately after class, Bolt."

The usual classroom bustle suddenly stopped.

"You, Nosov, will come to my office after class as a witness."

"What did I do?" Max muttered. But VIP had already turned back to the blackboard to write the pages of the next day's homework assignment.

During the 40-minute session with VIP, Alex confessed that she had indeed whistled but hadn't admitted her guilt from fear, which of course meant that she was a coward too. The iron logic of it flowed like water from one pool to another. It was clear to Alex that finding a way to save her skin was more important than either the truth or honour, and that if she accused her friend and betrayed him (even if he had just done the same to her), she wouldn't ever be trusted with anything, least of all math, "the noblest of sciences." Soiling it with impure, morally compromised hands was unthinkable, VIP had said. Didn't Alex understand that? Unable to think of a reply, Alex nodded.

VIP then told her that her parents would have to be informed immediately, and handed her record book to her with the order to bring it back with their signatures by next Monday. Alex nodded again.

In the space for "Teacher's Comments," VIP had printed in bold: "You are urgently summoned for a meeting with the mathematics teacher to discuss your daughter's imminent expulsion from the class on moral grounds." The day was Wednesday. She had until the following Monday.

218 MARINA SONKINA ~~~

# 4

The house was empty when Alex got home. Her father must have gone to his office at the Academy of Sciences, and her mother to one of her many meetings. Breathing in the familiar odours of home — of freshly ironed laundry and her father's tobacco and her mother's perfume — made her only more aware of her betrayal of her parents, of Katya, and even her dog, Kerry. She went to her bedroom and locked the door behind her. Still wearing her school uniform, she curled up on the daybed and pulled the coverlet over her head, wrapping her braids around her eyes to hold the tears back.

Showing VIP's note to her parents was out of the question. She had to come up with something better, but what? There was Chvanov, the compulsive counterfeiter from the year ahead of her, forever emending record books from love of his art. He could easily make the summons disappear. But could he erase it from VIP's memory? Tell Goop about it? But to involve him in the trivia of her life would spoil their special relationship and lessen his regard for her. Perhaps tell her father in private? But that was unpromising too, since, unable to make decisions on his own, Professor Bolt would surely delegate the matter to her mother, which would inevitably lead to rage, door slamming, and perhaps even the end of Alex's voice lessons, her greatest fear.

What if she hid the record book and then told her mother on Saturday that she'd left it at school, and then on Monday she could get sick and secure another day. And then on Tuesday, the day of the appointed meeting, she could tell VIP that her parents couldn't come. Taking temporary comfort in that dubious reasoning, Alex listened to the sounds of the apartment, of drawers opening and closing and other activity in the kitchen as Katya got supper ready. Then she heard her parents come home. And then the doorbell rang and several voices were heard in the hallway. It must be company for supper.

So why did he say that she whistled, Alex thought pressing her head into upholstery of the sofa. Why did he do such a hateful thing? She remembered how last spring she had brought him a small box of Turkish delight, a rare treat delivered to their home as part of a special ration. Using the inside of his foot, Max was kicking a small stone by the schoolyard fence. Alex had gone over to him and silently handed him her present.

"Ah, Marsh Gas, it's you and no other," he said as he continued to kick at the stone, picking it up and dropping it again with his foot. "What's this?" She had no idea why he called her that. Everyone at school had a nickname, but the one he came up with for her was easily the strangest.

Finally, he kicked the stone away and took a piece of candy from the box, licked the powered sugar off it, sniffed it, and put it back in the box. Then he took another piece, licked the sugar off it too, and stuck out his tongue all the way so she could see its red central groove.

"You think I'm some little winkie-dinkie? Take your junk away! Or even stick it up your ass, nutty Marsh Gas."

Why did she like him so much? Why, even after that incident, did she try to help him with his school essays? "You're terrific," he said after receiving a 5 and the comment "excellent" on one of them. And then, to confirm his friendly feelings, he had pinched her painfully. But now it was clear to her that he must have hated her all along. She didn't want to admit it to herself, but now she knew.

She shuddered under the coverlet and her palms started to sweat. She was worn-out with fear. Withdrawing into sleep, she dreamed of warm water washing all over her as she and her brother swam together, shoulder to shoulder, before getting out of the river to lie on the warm sand near their dacha. In her dream she loved her brother and admired him and happily felt his arm around her, protecting her.

He was telling her about something, about some easy trick she could use to solve all math problems, once and for all, a trick she'd always known but just didn't realize that she knew. "It's simple," her brother said. "We need to find a seed."

"A seed? What kind of seed?"

"A hemp seed like the one in 'The Black Hen.'"

She was surprised and delighted that he knew her favourite fairytale from childhood. The Black Hen, who turned out to be the ruler of a kingdom of underground people, was saved by the little boy, Alyosha. The hen rewarded him with a magic seed that would free him from all homework. As long as he kept the seed in his pocket, he would know the answer to any question at school. But he betrayed the Black Hen's secret and the seed lost its power.

# 5

The second class on Thursdays was physical education. Which in the winter meant 45 minutes of cross-country skiing around the schoolyard with barely enough time to change back into school uniforms, since between physical education and math, the next class, there was only a ten-minute break. When Alex stepped outside with her skis, she was blinded for a moment by the bright glare of white snow against the steel-grey sky. On seeing Max putting on his skis, the blood rushed to her cheeks. She needed to talk to him, to ask him why he had lied. But then she hesitated.

"Get away from me, Goofball!" he yelled, throwing a ski pole at her and harmlessly hitting the padded sleeve of her jacket.

"But why? Why did you say that? What have I ever done to you?"

"Don't even talk to me, you fat pig!"

"I am not … I never did anything …"

"I hate your mug! Don't you get it?" He pushed off with his poles, joining the other students on the crystalline white tracks.

After going around three times, Alex brushed off her skis, returned them to the shed, quickly changed, and ran to her math class. Her hair still uncombed and her cheeks red from the cold, she came to a stop in front of the open classroom door. Hadn't VIP make it clear that she wasn't to return to class until the meeting with her parents had taken place? A familiar sense of hopelessness overcame her and she started to feel sick.

"Are you coming in or not? There's a lot of work to be done before tomorrow's test. You had better come in." VIP's voice sounded almost friendly and Alex entered the room.

Ten minutes into the class VIP called Alex up to the blackboard. Standing in front of the rest of the class and watching her own trembling hand, Alex picked up a piece of chalk from the blackboard shelf. Then she felt a tickling sensation in her nose, an invariable precursor of tears. VIP stated the conditions of the problem. The class fell silent, waiting for Alex's next gift of involuntary entertainment. She stared at her own blackboard scrawl, none of which, numbers or signs, was comprehensible to her.

"I can't do it," she whispered paralyzed with fear. "I don't understand any of it. I can't."

"My goodness, what a *milksop* you are, Bolt!" VIP said emphatically. "Just a worthless, worn-out thing of no use to the world at all. Then she added: "An *amoeba*," implying an even more radical lack of merit or substance. "A nonentity, a good-for-nothing cipher! The country needs qualified engineers. It needs nuclear physicists to develop peaceful atomic energy. It needs cosmonauts to conquer space. Maybe Bolt thinks that the Soviet people don't need mathematics? Or maybe she thinks that she can somehow take from society without ever giving anything back?"

No, Alex said, she didn't think that at all. She didn't want to take away from other people. She didn't know why she was the way she was, why she was unfit for math, the only thing in the world that mattered.

# 6

Alex wasn't supposed to open the door to strangers when home alone. Listening to the assertive ringing of the bell and pressing her eye against the peephole in the door's leather-padding, she saw a woman with a small child in her arms.

"Help a fire victim! Spare whatever you can! Don't begrudge! Old clothing, shoes, in God's name!"

"Fire victim" was a dark phrase that meant the destruction of a home. Such people were among the poorest of all. Somehow, fires never seemed to dispossess the rich. Since early childhood, Alex had always pictured fire victims with blackened faces and charred skin, but she had never seen any. And now only the front door separated her from two.

Through the peephole Alex could see only the child and the dirty calico headscarf covering the woman's head and the lower part of her face.

A flat monotone came from the other side of the door: "Please help those in need!"

Alex opened it without unhitching the chain and saw a swarthy dark-haired woman in a crooked scarf, an oversize man's jacket, and a gaudy Gypsy-style flared skirt. She was barefoot. The sight of bare feet in the middle of winter impressed Alex and she removed the chain and opened the door a little wider.

"I'll see if I can find something warm for you," she said.

The woman and the child immediately came inside. Alex hadn't meant them to, but now it was too late. A rancid, alien smell invaded the hallway. The woman unwrapped the child's dirty rags and set down on the floor what turned out to be a little girl of around four. The shiny black buttons of her serious, unblinking eyes stared up at Alex. The mother's gaze, however, looked ceaselessly around, taking in every detail.

On the wall opposite her a mirror in a gilded frame with plump cherubs spoke of the comfortable, easy circumstances of the Bolts' lives. An ottoman with carved legs stood in a corner of the spacious hallway, the warm red velvet of its upholstery matching the pink wallpaper flecked with golden sparks. The pendant grape-shaped light bulbs of the hallway chandelier bathed the woman and child in a golden glow. The woman's nostrils flared. Katya had been baking cinnamon buns that morning.

"She hasn't had a crumb all day," the woman said, pointing to the little girl. "I can see that you're a good soul. Give the little one something to eat."

"I'll see what there is in the kitchen," Alex uneasily replied, since she was afraid of leaving them alone in the hallway.

The woman apparently sensed that and pretended to take offence. "Scared? Then don't get anything. We're fire victims not beggars or thieves of some kind. Left with nothing at all, just the clothes on backs as you see us now."

"I don't have anything your size," Alex mumbled, startled by the woman's sudden change of tone.

"I'm sure your mama has something warm ..."

"Yes, there's her fur coat, but I can't give that to you."

"But why not, sweetheart? You'll get it back, my pretty one, I swear on the life of this child. As soon as I drop her off at my sister's, I'll bring back everything you give me. You want to see how Gypsies live? Then come with me!" The woman pulled the little girl's head toward her hip and both of them stared at Alex.

After making a quick mental measurement of the woman — she was exactly her mother's height but half her size — Alex went to the armoire and ran her fingers through the things in it: a rain coat, a leather jacket for early spring, her mother's mink coat, and some enormous jackets of her father's. She hesitated for a moment and then removed the mink coat from its hanger. The woman tested its weight on her arm and then wrapped it around herself and twirled in front of the mirror. "It fits well, doesn't it? Now how about some shoes I could wear?"

Exactly at what point did Alex completely yield to those forces now beyond her control? She got out several pairs of shoes from the armoire drawer. But they were all too small for the woman's large feet. Then the woman pointed to Alex's father's fleece-lined snow boots and quickly slipped them on.

"God will send you a good husband for your kindness," she said. And then she picked up her little girl and was out the door and on the stairs before Alex realized what had happened and ran after them.

The woman and girl went around the building into the courtyard and then across it and out through a narrow archway to another building and then through another courtyard. The woman loped with long strides in her new snow boots and loose-fitting mink coat. She paid no heed to the little girl, who was even so easily able to keep up with her. They were rapidly moving farther and farther from Alex's familiar neighbourhood. As they were passing a row of metal storage sheds with construction materials scattered nearby, Alex tripped over a piece of wire hidden in the snow and fell hard on her face. She had by then no idea where she was, but oddly enough curiosity had replaced her initial fear. She felt vague excitement, even a kind of bold impatience.

The woman and the girl crossed over some old streetcar tracks and entered what looked like an abandoned barracks. Alex went over to it, and through a partly open dirty window on the ground floor she saw a room with dirty rags by the door and no furniture. When she followed the woman and girl inside, she smelled the same reek that the woman and the girl had brought into the apartment. The room itself turned out to be crowded with people. Swarthy children with curly black hair were running wild around women sitting on the floor and waving their arms as they argued with each other in an incomprehensible guttural tongue. Just as Alex was entering the room, a man suddenly blocked her path. He must have come in through another door that she hadn't noticed in the semi-darkness. The "fire victim" angrily shouted at him and then they started fighting over the coat as the man tried to pull it off her while she tried to prevent it. In the end he slapped her hard.

"You better take the coat and run, girl! Run!" the woman shouted at Alex. The coat flew over the heads of the fighting man and woman in Alex's direction but was caught in the air by the man's outstretched hand. And then, before Alex could react, he grabbed her with his other hand and pulled her at a run out of the room. As they ran, he draped the coat over her. Strangely, she wasn't afraid. Bundled up in the fur, she felt warm and cosy.

They finally stopped in front of a large section of conduit pipe left on the ground, its dark opening vivid against the white snow. Scraps of the insulation material covering its surface fluttered in the wind. The man bent over and entered the pipe, still keeping a tight grip on Alex. Once inside he placed a round piece of plywood in front of the entrance and then put her down. Total darkness enveloped them. A shiver ran down her back. She felt strangely detached and curious at the same time.

"We'll make it warm for you," the Gypsy said. The sound of his rough voice was appealing.

He lit a little oil stove. Its small flame relieved the darkness, casting triangles of flickering light on his sharp features and mass of matted curly hair.

Alex was mesmerized by his face, so close to hers, and by his smell, and by the rustling, whispering sound his feet made as he moved about. The other end of the pipe must he covered with last year's frozen leaves, she thought. Every sound he made had its echoing twin as if glass was being broken. If she closed her eyes, it even seemed like the interior of a church. She was startled from her reverie when the Gypsy kicked some wooden object, a crate as it turned out, and then sat down on it with Alex in front of him.

"Scared? I won't do you no bad if you be good."

"But I'm not scared," Alex pluckily replied, knowing in her heart that it was true. "Why did you slap the fire victim? They lost everything in a fire."

"What fire victim? That was my wife!"

"Your wife? Is the little girl your daughter, then?"

The Gypsy burst into laughter followed by a sharp hacking cough.

"Oh, sure! Like I'm rich or something? She borrows the kids for begging. And you, little miss madam, you no meddle in Gypsy business, get it?" His eyes narrowed and gave off a menacing glint in the weak light. "Want something to drink?"

Alex shook her head, the defiance suddenly gone from her face. The Gypsy got to his feet and groped for a bottle. He drank what was left in it and tossed it into the darkness and leaves at the other end of the pipe. Then he passed his hand over the coat, feeling the soft fur. "Nice coat! Your mama's? You must be rich, eh?"

"No, we're not rich and I have to take the coat back," Alex said firmly. But almost immediately she was overcome with fear.

"You want the coat back? Mama will get mad, eh?" He put his arms around her and squeezed her until she couldn't breathe. "Here's how it work. You get coat, I get what inside."

Alex didn't understand.

Then he quickly and expertly checked the coat's pockets, turning her around as if she weighed nothing, a mere toy. He found some rubles and put them in the pocket of his shabby jacket. "These be mine. The coat you take." And then he set her on his knee and gently rocked her while humming something. She knew he was dangerous and was afraid of him, yet at the same time she didn't care.

The harsh edge of his voice, the wildness of his face, the probing of his hands excited her. And when his hand slipped inside the coat and then deeper under her sweater, she didn't resist but continued to feel the same passive curiosity and indifference, reacting only as his hand moved toward her bra. She was afraid he would find the cotton wool stuffed in it for the technical translation teacher. But it was too late. The Gypsy's hand was already painfully squeezing her breasts. She cried out, but he silenced her with his rough, chapped lips, covering her whole face, and took one of her nipples between his sandpaper fingers. She cried out again and for a time seemed to lose all sense of reality.

But the movement of his hands stretched her nerves like strings to their limit, so that every smell or sound or touch seemed to resonate within her entire body. But what completely brought her back to reality was the weak fragrance of *Red Moscow*, her mother's favourite perfume, emanating from the coat. She kicked the coat away, trying to free herself from her mother's abrupt intrusion.

Then she was lying in the man's arms with nothing on but her woollen tights and her woollen camisole, its buttons undone. The Gypsy's hands searched her body hungrily, now stroking the inside of her thighs. "You one fresh little bun, nice and soft!" For the first time her chubbiness was a source not of scorn but of pleasure to someone. Now she wanted him to know everything about her, wanted him to hurt her nipples, her lips, her thighs.

He raised himself up without releasing her, reached over to where she had kicked the coat, and wrapped it around her. And then he kept rocking and fondling her until she drifted off again. Her trance came to a sudden end when she felt a terrifyingly sharp pain between her now naked thighs. She shrieked, but he suppressed her shrieks with his biting kisses. She fought him and cried out again and again until finally he let go of her and the pain stopped. Then he groaned and forced her hand between her legs and back and forth over her belly and thighs, now covered with something wet and slippery. And then he roughly pushed her away. She began to sob, at once frightened and repulsed, thinking that the slippery fluid was her own blood. Or maybe his blood, which would mean that she'd done something terrible to him.

Then she heard his curse, then laugh and hacking cough and sobbed even harder from bewilderment, until he took her in his arms again and they both lay still for a while. From the world outside came a continuous, all-encompassing sound. The weather had changed, replacing the wet snow with the steady beat of rain against the metal of the pipe.

"Now you go home," the Gypsy said.

"I don't know the way," Alex murmured, still in a daze.

"What you mean?"

"I don't know where we are."

"Near bird market, stupid. You know bird market?"

"No."

"Jesus!" he said, chuckling. "How you get here, then, you goose?"

"I followed your ... wife."

The man fussed for a moment with something on the floor, then he blew out the stove and led Alex outside. The rain was now mixed with hail. "I'll show you how to get to market this time, and then you on your own."

She wanted to stay close to him, but he quickly moved away from her.

It was still daylight when they entered the pipe, but now it was dark. Her parents must have declared an official search, Alex thought, beginning to panic. They must have called the police by now and started to check all the hospitals and morgues.

They continued on their way, and then the Gypsy came to a stop.

"See those tracks? Go left and when you come to construction, go left again. You come to pipe tomorrow?"

She looked at his face partly hidden beneath the long bill of his cap.

"I won't be able to find it by myself."

He laughed. Then he touched her shoulder, turning her around. "You an idiot or what?" he said. "I meet you at market. You come after it get dark."

She nodded.

The market stalls looked deserted, with discarded

newspaper turning wet in the rain and the piles of shovelled snow now dark with dirt and excrement. On Sundays people bought and sold pets there: dogs, cats, hamsters, guinea pigs, and even a few birds. But the name still remained from the time when pigeon breeders had gathered there.

"You bring money. No money, no go."

"What money?" Alex asked, not understanding.

"Gypsy not work for nothing."

"How much should I bring?"

"What have you got?"

"Thirty kopeks for the movies, and some money for ice cream. About two rubles, I think. Is that enough?"

"You kidding? With fat pigs like your parents? I need at least five."

"Five rubles? Where would I get that?"

"How I know? That your business. No money, no fun," he said and left her standing under a buzzing, blinking street lamp.

She felt cold in the freezing rain and pulled the collar of the fur coat around her throat to protect it. Then she realized that if the coat got soaked, her mother would know that she had used it, so she took it off, rolled it up, and waddled off home, the rain and hail beating against her cardigan.

# 7

The courtyard of Alex's building was deserted. To avoid bumping into any neighbours, she took the stairs up to the eighth floor instead of using the elevator. She quietly opened the door to the apartment with her key and slipped inside its brightly lit hallway. No one had missed her. Judging by the cheerful banter coming from the dining room, her parents had company. Without looking to see, she went to her room and took off her wet clothing, tucking it out of sight where Katya would be unlikely to find it. The sight of her own nakedness in the shower filled her with shame. She noticed a bruise on her thigh and hurried to dry herself and put on her robe back on. The cleanliness and soothing coolness of the bed sheets gave her some comfort, although the pleasant sensation lasted only a while. Her skin had begun to burn and she found it hard to breathe. "I did catch cold, after all!" she thought with sudden relief. If her mother or Katya should ask, she could say that she'd been sick in bed the whole time and for that reason couldn't come out to greet their company.

What had just happened to her overwhelmed all the other troubles that Alex was facing, or at least what had passed for troubles: her unfinished homework, the note from VIP summoning her parents for a conference — all dwarfed by comparison. The pipe had obliterated Alex's past, but it had also brought new worries. What if it turned really cold and her mother decided to wear her coat? She needed to clean it somehow. Unsteady on her feet, she got up and looked out the window. It was still drizzling, which meant that it was above freezing. That would give her some time. The next morning, her mother felt her forehead, agreed that she was sick, and went off to one of her meetings.

Alex waited until the apartment was quiet again with that special, late morning calm that followed the fuss and bustle of everyone getting ready for work. After listening to make sure that Katya had left on her regular visit to the market, Alex got out of bed and staggered over to her piggy bank. After losing count several times, she was finally able to make a fair estimate of how much she had — a total of almost nine rubles.

The dry cleaner said it would only be three rubles and promised to have the coat ready in a week at the earliest. Alex panicked. The woman looked at her for a moment, and then said: "Come back in four days. That's the best I can do."

Later that afternoon, when her mother returned home, Alex was already feeling much better, well enough, she said, to visit the school friend with whom she always studied for math tests.

"I may have supper with her too," she said casually.

"But you were sick only a few hours ago," Katya said.

"The test's tomorrow, an important one," Alex said, averting her eyes.

It was a miracle that she managed to find the bird market at all, and she was only able to do so after wandering in and out of courtyards and crossing the tracks several times. Finally in the dusk she made out the figure of the Gypsy leaning against an empty booth. He had been waiting for her and watched her eagerly as she came over to him.

"So, you came back, missy! How much you bring?"

"About six rubles," Alex said. "It's all I have."

He counted the money, put it in his pocket, and signalled for her to follow him. She looked around, hoping to memorize the route. He entered the pipe first without looking back to see if she was following. When she stumbled over some bricks by the entrance, he turned around, said: "Shh! Quiet!" and pulled her into his arms. Then he sat down with her on the crate again and began to rock her back and forth.

Playing a game with herself, she pretended that she was a little child and was supposed to be passive and pleasantly powerless in his arms, the way she had felt the day before and the way, she sensed, that he wanted her to feel.

He unbuttoned her top and pushed her bra down around her waist. "Tits are still too small, huh?" he said, kissing her nipples. She lay semiconscious in his arms.

To cover her tracks at home, Alex made up various stories: a classmate's nonexistent birthday party, a school trip to the theatre, and, finally, her voice lessons, two of which she had already skipped, claiming to be sick. Her dog, Kerry, was becoming a nuisance. He seemed able to read her mind and would whimper and whine whenever she was about "to go to the pipe."

The fear of discovery was wearing her down. Financing her adventure demanded an ingenuity she lacked. Her tiny allowance wasn't enough to satisfy the Gypsy. She borrowed money from Katya and, when that source dried up, she took ten rubles from her father's wallet.

She must have visited the pipe five times by then but still didn't know the Gypsy any better than on the first day. He remained aloof and rarely spoke. But now she needed him and sometimes she would sulk like a small child to draw him out. He would scoff and laugh and rock her, but that was the nearest she could get to anything like tenderness from him. On the way back from the pipe, he would whistle. What followed the rocking prelude always filled her with horror, for nothing had prepared her for the ferocity of human lovemaking. Her own readiness to participate shocked her even more. She had eagerly flung herself into "that," and now her body was taking its revenge. She felt weak, sickly, barely able to walk, yet full of an unrelenting desire for that stranger. Sometimes she managed to suppress her fear by imagining that she was just an observer, that she was located somewhere outside her body, which was on temporary loan to her master.

But her earlier sense of being an outsider had passed. Now she wanted the Gypsy and counted the days and hours until their next tryst. She was resentful that he had a wife and pretended he didn't. And then she admitted it to herself and pretended that it was interesting and mysterious, like the picture in one of her father's art books: a harem, languid women reclining around a fountain, getting massages from their black slaves as they waited, waited to serve one man. She imagined herself as one of them, lustful and carefree. But there was also the fear that she would soon run out of ways of getting money and he would forbid her to come to him. As if tempting that possibility, she suggested it.

"What if I can't come tomorrow?" she asked the Gypsy, stroking his black curls.

"Oh, you'll come. Where else would you go?"

"But what if I can't find any money next time?"

"You'll find it, all right."

She obeyed him and found it. She wanted to.

Disaster finally struck from an unexpected quarter. Alex was sitting in her room over her homework and staring into the distance while thinking about the Gypsy, when she suddenly heard the sound of angry voices in the hallway.

"But I didn't take it anywhere, I swear!" Katya said.

"Then how do you explain the cleaner's identification tag on the collar?" Alex's mother said.

She was accusing Katya of removing the mink coat from the apartment, perhaps even wearing it herself, and then taking it to the cleaner's, something that would certainly have been forbidden, since everybody knew that cleaners could replace real fur with fake.

"I didn't touch it, as God is my witness," Katya swore.

"You work in a respectable home. I can send you back to your village anytime, if that's what you want."

Alex pushed back her chair and ran out to the hallway.

"Leave her alone, Mama! She didn't do anything. It was me! I took the coat to the cleaner's."

Her mother stared at Alex for a long time.

"But why? You didn't wear it, did you?"

"No, I lent it to the Gypsy."

"What do you mean, *the Gypsy*?"

"Just that. The Gypsy wore it. They were fire victims. They lost everything in a fire. I had to help them, didn't I?"

For a moment, her mother was speechless. When she recovered, she brought her face close to her daughter's and said flatly, barely letting the sound pass through her lips: "He was killed, but you're alive? Why? Where's the justice in that?"

# 8

Valentina Ivanovna Popova had taken up mathematics merely by chance. She had grown up in a family of construction workers in a little provincial town three hours from Moscow.

Although strong and lean and an excellent track athlete who could beat any boy, none of them were attracted to Popova, for some reason preferring anaemic, empty-headed girls instead. She found relief during most of her adolescent years in collecting and classifying amphibians, intending to become a batrachologist, until an apparently minor event changed her life forever. As was the practice around the end of every September, the students of her school were taken by truck to a chronically understaffed collective farm to help bring in the harvest, this time by digging up potatoes from the hard, cold earth with a group of boys and girls from Moscow sent to work with them.

The *Soviet Dawn* collective farm was an hour of dirt-road bumps and ruts from Popova's school. With boisterous cries and whistling, 20 tenth graders climbed into the back of a rickety old truck, the boys taking their places on the side benches and the girls sitting on their knees. Every bump provoked excited screams. Popova was the only one sitting in the back with her legs hanging over the truck's open tailgate. Unaffected by the general hilarity, she watched the dirt road running away in front of her and swore to herself that one day she would prevail over those inane hedonists and over the city children too. And especially over the girls the boys found attractive, and she would do so by excelling in an area where those ninnies would never poke their noses. And then and there she decided to become a mathematician.

For a long time Popova's efforts were unavailing and her marks remained middling at best. Even with her impeccable social background (her parents were both proletarians), it was still doubtful that she could get into the Moscow State University Department of Mathematics, the best in the country. But she tried anyway. Failing the entrance exams the first time, she took them again the next year and failed again. But that didn't discourage her. The standards of the much less prestigious Pedagogical Institute weren't so strict and she was ultimately accepted in its Department of Mathematics to train as a school teacher. But to her great disappointment, the overwhelming majority of students in the department were girls, with the small minority paying as little attention to her as before. But she persevered, despite her dislike of the subject, eventually becoming a leader of the Communist Youth Organization and serving in her final year as Secretary of the Institute's affiliate. She was efficient, disciplined, and self-assured. Many of the other students were afraid of her, even though what she wanted was neither fear nor respect but affection. She began organizing nature outings and camping trips with bonfires under the starlit skies. She also led special trips to lakes and ponds to identify different species of frogs and water insects, and she strummed a guitar around those same bonfires, singing folk songs in her characteristic whinny.

In five years Popova graduated from the Institute with a master's degree and teaching certificate. By that time most of the girls in her year had got married, and several of them were even nursing their first children, while Popova remained a virgin. On the other hand, her Communist Youth activism assured her excellent job opportunities and she was sent to a boarding school for the mathematically gifted. The school was in a forest 100 kilometres closer to Moscow than her childhood home and thus meant a significant geographic promotion for her. And then, after a time, she was invited to teach in Moscow itself, which gave her a coveted residence permit and, because she was a teacher, a room in a communal apartment near Paveletsky Station without the usual wait.

In her classes, Popova invariably favoured the boys over

the girls, regarding the latter as silly, petty, and innately incapable of learning mathematics. She managed, as a rule, to win the boys over, forming something like a comradely bond with them. All the same, she remained hopeful of "personal happiness," as it was called in the New Year's greeting cards of the day. To expedite its arrival, she took up tennis, an uncommon game in the 1950s with courts reserved mainly for the elite. Since the majority of the players were men, she reasoned that the statistical chances of an auspicious encounter should be extremely high. And she wasn't in that reasoning altogether mistaken. The men were happy to team up with her, considering her a good sport. Yet at the age of 35 she was still a virgin, and by 40 she had given up any hope of marriage.

For Popova, Alex, the girl with a boy's name, was an aberration and not to be tolerated. There was in her lazy passivity, in her unassailable perplexity, and above all in her clumsiness — in the way she tended to knock everything around her into disarray, something that offended Popova to the very core. Unfocused and disorganized, the girl seemed to be sleepwalking through life as if she had all the time in the world, whereas no one does. To live without any purpose was inexcusable to Popova. Mathematics was a vast subject, so vast that it could never be mastered in a single lifetime. Popova herself had achieved what she had by dint of sheer hard work, sacrificing everything for the sake of her science, whereas that girl was looking for an easy way and would even lie if it suited her purposes. And there was her last name too. Bolt? Was that Jewish or German? And her father, the principal had intimated, was a big fish of some kind. Oh, those people are so sure they'll prevail! Only not this time. And certainly not over her! If the parents wouldn't teach their children to accept responsibility, then the school would have to take appropriate measures on its own. And so with quiet resolve, the way she made all her decisions, Popova assured Alex's expulsion from School No. 1. By failing her in mathematics.

# 9

When Alex's father appeared in her office one afternoon, Popova politely asked him why it had taken him so long. Her summons had been sent almost two weeks before. When he heard that, Professor Bolt's his eyebrows rose: he had never seen any note, he said, but had come on his own initiative because he and his wife were concerned about their daughter's lack of progress.

"Her marks are surprisingly low, given the enormous amount of time she spends on your assignments," he said to Popova, while quickly looking her over and casting down his eyes . "Three hours a day, on average, and sometimes more. My wife and I have been wondering about the reasons for her lack of success. Well ... it goes without saying that your view of the matter is crucial."

There was a pause. "Comrade Bolt, let me ask you something. In your line of work, are you judged by the results or by the amount of time you put into them?"

"Well, the answer to that is clear enough," Bolt said, acknowledging Popova's point. "But let me stress that we really do need to consider any child's development in its totality. And from that point of view, my daughter's other subjects have been suffering. Because of her heavy math assignments, she has had no time for anything else. She's been taking voice lessons after school, as you may know, and she seems to have some talent."

"Voice lessons? Now that surprises me!" Popova replied with a grave expression. "Don't you think it would be better for your daughter to avoid extraneous activities and focus on what's important? With the problems she's having with math? Focus on what will ensure her continuing presence in School No. 1?"

"Yes, of course, of course, I do," Professor Bolt rushed to assure his interrogator. "But perhaps I didn't express myself clearly enough. Our daughter has a special talent for singing. It would be devastating to her if we took away such an important part of her life. But if you think the danger of her failing your class is a real one, then we'll certainly ... well, we'll have to take that into account."

"Do you know why I had asked you to come in, Comrade Bolt?" Popova asked.

"Her poor performance in your class obviously needed to be ..."

"That's only half of it," she said, interrupting. "I asked you to come because of her morals. Your daughter's morals have become a matter of serious concern to me, and you and your wife needed to be informed of that."

"I beg your pardon?"

"Your daughter has proven herself to be an inveterate liar, and that simply will not be tolerated in my classroom."

"I'm afraid I have no idea what you're talking about," he said. "But let me return to the main issue of her math performance and be completely clear about it, since it's a matter of the utmost mutual concern. I looked through her exercise book and I think, well, it's my own personal opinion, obviously, but I think ... I think ... she should be given less homework rather than more. Inundating her with impossible amounts of work would seem to be counterproductive. And in fact, a basic principle of pedagogy is that it's better to look at a smaller segment of the material in depth than to ... Well, it could be that teaching logarithms and calculus at her grade level is premature ..."

Popova briefly shuffled some papers on her desk. When she lifted her head, Professor Bolt saw that her face was covered with red blotches. "Are you a mathematician, Comrade Bolt?" she asked. "A teacher? So that you think nothing of telling me what and how to teach my class?"

"I'm sorry. I certainly didn't mean to criticize your methods. I was merely asking you to consider a possibility. But tell me, if you will, what you think our daughter's problem is in comparison with the other children."

"I've already indicated that, but I'll do so again. There are many, and I do mean many, things wrong with your daughter. She has no interest in mathematics. It makes not difference to her whether I say minus or plus in an equation. But that's only half the trouble. I can work with children who lack natural talent, but I cannot and will not tolerate hypocrisy and lies, yes, lies! You daughter is a cunning manipulator. She plays the innocent very well and tries to garner pity with tears and whining whenever it suits her."

"What do you suggest we do?" Professor Bolt asked, completely dumbfounded.

"At this point, I have no suggestions. You might try a tutor, but I doubt, with your daughter's other serious problems, that anything will help at this point. Things have just gone too far."

All of a sudden the Bolts found themselves completely adrift on an ice floe, cut off from the familiar solidity of their lives. No other concerns could compare with the news of their daughter's impending failure in math and with it her automatic expulsion from School No. 1. What made things even more painful was that they were entirely alone and without recourse in their private tragedy. Friends merely shrugged their shoulders, as the matter obviously couldn't be dealt with by taking it to the school principal with an appropriate gift. And because Professor Bolt had himself gone for a conference with the math teacher, he regarded the whole affair as a personal failure. Why had he allowed that woman to intimidate him? Why hadn't he told her what he meant to: about his experiments in cognitive development? Contrary to standard Marxist dogma, he believed that nature, that is, genes and not class, shaped personality, but that nurture, that is, a benevolent, caring environment, could modify the genetic foundation. Give a weaker student additional time, stay after class with her, if need be (it was your obligation as a teacher), and you'll see improvement. But he was a gentleman and found it impossible to argue with any woman, whether a teacher or his own wife.

## 10

To her father's surprise, Alex accepted the decision to cancel voice lessons with indifference. He had suggested that they go for a "good vigorous walk," as he called it, though really meaning a private chat with nobody else around. But a raw, hard wind was blowing and it was too cold to walk, so they sat down on an icy bench in the courtyard of their building.

When he asked Alex about her situation at school, she shrugged her shoulders: there was nothing new to report. She kept moving the tip of her boot back and forth in the snow with a vacant expression on her face, hands thrust in her pockets, so that her father couldn't really tell if she was listening. His prominent eyes started to water in the wind and he looked away. She knew she was being rude but couldn't help it and felt ashamed. If only she could throw her arms around him and beg for his help and tell him that she had stolen money from him and would do it again, and plead with him to do something, to lock her up, if necessary, but keep her from going to that man again! He could do none of those things, she knew that. She was alone and no one else could help her.

She suddenly felt very tired, as if she had aged immeasurably, and she said that she was cold and wanted to go inside. While they were waiting for the elevator, she finally broke her silence. Looking at the wet toes of her boots, she murmured that she would try to apply herself, that she would do her best to keep from being expelled, a promised that she knew he wanted to hear.

Her unspoken confession tormented Alex, but when the day was finally over and she was able to crawl into bed and hide her head under her blanket, it occurred to her that she didn't need her father to rescue her from her troubles, that she could do so herself. All it would take was not going to the pipe ever again. The idea came as a revelation. Just not go! But then she wondered if that wouldn't be cowardly. She felt hot and pulled the blanket away from her head. No, she would have to see the Gypsy one last time to say good-bye. After that, she would turn a completely new leaf.

# 11

The snow on the sidewalks, not cleared over the long months of winter, was hard packed and slippery. Though Alex's visits to the pipe had changed everything and she was no longer a child, she remembered how she liked to run and slide across the snow. And now she resumed that childish fun as if reclaiming her earlier freedom. Balancing first on both feet and then on one seemed to give her infusions of courage. It was snowing and the snow quickly covered the tracks left by her run and slide. She brushed the snowflakes off her sleeves and collar and laughed to conceal her anxiety about the task ahead: removing the burden of the pipe from her life, for she knew she was on her way to the bird market for the last time.

When she saw the booths in the distance, Alex's heart started to pound. She looked hard through the blur of falling snow for the Gypsy's lean, familiar figure, but he wasn't there. She breathed in the cold air with relief. The wait would give her time to calm herself. By her feet two sparrows were bathing in a muddy puddle as the fresh snow fell on them. Their exuberance was a sign of approaching spring. She waited. He had always come first, and leaning against a booth with his legs crossed, immobile, would squint at her in the distance, greeting her approach with his eyes. She looked at her watch. He was half an hour late. She waited a little longer, glanced at her watch again, and then suddenly realized that he wasn't coming at all. She recoiled into herself in dismay. To be back in their pipe amid the rotting leaves and sweet odour of decay was all she wanted now. She wiped her runny nose with the back of her mitten. The sparrows continued to take their snow bath as if nothing had happened. What was his name? She had never asked and he had never told her.

She waited a few minutes more, and then gripped by growing fear she took off at a run toward the tracks and past the chaos of the abandoned construction site. A cold gust blew off her beret. As she bent down to pick it up, she saw the frozen remains of a crushed pigeon partly covered by the snow. Averting her eyes from the sight, she stood up. And then there it was before her, their pipe, its forlorn opening now cluttered with crates and other rubbish, including a broken tricycle, one of its rear wheels suspended in the air.

Seeing it, she turned and ran as fast as she could.

When she finally reached her building and opened the door to the apartment with her key, she was confronted by her mother. They stared at each other for a moment. Alex was the first to lower her eyes.

"I won't ask you where you've been or what you were doing. I don't want to know," her mother said, clearly enunciating each syllable. "But I would ask you *not* to leave your menstrual pads in the trash bucket. The dog likes to chew on them."

"I'm sorry," Alex said. "I'm really sorry."

## 12

In the days that followed, Alex virtually stopped eating. Lying awake in the darkness she tried to visualize the Gypsy's face, but it was hard to remember exactly what she missed most of all about him: his touch, his kisses, his fondling hands. Toward morning she would fall into a deep sleep and hardly wake in time to go to school.

She now felt irrevocably separated from the world around her. Her classmates, especially the girls with their petty interests and quarrels and silly intrigues, seemed to her like creatures from another planet. Max was simply an aberration. How could she ever have been attracted to him? His taunting no longer had any effect on her.

The sweet and nasty secret locked inside separated her from the world around her and, at the same time, connected her no less to life's essence, to the core of life's delight and misery. Now she knew what desire was and what it meant to be racked by it. She had lived through a loss and suffered from it.

She was tormented by unceasing restlessness. The sensation of the Gypsy's touch pursued her, poisoning her waking hours. Languidly, she submitted to a ghostly orgy of emotion and need that excited and exhausted her. Mostly she felt weak, but sometimes those bouts of frenzy fuelled by fasting took complete possession of her, and those were the worst days, for then she didn't know what to do with her body and wished she no longer existed. Bitterly she entertained fantastical plans of avenging herself on the man who had so cruelly betrayed her, forgetting in those moments that she herself had meant to give him up, and that he had simply done so first.

Spring was late to arrive that year. The patches of snow on the pavement shrank slowly, gradually exposing the litter that had accumulated and then been buried over the long winter months. The trees were still bare except for a few tiny buds. An urge for movement, for fresh air began to

stir in Alex. An enormous icicle dripped from the low eave
of the wooden shack in their courtyard. Obeying a childish
impulse, she put her shoe under it and watched it turn wet,
drop by drop. Then she waited until the icicle fell to the
ground and broke with a glassy sound.

Finally, the spring academic break arrived. Alex's parents went to Leningrad for three days and Alex was left in
Katya's care. With no classes to attend, she started to feel
a bit better. A strange void replaced her earlier conflict and
desire. She cleared her voice and tried to sing a few notes.
But they sounded false, broken, and she wanted to be done
with singing and not to think about it at all.

For the first time in many months she felt like eating
again. She decided to buy herself an ice-cream bar, something she never allowed herself during her intense voice
training. Standing on a street corner and licking the bar's
chocolate coating from the ice cream underneath, she
gazed at the people around her, most of whom had begun
to shed their heavy woollen caps and coats and with that
winter's bleakness.

A woman in a warm-up jacket and pants with a tennis
racket under her arm hurried past. Alex looked at her again.
It was her math teacher! But almost unrecognizable. Lean
and strong, VIP looked youthful and somehow more like
her real self. She didn't see her student, or perhaps just
didn't recognize her, now that Alex had lost weight. And
then VIP disappeared into the crowd.

As she licked the last of the ice cream bar from its stick,
Alex thought about that chance encounter. A tennis racket!
Just as she herself did, her teacher had a secret life. Didn't
that make them accomplices in some sense? Alex's gaze fell

on the wire fencing around some trees that had been plant-
ed next to the sidewalk. The ground inside the fencing was
littered with cigarette butts, bottle caps, and pieces of
broken glass. Alex added her ice-cream stick in the litter,
examining as she did so the tree's skinny trunk tied to a
stake. It wasn't so much a tree, really, as a stunted branch
stuck in the earth. Without its stake, the tree would have
toppled over. But the stake was stronger than the trunk of
that puny tree and gave it the support it needed. That's how
it is with me and VIP, Alex thought. I'm crooked, and she's
trying to hold me up straight. She's giving me a chance to
grow. And she has to be strong to do that, to overcome my
stubbornness, my lies. I was lying to everybody, and she
somehow sensed it. How is it that I failed to see what is so
clear to me now, Alex wondered. VIP had wished me good
all along. She acted from selflessness, from generosity of
heart! But I was stubbornly blind. She was waiting for me
to wake up, but I refused to. And yes, she had to be strict
and even unpleasant and rude, since she believed in the
future of small trees, in my future.

After she got home, Alex wrote in her diary:

*My eyes have finally opened!! I was corrupted from the
start and VIP sensed it! We're used to being punished
for the past, but VIP punished me for my future. And I
deserved it! I had no will power! I lacked principles. She
was clairvoyant. She knew everything about me:
Stealing from Papa, going to the pipe! She punished me
for my wrongdoings without naming them, thinking
that I would take her hint. Yet even while punishing me,
she still cared. She called me up to the blackboard to*

*fortify my spirit, to challenge me, so I could acquire the strength to fend off my perversity myself. But I kept rejecting her helping hand!*

All the rubble, all of life's debris: the broken glass on the pavement, the pigeon frozen in the snow, the drunks lying in the ditches in the morning, the shouting and fighting, the little girl borrowed for begging, the lie about being fire victims, the Gypsy fighting with his wife and then carrying her off right in front of her, her mother with her Women's Peace Committee, all of it stood in front of her in a new, clear light. *I took part in all that seamy underside of life,* she thought. *A wayward daughter inflicting herself on a respectable family.*

There was only one place where that impurity was banned: the crystal kingdom of mathematics, a kingdom of order and truth, where VIP ruled. *VIP invited me to partake of that purity. And I, Alexandra Bolt, refused to do so.*

〜

Having at last awakened to the truth, Alex now noticed things about VIP that had eluded her before. How orderly, in two neat stacks, her books lay on her desk were! How elegantly, in perfect alignment with each other, the numbers and symbols emerged on the blackboard as she quickly covered it with formulas! How intelligently her eyes gleamed behind the thick lenses of her old-fashioned glasses! And how touching was her slender, slightly bent figure, leaning forward as if trying to keep pace with the speed of her thought, and how moving her face, its grave expression

conveying the clarity, immutability, and resolve of mathematical truth. Yet, she was humane too. She had a fine
sense of humour. She made the whole class laugh. And she
lived by her principles, unlike Alex's parents, who always
watched to see which way the wind was blowing. No, Vera
Ivanovna was never afraid to speak the truth.

Alex gazed at the dust motes suspended in the shafts
of sunlight coming through the window and at the way it
dappled her teacher's old-fashioned laced shoes and heavy
stockings. What did it matter, the way she dressed? Genius-
es are not of this world. All Alex had at her disposal was the
dirty little two-cent secret of any adult. Vera Ivanovna, on
the other hand, possessed true knowledge. She could cal-
culate the moon's phases, the path of a satellite, the slope
of a bridge's arc, the configuration of a nuclear reactor, the
mass of the earth's molten core, the spinning of atoms and
galaxies. Alex understood none of those things, but Vera
Ivanovna did.

To be like Vera Ivanovna wasn't possible, but for Alex
to tell her that she bore no grudge, that she had admired
her all along, that's what she wanted now more than anything else in the world.

# 13

Alex looked forward to International Women's Day with
particular excitement that year. It was the custom to bring
female teachers flowers in honour of the occasion. But Alex
resolved to give her flowers to Vera Ivanovna privately, out
of sight of the rest of the class.

It took Alex a few weeks to determine that VIP lived nowhere near Lenin Prospect, the neighbourhood for the privileged where she herself lived. No, VIP lived a long subway ride from the centre in a rundown old building, a hive of shabby communal apartments.

On the fourth floor, among the many names scribbled in different hands on the door plate, Alex found the cherished name: *Popova Vera Ivanovna.* She hesitated. And as she wavered, she smelled the delicate fragrance of the bouquet of mimosa in her hand, then wiped the tip of her nose with her sleeve, in case any pollen had rubbed off on it from the tiny flowers. As she was about to lift her hand to press the doorbell button, the door suddenly opened and VIP stood before her in old slippers and a robe with a trash bucket in her hand. They stared at each other in surprise.

"What are you doing here, Bolt?"

Speech failing her, Alex held out the bouquet of fresh mimosa to her idol. A small congratulation card had been inserted in it.

"For me? But why?"

"It's the 8th of March and I thought ..."

"I know what day it is. But students usually bring their flowers to school," VIP said, looking at Alex with curiosity. "And how did you get my address, anyway?"

"The music teacher gave it to me. I just wanted to thank you for everything you've done for me. Please take them." Alex held the flowers out to VIP again. But she was in no hurry to take them.

"You're thanking *me*? You don't think that might be inappropriate given the seriousness of your situation? You do know how serious it is, don't you?"

"Yes, I do."

VIP started to move toward the stairwell.

"Please, take them, Vera Ivanovna! I simply wanted you to know ... how much I appreciate what you ... what you've done for me!"

Popova put the bucket down and stared at Alex in astonishment.

"First your father comes to try to persuade me to put you in a privileged position by giving you less homework than the others. And now, failing that, the family has decided to bribe me with flowers. And of all people, sent you on that mission! Do you know what that kind of behaviour is called?"

"I didn't ... We didn't mean to ... " Alex mumbled. VIP stared at her for a moment and then turned around and started to walk away. Alex ran after her: "Vera Ivanovna, my elder brother won first prize in the All-Soviet Mathematics Olympics. He was accepted into the Moscow State University math department when he was only 14! What I mean is that our whole family has always admired math."

VIP stopped and turned around. The mention of the Moscow State University math department, the unattainable dream of her youth, rankled. She gave Alex a sceptical look.

"I've been on the Olympics Committee the last five years. I don't remember anyone named Bolt."

"I'm not sure what year it was exactly."

"So now you're counting on your elder brother to rescue you? Or is this another story you've made up?"

"Vera Ivanovna, you can expel me. I know I deserve it. But all I care is that you believe me!" Alex dropped her eyes, trying holding back her tears. VIP tightened the belt of her robe.

"How can I trust you, Bolt, if you lie as easily as you breathe? You say your brother won first prize, but don't remember what year it was?"

"My brother died before I was born, but if you want, I can bring his Olympics certificate. He made some mathematical discovery during the competition. That's why they accepted him at the university at 14 without exams."

VIP removed her glasses and rubbed her forehead.

"You're a strange girl, Bolt, and of course I'm sorry about your brother if what you're telling me is true." She paused and put her glasses back on. "But you should understand that it doesn't change anything."

"No, of course not, I understand. I just wanted you to know it was true ..." Alex said, her lips starting to tremble.

"Goodness, Bolt, get a hold of yourself! If you're going to cry over every little thing, how on earth will you ever live your life? When I was your age, I wanted to study amphibians. You know what they are? Creatures that live both in water and on land. Take tree frogs, for example. They live mostly in the tropics. When the time comes, they have to drop their eggs from the trees into ponds. The tadpoles from the eggs are helpless. Water snakes love them, fish love them, even young crocodiles do, and they have very, very little chance of survival. Hundreds, even thousands of them die! But out of that number a few do survive. We have to be like those few surviving tadpoles. Do you understand?"

And then VIP suddenly reached out and patted Alex on the shoulder and their eyes briefly met. Alex's turned moist with gratitude. VIP had reached out to her, their souls had touched in mutual recognition. VIP then quickly turned away, picked up the trash bucket, and set off down the stairs.

Alex remained standing where she was, holding the unwanted mimosas to her chest.

# 14

Alex watched the trees flickering past the window of the train carrying her on the Kazan line from point A, Moscow, to point B, Istra, and the Bolts' abandoned dacha. The car was nearly empty, since for most people it was too early in the season to leave the city. She stepped onto the deserted Istra platform, crossed the tracks, and followed the familiar path through the woods to their dacha. It was colder than in the city, and pockets of partially melted snow remained in the deep shadows of the firs and spruces. The sudden silence of the woods following the train's noisy departure was spooky. Soon Alex came to a familiar glade. Standing at its edge was an old birch on which Germans had inciner-ated a partisan during the war. If you squinted hard enough, the kids from the local village told her when she was a little girl, you could see the charred outline of the partisan's body through the tree's white bark. That made the glade danger-ous, they said, for souls never leave the places where they part from their bodies. They hover invisibly, waiting for to take revenge. Alex began to sing quietly under her breath to overshadow the frightening thought.

The dacha stood on the shelf formed by a steep bank of the Istra river, several meters away from where it made a sharp turn before falling into an artificial lake. Old firs stood in front of the dacha, and the shallows below were still covered with sedge from the previous year. The hand-carved gingerbread trim of dacha's weathered grey porch was still intact — roosters intermingled with diamonds and squares — and the cache of firewood under the porch was still there too, untouched in many years, its pale logs adorned with spreading medallions of lichen.

Alex found the front-door key still hidden in a metal box stuck between the logs. Using both hands, she forced it into the rusty lock and at last opened the door. The long neglected, grave-cold dacha reeked of mildew. She stood by the door for a while, at first not knowing where to start her search. Over years, her father had brought his dead son's belongings to the dacha away from his wife's sight, storing them in what they all called "Alexander's room." Anxiously, Alex decided to begin there. The furniture, unused for years, looked forlorn. The drawers of her brother's wobbly desk wouldn't open until, finally, she forced them to. They were filled with warped notebooks, drawing pads, old atlases, stamp albums, and rusted pen knives. She went through everything piece by piece, looking for the Olympics' certificate. She opened several boxes in a corner of the room. They contained old cameras and compasses and two chess sets. She sat down on the floor and surveyed the chaos around her. She didn't feel the cold any more, just hunger. A sheet of paper lay separated from the rest, as if it had been wafted from the pile by a discerning gust of air. She picked it up. "The Book of Nature is written in the language of mathematics" (Galileo Galilei). It was a loose page from her brother's diary. Alex continued to read. "Chateaubriand believed that love is a terrible burden. I think I understand him. If you love, or become an object of love, you allow an intruder to enter your soul. Love takes possession of you, you give up your freedom, finally losing your own personality. I will avoid that at all costs. May 18, 1953."

How old was he when he wrote that? And who was Chateaubriand? A wave of self-pity passed over her. Her brother didn't want to be loved, yet he was. It's easy to love the dead. If she were dead like him, she would be loved too. But what if she weren't, even then? She would never know. She shivered, recalling the incinerated partisan and his restless soul.

It was starting to get dark. An old kerosene lamp covered with dust stood on the shelf in her brother's room, but she didn't know how to use it. If she started going through the things in the room now, she would miss the train back to Moscow. Better to come back again over the weekend to continue her search for the certificate. She felt VIP's benevolent hand on her shoulder. A blessing. One tadpole out of thousands.

Alex locked the front door, put the key back in its metal box, and returned it to its hiding place among the logs. The sky had partially cleared, revealing a streak of fading gold. Further downstream, at the bend in the river, the water reflected pearly-pink light like a gleaming shield. The path sloped down toward the bank, then up again. Alex climbed to the bluff to see the sunset better. Far in front lay the lake framed by the dark crowns of firs, with the river breaking into separate streams at its mouth and forming little sandbars. The sun had partly slipped behind a dark heavy cloud, and the water had turned a menacing grey. As she watched the rapidly changing light on the water, Alex noticed a leaf floating past. She followed it with her eyes, fascinated by its agile zigzag, as if it were a living thing, until it was carried by the accelerating current into an eddy, where it disappeared and then suddenly emerged again. She bent down to better follow the leaf's movement, but her right foot slipped from under her on the icy ground. As it did she reached back to grab the faded stalks of grass behind her, which immediately came loose in her hand. Her foot began to skate down the bare face of the cliff and she slid all the way down into the river, its icy chill of the water penetrating her as if she had been stabbed. She screamed in fear, and then the water filled her gaping mouth. She had never learned to swim, and frantically, helplessly she flailed her arms and legs, struggling to stay afloat. The silent river was in no hurry, however. It let her struggle for a while and then gently, indifferently, pulled her down into its depths and toward the waiting lake.

The search for Alex was unavailing. Her mother took to her bed, inveighing against the injustice of a fate that had snatched one child and then another from her loving hands. Within days Professor Bolt turned completely grey and begun to mumble, the shaping of words requiring too much effort. Kerry refused to leave Alex's bedroom and stopped eating. Cleaning Alex's room, Katya found the bouquet of dry mimosas stuck without any water into the red Venetian vase. A small greeting card with the smiling face of a woman surrounded by a wreath of flowers fell out. Katya put on her glasses to read it.

"Dear Vera Ivanovna! Happy International Women's Day! I wish you health, happiness, and achievement in your noble work of educating new generations! With great respect, your student from grade 8B, Alexandra Bolt."

A bit of fluff fell out of the vase onto the kitchen floor. It was a dead moth.

# ⟨ ABOUT THE AUTHOR

A former professor of Russian Literature at Moscow State University, writer and scholar Marina Sonkina now lives in Vancouver. She divides her time between teaching, writing, tango dancing and taking her students on culture trips to Russia. Marina's previous collection *Lucia's Eyes & Other Stories* was also published by Guernica.

Printed in July 2015
by Gauvin Press,
Gatineau, Québec